Deadly Sacrifices

BRIDGES DELPONTE

This novel is a work of fiction. All of the characters, organizations, names, places, and events portrayed in this novel are either products of the author's imagination or are used fictitiously. Any resemblance to actual events, locales, or persons, living or dead, is entirely coincidental.

To my dearest friend
Mary E. Sawicki, Esq.
for always doing the work of the angels
by selflessly dedicating her life to protecting
children and persons with disabilities from abuse.

ACKNOWLEDGMENTS

I offer my special thanks to my fellow authors, Pat Wakeley and Christine Eskilson, Esq., who read and critiqued this mystery from the very first chapter. For many years, Pat hosted a writer's group in Arlington, MA that really pushed me forward with honest, no-nonsense feedback and solid encouragement for new writers. There would be no mystery novel without the insights of Pat and Chris. I wish to acknowledge and thank wonderful readers of earlier drafts of this mystery for their helpful comments and support, including Charlee Allden, Michelle Bakay, Professor Robert C. Bird, Dr. Ronni L. Goldsmith, Professor Anne-Marie G. Hakstian, Dolores Fallon, Professor Jennifer L. Gillan, Jean Osborn, the late Alice S. Ponte, Christine Ponte, David Riddell, Ruth Riddell, and Marguerite Ulrich. I also thank Jeannette de Beauvoir of Customline Wordware for her superior copyediting skills. Lastly, I am grateful to the Florida Writers Association for honoring *Deadly Sacrifices* with a 2012 Royal Palm Literary Award (second place—unpublished mystery) and their continuing support of Florida writers.

Also by Bridges DelPonte

Bridles of Poseidon

To learn more about Bridges DelPonte and her writing,
visit her web site - *http://www.bridgesdelponte.com.*

CHAPTER 1

You always remember your first time.

My first happened in St. Stephen's church, directly beneath a statue of the Virgin Mary, right after morning mass. I studied the body bathed in a golden glow of flickering votive candles. Somebody had done a damn good job of bashing in Miriam Carpenter's skull. Her blond hair ran red with blood, snaking in a sludgy river toward a confessional box. A string of rosary beads remained coiled around her limp left hand. Her right arm and leg lay sprawled across a green velvet kneeler. Normal people would turn away, but I couldn't help myself. I needed to see everything.

"Do you want some?" asked a forensic specialist.

His impossibly large ears stuck out from his shaggy mop of brown hair. A wooden pew creaked as he climbed up next to me and clicked off photos of a brutalized woman.

"Some what?"

"Souvenirs of your first homicide."

It was my first homicide case, but not my first murder investigation. I'd already spent years scouring police reports and following up any tip which occasionally got posted on a web site I set up five years ago about her unsolved murder.

"Marguerite Montez, DA's office. Everybody calls me Monty." I gave his hand a firm shake to let him know that I might be the new kid, but I wasn't a pushover. My wrist still ached a bit from last night's experiment with those furry handcuffs.

"Phil Bauer, forensic photographer. I do weddings and bar mitzvahs, too." He smirked.

FlashPhoto Phil? A good moniker to remember his name.

"You know, we haven't seen a gal in homicide for a while." He clicked two more photos. Gotta be at least three years ago."

"Actually, it's been five years."

The first and last female homicide prosecutor in Charles County had gone down in a blaze of scandal. After a couple of big wins, she got canned for doing naked lap dances in chambers for a very married district court judge during a triple homicide trial, and then still losing her case. In her wake, I had to fight hard to break into the all-boys clubhouse at the Charles County District Attorney's office.

"I'm glad you're paying attention, Monty." He jumped down. "Most ADAs don't tune in until they get our final reports. Then they bitch about anything we missed. Gives them an escape hatch if they lose."

"I'm not looking for an escape hatch."

"Not yet anyway," he said. "So do you want any personal photos, Monty?"

"No, thanks. This one will stick with me."

I spotted Rick Connelly, chief homicide detective, taking it all in from the front altar. His dark blue suit strained to contain this massive bear of a man with hulking shoulders, a mammoth chest, and immense hands. His close-cropped white hair framed his round face and green eyes.

"Hey, Monty. Congrats on getting kicked upstairs." Connelly offered the gentlest of handshakes and the strongest of Boston accents. "I hope you're not going to start pestering me about that cold case. I got enough new stuff to work on."

"Not to worry. I'll stay busy learning the ropes on this case." But I planned to nag his department after I settled in.

We walked back to a side chapel and Connelly immediately took charge of the forensic team swarming over this crime scene. I listened carefully to pick up some tidbit that I might be able to use in Ginny's case.

"Getting any prints off that railing?"

"Yeah. The whole damn congregation," said a male tech.

"What about hair samples?"

"Blonde. Brunette. Redhead. Toupee. You name it. ME's gonna have to check her body to see if anyone got up close and personal." The female tech raised a tiny gold item between tweezer

4

pincers. "This is the only other loose thing. A little angel pin. Found it under a kneeler."

"An angel pin in a church. Hardly a breakthrough," Connelly said. "Tell me some good news on blood spatter."

"Gotta decent blood trail to a side exit. Stops near a blue dumpster outside. A few uniforms are combing the trash. And a nice partial boot print near our victim, too."

"Good stuff," he said. "You got all those key angles, Phil?"

"Yup, chief."

"Take some extras from that main altar. I want the whole church. Front to back." Connelly crossed his arms over his chest and exhaled slowly, examining this scene in silence. "My youngest is supposed to receive First Communion this year."

"Are you and your family parishioners here?" I asked.

"No, over at St. John's. Only my wife and kids. Not much of a churchgoer myself."

"Me, neither." The Almighty and I hadn't been on regular speaking terms for some time, despite a diagnosis that should've brought me to my knees two months ago.

"Any witnesses?"

"No eyewitnesses. But an elderly lady and her grandson found her body. They're at District Two giving their statements."

A beat cop pulled Connelly aside and murmured into his ear.

"Okay. I'll handle it," Connelly said. "Looks like the pastor wants to bless her body or something. Shouldn't let him in. But my wife tells me he's gonna be the next archbishop, so we don't want to ruffle any feathers."

We both knew that even wounded, the Catholic Church remained very powerful. The priest walked over, dressed in black with his white clerical collar peeking out from under his scarf. Wet snowflakes glistened on his woolen coat. With his boyish face and full head of light brown hair, this fortyish pastor seemed young for his post.

"Father MacNamara, I'll have to ask you not to disturb anything. We're still collecting evidence from this scene," Connelly said.

"Yes, I understand. I've known Miriam since childhood. Her family will be devastated."

Connelly escorted the priest closer. As he neared her corpse, I read the horror on his face. His right hand trembled as he raised a wooden crucifix over her body. He whispered prayers and made a sign of the cross. In an instant, I was thirteen years old again, clutching my dad's hand and crying my eyes dry as Father Avila blessed Ginny's coffin at her funeral mass. Echoes of the somber tones of St. Anthony's church choir and the pungent scent of incense felt palpable to me.

"Lord, have mercy on us all." His voice cracked with emotion. He fumbled in his pocket for an asthma inhaler. After a swift puff, he took in two or three gulps of air.

"You okay, Father?" asked Connelly.

The pastor drew in several deep breaths, but made no reply.

"I'm sorry, Father," Connelly said. "I know this must be a difficult time. We're gonna need to ask you and your staff some questions. Routine stuff."

He nodded. "Please feel free to come over to our rectory. Bless all of you in your investigation." Once more, the priest marked a sign of the cross, his hand still shaking.

After the pastor left the church, Bill O'Brien waddled in, slurping coffee from a Styrofoam cup. His broad belly peeked out of his rumpled winter coat. A crusty veteran homicide prosecutor, he hated being shadowed by anybody and largely ignored my existence. In the past week, he mostly communicated with me through yellow sticky notes, reeking of Marlboros.

O'Brien scanned the scene and then grunted "hello" to us.

"Two of you here this early?" Connelly whistled. "Quinnie-boy must be getting pretty nervous."

"Election years are always tough," I said diplomatically. "He'll pull through."

At least I hoped so. My boss, Frank Quinn, lagged way behind in recent polls about his re-election as District Attorney. He'd gotten slammed in *The Catholic Sentinel* for prosecuting nuns chained to abortion clinic doors and for not locking up AIDS activists who showered condoms on the faithful after midnight mass. Then that Father Dan case. Sodomy and altar boys made good copy. Quinn's approval ratings took a nosedive for not hauling in pedophile priests fast enough, losing support from both urban liberals and suburban conservatives in this hybrid county. And now, a thirty-something soccer mom and choir member clubbed to death in her church. Our office couldn't afford to screw this one up.

"Next of kin been notified, Connelly?" asked O'Brien, breezing past me.

"Not yet. Her husband's out on a job site for a new subway line. We're tracking him down now."

O'Brien glanced at his beat-up Timex.

"I got a probable cause hearing in an hour. I hate notifications. No good with all that touchy-feely crap." Without looking at me, he jerked his thumb in my direction. "Take Miss Marple with you." He smirked.

"No problem, Perry Mason," I said.

O'Brien might mock me now, but my hard work and bulldog tenacity would do all the talking for me. Miss Marple, my ass.

CHAPTER 2

Notification is too benign a word for telling a guy his wife got clobbered to death in a church. My heart thumped faster as we drove up to a set of construction-site gates. A big orange metal sign clattered in gusting winds against a rusty chain link fence, cautioning, This Is A Hard Hat Area. All Visitors Must Report To Hockings Construction Trailer. A second sign warned, Blasting Area. Turn Off Two-Way Radios and Cellular Phones. Listen for Blast Alarm. As our squad car drove over a small dirt pile, its tires spun in muddy slush, letting loose a high-pitched squeal like a dentist's drill.

"Better shut off your radio, Healey. Don't want to become a permanent addition to this subway station," said Connelly.

Officer Healey reached for his radio and told central dispatch why he needed to go offline.

"Good. There's Saint Cyr." Connelly pointed to a guy who looked like he tumbled out of a Ralph Lauren ad wearing cowboy boots, faded jeans and a camel hair coat over a white Oxford shirt. "A visiting detective from Québec, Monty. Part of a police exchange program. We're both learning some good stuff."

Saint Cyr stood over six feet tall with a muscular build and thick blond hair. Leaning against a brown sedan, he was sketching in his interview notebook. Healey parked beside him in front of a gray construction trailer resting on concrete blocks. Light snow blew around this unpaved lot.

"Watch your step," Healey said. "It's pretty slippery."

I clenched my scarf and focused on not falling into the mud to distract myself from our bleak reason for being there.

"How did your interview go with those witnesses?" asked Connelly.

"Interesting and strange. I met many difficulties. I'll speak to you later," said Saint Cyr.

"Detective Gérard Saint Cyr. Québec City Police. Marguerite Montez. Charles County Prosecutor's Office," said Connelly.

"Nice to meet you. Call me Monty."

"But Marguerite is a lovely French name," he said.

His easy smile made his skin crinkle around his cobalt blue eyes. AngelEyes? Nice nickname, but I wasn't going to make Lori's mistake of mixing business with pleasure. I planned on keeping my pantsuit on, for now, despite his cute French accent.

"Folks, I'll handle any notification. Healey will take notes," Connelly said. "I want you both to observe this guy's demeanor and let me know what you think."

Connelly rapped on an aluminum trailer door. A pale man with a buzz cut ambled out. He wore a thermal vest over a faded flannel shirt and dirty overalls.

"Yeah?" He eyed us warily.

Connelly held up his detective's shield. The man squinted at the badge.

"You with INS?"

"No, we're not interested in illegals. We're local cops," said Connelly. "And you are?"

"Balboni. Nick Balboni."

"Mr. Balboni, we're looking for Patrick Carpenter. Know where we might find him?"

"No trouble with his son, I hope."

"His son?"

"Yeah, his boy's been pretty sick with cancer or something. Just a kid. Like fourteen years old."

"No, not his son. Here about something else. Is he around?"

"Yeah, I think so. Haven't seen him since this morning."

"When was that?" asked Connelly.

"Around six o'clock. I think he's in the tunnel doing some prep work." Balboni pointed toward an enormous black gash in the ground.

"Can you get a hold of him for us?"

"If he's in the tunnel, I can go get him."

"We'll come with you," said Saint Cyr.

He shook his head. "Nope. Nobody's allowed underground unless they're on the job or got state permission. Orders from our union and insurance people."

"It's an emergency," said Connelly.

"No exceptions. Be back in about five minutes. Okay?"

"That's fine."

Balboni pulled on a pair of green rubber boots and a blue slicker and stuck a hard hat on his head. "The trailer's kind of a mess, but it'll keep you dry," he said. "There are a couple of chairs. Coffee machine. Help yourself."

He clomped down the trailer's steel steps. We watched Balboni stomp through sludge to a cavernous tunnel until darkness swallowed him up. As we stepped inside, three fluorescent lights with exposed wiring lit a sloppy trailer office. A rank scent of mildew hung heavy in the air. Wet rain slickers, thermal vests and gloves were piled next to a dented space heater. Several pairs of thick rubber boots in brown puddles crowded out most of the floor space. Two gray metal chairs sat in front of a desk covered with stacks of rolled construction plans. A red-white-and-blue bumper sticker plastered on the end of a row of green file cabinets proclaimed, "Proud to Be Union." I counted five scraped-up hard hats dangling from wall hooks. A filthy coffeepot gurgled on a corner table.

"Would you like to sit, Marguerite?" Saint Cyr asked.

"No. It's okay. I'll stand." I didn't want to park myself on any hazardous waste.

"I'll take a seat." Healey plopped into a metal chair.

"Feet killing you from sitting in your squad car all morning?" Connelly asked.

Healey rolled his eyes. "No. We gotta two-month-old. Kept us awake all last night. I'm dragging ass."

"Now you know why some species eat their young," Connelly said.

Healey laughed. "You got any kids, Saint Cyr?" he asked.

"No. Never married."

"Never married doesn't mean you don't have kids."

"No. No wife. No kids."

"How about you?" Healey asked me, not one to know when to

stop asking questions.

"No. No wife. No kids."

I had no plans to tell them about my brief but painful stint as Wife Number One of Ted Kiley, a now-famously flamboyant defense attorney. I didn't want to expose my poor taste and lousy judgment all at once.

"Enough questions, Healey," Connelly said, rescuing me from further interrogation.

I stared out a foggy trailer window. Two blurry figures emerged from the subway tunnel's mouth. I spotted Balboni escorting a man wearing a heavy over-sized rain slicker and yellow rain pants with rubber boots up to his knees. As he got closer, I noticed a dark beard jutting out from under his white hard hat.

"Here comes Carpenter," I said.

I felt my stomach tighten at the prospect of crushing this poor guy with news of his wife's murder. A flash of my murdered friend Ginny's mom, Angelina, crossed my mind. Mrs. Viera, a ghost of a woman, continued to roam aimlessly through our neighborhood searching for an end to her living nightmare. Yet I didn't have long to feel sorry for Carpenter. He suddenly broke away from Balboni and bolted toward a beat up pickup truck.

"My God, he's taking off!" I yelled.

"What the hell?" Connelly looked out a trailer window.

Carpenter jumped into his truck and started it up. His pickup's wheels whirred in the muck as it fishtailed out of the lot. Healey scrambled to his feet. Saint Cyr almost knocked me over as he raced for the trailer door. We tumbled down its steps like clowns falling out of a tiny circus car. Healey crashed into Balboni and fell to the ground, covering his uniform pants in mud.

"Goddammit, that bastard is dead meat," said Healey.

We bounded toward Healey's squad car. Saint Cyr jumped into his sedan, jammed his police light onto its roof, and peeled out of the site. Healey hit his siren and lights as we trailed Saint Cyr. Connelly flipped on his radio, barking out the color, make, and plate number of Carpenter's truck. Our squad car skidded in mud and bounced over some potholes, past metal gates on to busy urban streets. Carpenter sped on Atlantic Avenue alongside Boston Harbor with Saint Cyr roaring right on his tail. A recent subway project converted these streets into a twisting obstacle course of orange cones, jersey barriers and quick lane changes. Carpenter zigzagged through bizarre traffic patterns and charged ahead, but he couldn't shake Saint Cyr.

"Stay with him, Healey," yelled Connelly.

Healey punched his accelerator and we started gaining on Saint Cyr and Carpenter. Our squad car dashed along the crooked street, its blue lights flashing and its siren wailing. We whizzed around sharp turns and rumbled over uneven pavement. Pedestrians leapt out of our path near the Aquarium. Healey nearly brushed the bumpers of every car trying to scramble out of our way. We hurtled past Faneuil Hall, Columbus Park, and the North End's backside. I stopped breathing somewhere around Lewis Wharf. Up ahead, two squad cars crawled through snarled traffic coming over Charlestown Bridge heading toward us.

Carpenter tore through a red light at the bridge, clipping a blue Toyota's tail end and sending it twirling like a baton in the intersection. This whirling car whacked Saint Cyr's sedan, shoving it into a fire hydrant. We zipped past them, heading into dangerous territory near the old Boston Garden on Causeway Street; once a narrow cow path, now locked in the eternal gloom of a subway overpass. Healey never let up on the gas as he careened around huge concrete highway footers. My right shoulder kept banging into a rear car door with every turn. It hurt like hell, but I didn't dare make a sound as I slid across the rear bench seat like a hockey puck.

I gripped a passenger handle even tighter just as Carpenter's car spun out and smacked into a highway stanchion. Our fender caught an edge of his truck bumper, sending us soaring into the air. Healey's squad car smashed into stone steps at the O'Neill Building. Shrieks of buckling metal pierced the morning stillness. As we jolted to a stop, my shoulder felt like it had jerked out of its socket. Connelly lurched forward, banging his head into a dashboard. He slumped to his side, blood trickling from his forehead. Steam began to rise from under our squad car's hood. I searched for a pulse as Connelly's blood dripped on my fingers.

"He's alive!" I yelled. "I'll call it in. Go get Carpenter!"

"I'm going to kick that guy's ass," Healey roared. He threw open his squad car door.

Our crash jammed my door shut so I climbed over a console

and tumbled into the driver's seat. I grabbed Healey's radio. "We got an officer down. Officer down. Causeway Street. O'Neill Building. Send an ambulance! Now!"

Connelly's breathing seemed labored so I loosened his tie and popped two top buttons on his shirt. I yanked off my scarf and pressed it against Connelly's forehead to help staunch his bleeding. Through a rear window, I watched Healey sneak toward Carpenter's pickup. Two other police cars surrounded his truck, its front end squashed like a flattened beer can. These officers leapt out of their cars with guns ready to fire. I caught sight of Saint Cyr running toward us with his gun cocked skyward.

"Out of your truck, Carpenter! And I wanna see your hands up!" shouted Healey.

There was no movement inside. He repeated his demand, but nothing happened. Healey crept up, flung open the driver's door and poked Carpenter's shoulder. But he still didn't move. Grabbing Carpenter by his dark hair, Healey pulled his head up. Fresh blood covered Carpenter's face and beard.

"He's still breathing," said Healey.

In an instant, ambulances, fire trucks and more police cars flooded Causeway Street. Notification. Not quite the touchy-feely thing it used to be.

CHAPTER 3

After waiting four hours, feeling like my left arm barely dangled from my shoulder, an overworked ER doc decreed that I'd live to prosecute another day. She offered to write me a prescription for pain pills for my bad muscle strain and deep bruising.

"They'll help you sleep," she said.

Sleep and I had remained complete strangers for nearly two months, since my diagnosis and my new dopamine meds. But knowing my lousy family history with narcotics, I declined her tempting offer. The ER doc told me that Connelly had suffered a mild concussion and needed to stay and enjoy their hospitality overnight.

Unfortunately, Carpenter slept in a coma in intensive care.

The office was only a couple of blocks away so I decided to walk. I braced myself for a blast of artic air, but it felt refreshing to flush the hospital's stale antiseptic smell out of my lungs. I entered City Square, a brick plaza in front of Charles County Judicial Center. Blue sawhorses, strung together with bright yellow police tape, corralled curious onlookers under a gray January sky. A half-dozen police cars were parked at side angles, their blue lights flashing and their radios crackling in the frigid air. I wondered who was patrolling the rest of the county.

O'Brien hustled over to me and grunted, "Where've you been, Nancy Drew?"

Before I could answer, he said, "Let's go. It's show time!"

I spied one of Quinn's political handlers clutching a clipboard. He fussed over several RE-ELECT QUINN signs placed with campaign volunteers in a gathering crowd. A thick knot of tangled wires and a bank of microphones covered a makeshift podium on a top courthouse step. He strode over and seized my arm barking in rapid-fire bursts into my right ear.

"When Mr. Quinn approaches those microphones, you stand to his right. A step or two back, not right behind him. He'll introduce you. You step forward. Nod your head. Then step right back. Look serious. No waving. No smiling." He turned toward O'Brien.

"Spare me. I'm no virgin."

"Coats off, folks," he said. "We want your clothing to scream tough prosecutors, not bundled-up commuters."

Handing my winter jacket to one of Quinn's media lackeys, I shivered beneath my traditional battle dress, a simple white blouse and black pantsuit with matching pumps. My unruly, dark brown curls were pulled back into a tight bun, my ears punctuated by unremarkable earrings. I allowed myself a touch of matte blush over my mocha skin and a neutral shade of lipstick. No ruby lips, no dramatic eyeliner, no clattering jewelry. Sister Mary Vincent would be pleased to see her once-defiant student in her proper legal habit.

Quinn stepped out of the courthouse and surveyed the scene.

"Looks good," he said to his political operative. "Live TV?"

"Of course, Frank. We better get started. And remember, don't shift on your feet. Makes you look anxious," said his aide.

Quinn's adviser scurried away and gave each cameraman a thumbs-up. The DA strode toward a bank of microphones, flanked by beefy uniformed police officers. I squinted at a sudden white gush of TV spotlights. Quinn didn't even blink. My lips quivered as I fought to suppress an unexpected toothy, nervous grin. I shuddered to think how many pounds live TV would pack on to my already curvaceous body, shaped by a lifetime of bakery treats. Was it too late to join a gym? Frantically gesturing for O'Brien and me to move closer, his aide choreographed us as Quinn's backup singers, the Quinnettes. As red camera lights blinked on, his handler cued Quinn to start his speech.

"It is with great sadness that we find ourselves investigating a senseless murder within the sacred walls of St. Stephen's Church. Another assault on our values and respect for law and order in our Charles County community. It is crimes like this horrific murder that I hope will move our state legislature to pass a death penalty law that I support in these violent times."

He waited for scattered applause and began waggling his right foot behind him. His handler scowled at Quinn who immediately stopped jiggling his foot.

"My office is working with the Charles County police to investigate this terrible crime. Our fine working relationship with law enforcement, achieved through years of hard work and collaboration, will lead to a successful prosecution of the perpetrator of this heinous act."

He fixed his stare on O'Brien and me, solemnly anointing us as his most trusted advisers.

"I'd like to introduce the two prosecutors who will handle this case. First, Bill O'Brien, deputy district attorney, who's been successfully prosecuting homicide cases for over fifteen years."

O'Brien took two steps forward, nodded and returned to his initial spot.

"And a promising new prosecutor in our homicide unit, Marguerite Montez, will be assisting him."

I mimicked O'Brien's moves. Promising. I felt pretty puffed up as I stepped forward then back. Promising. Yet a pinprick of reality burst my little bubble when I noticed his political aide holding up a white cardboard sign with my name scrawled across it. Damn it. Quinn didn't even know my name. But I planned to make sure that he did before this case was over.

It was nearly four o'clock and my shoulder throbbed with pain. I should have called it a day. But instead I decided to catch up with Saint Cyr and company tossing the Carpenters' home for evidence. The Blue Bomb, my Dad's old '67 Chrysler Newport, chugged all the way to their Watertown home. When we were kids, my sisters died of shame when Dad picked us up in the Bomb. But I loved it. After he died two years ago, I inherited her along with his Teamsters key chain. Since his glorious Bomb lacked power steering, my shoulder howled in pain with each spin of her wheel. Despite my soreness, I felt it tugging at me again. It was on my way to Carpenter's place so I decided to stop.

A shrink would tell me not to do it, but I didn't have one on speed dial and pulled onto a sandy shoulder near the Charles River. I hadn't been there in about six months, which showed a lot of restraint for me. Taking a deep breath, I stepped out of my car and picked my way along a grassy path to a sloping riverbank. A blueberry bush's snarled dark tentacles grew wild over a corroded outflow pipe. My heart didn't pound anymore and no tears filled my eyes when I stared at it. My feelings of shock and grief had long ago morphed into erratic spasms of anger, frustration, and emptiness.

At age thirteen, life's brutal arbitrariness had stamped out my innocent Catholic upbringing filled with vigilant saints and kindly guardian angels offering their benevolent protection. After weeks of plastering homemade posters on telephone poles and attending painful candlelight vigils of weeping family and friends, a public works team discovered Ginny's tortured, lifeless body stuffed in this rusty tomb. And when it was all over, I realized that my impassioned prayers, lit altar candles and fervent novenas meant nothing. The randomness of violence and cruelty would happily rampage on without missing a beat.

It could have just as easily been me taking our favorite shortcut home after a late dance practice. But it wasn't me. It was Ginny. Her life ended, her family fell apart, her case never got solved. I got used to telling myself and other people that I became a prosecutor to honor Ginny, but that wasn't the whole truth. After her murder, I decided I didn't need God, the Church, or any of those holy holies anymore, for anything, not ever again. I realized we were all on our own and put my faith only in myself to protect my little sliver of this world. I'd use my street smarts and legal skills in the courtroom to make my neighborhood as safe as possible. No more falling to my knees and praying for any kind of divine intervention or heavenly protection from some unseen guardian angel that would never show up.

Yet my relentless efforts to go it alone had gotten me nowhere so far. After years of combing police reports and contacting investigators about similar crimes in other states, I wasn't any closer to finding Ginny's killer, and I still ached with guilt for not telling someone sooner. For nearly two decades, the Almighty surely reveled in being a wicked starting pitcher on the mound who knew how to taunt me with more wild curveballs than I could ever hope to bat away.

"You okay, miss?"

A trash collector, wearing an orange vest, momentarily startled me. He dragged a heavy garbage bag by his side.

"Yeah—yeah, I'm okay."

"Got car trouble?" he asked.

"No, no trouble." At least not of the automotive kind.

Pulling behind three police cars, I parked in front of a white Cape Cod home. Yellow crime scene tape fluttered in a bitter wind around this postage-stamp lot. Climbing out of the Bomb, I noticed several cops canvassing the working-class neighborhood for leads. I spied a Madonna statue on a half-shell keeping a lonely vigil over a worn-out swing set. I held the front door open for a cop carrying out a carton of evidence. Inside a black mailbox, I pulled out four envelopes, two from collection agencies.

I stepped directly into a tiny living room. Some plain white sheers drooped in its windows, flanking a beige couch, a beat-up vinyl recliner, and an old TV. Two cops examined the sparse contents of a wooden bookcase. I walked over to a mantel for a closer look at a wedding photo. She wore a simple white dress with a lace mantilla over her head while he stood stiffly in an ill-fitting blue suit. Another framed photo showed them standing with a boy and a girl next to Father MacNamara. The girl wore a First Communion dress. According to our records they were both only thirty-three. Yet the passage of time had judged Miriam more harshly than Patrick.

Passing through a dining room with its bare hutch and scratched mahogany dining room set, I almost overlooked a small room tucked away in an alcove. A mock license plate tacked to its door announced "Joey's Room" in raised letters. I walked in and found a sea of colorful bubbleheads, hundreds of them. Everything from sports teams to comic book heroes to jungle animals lined its walls and windowsills. Collecting them must've been a fun distraction for a sick kid. This array overwhelmed a twin bed and narrow bureau in his room.

"Unreal, isn't it?" said a technician. Holding up a jiggling Patriots football bubblehead, he tapped its helmet and it cheerfully bounced back and forth.

"Amazing," I said. "Somebody better call eBay."

Did an ill child really need the added pain of his mother's

grisly murder, likely at his father's hands? I didn't get it. I headed back through a dining room and a hallway toward their kitchen. Healey unexpectedly stepped out of an adjacent bathroom, magazine in hand. Not exactly the time for pleasure reading, I thought.

"Hey, how's Connelly doing?" He quickly ditched his magazine.

"He's okay. They're gonna keep him overnight to be sure."

"What about that bastard Carpenter?"

"Speed Racer's in a coma. Where are their children?"

"Joey and Bridget are with a grandmother."

"Which grandmother?"

"Father's side, I think," said Healey, scratching his head.

"That's not good, Healey. She might be filling their heads with alibis. Nobody from the wife's family around?"

"Yeah, a sister. But she's outta town. Won't be in until tomorrow or the next day."

"Damn it. Better beep protective services to start keeping tabs on them," I said.

"Okay, I'll call 'em, Monty."

I headed upstairs to a second floor. Two dormered bedrooms flanked each side of a small bathroom. Both bedroom ceilings sloped at sharp angles, ripe for plenty of unpleasant head knocks. One bedroom was a riot of pink, dotted with tacked on posters of tween heartthrobs. Three Barbies, in contorted positions, lay scattered across a fluffy area rug, next to a twin bed with its pink coverlet. An Irish step dancing schedule and several blue ribbons from dance competitions were taped to the edges of a white dresser mirror. Ginny excelled at all kinds of dance, too, especially rancho dancing. She would proudly swirl in her bright red embroidered skirt, crisp white blouse and multi-colored headscarf with a troupe of other young dancers at different Portuguese *festas*. Their clacking castanets and banging heels punctuated cheery bellows from accordions that still resounded in my ears. As the accordions ratcheted up their tempo, only a few skilled dancers could keep pace. And Ginny loved being the last dancer still standing by the tune's end as her audience cheered its approval. I often wondered if she'd become an insatiable pedophile's target because of it.

I heard Saint Cyr talking to someone else in the other room.

The Carpenters' bedroom doubled as both their sleeping quarters and an informal office. On one side, a mahogany bed with pineapple carvings stood between two matching dressers, one with a mirror. Several older black-and-white family photos sat on top of a dresser. A brown cross hung above their bed. Across their room, a mound of papers buried a black metal desk next to a file cabinet. Multi-colored pins fastened scraps of notes to a corkboard. Saint Cyr and a technician sifted through the Carpenters' records.

"Hi. How are you doing, Marguerite?" Gérard asked. He set down a pile of papers and walked over to me. "Nothing too serious, I hope, eh?"

"I'm okay, Gérard. Only strained my shoulder muscles." I felt better because he thought to ask. But then Canadians are the nice North Americans. "Connelly's being held overnight as a precaution."

"Yes, to his wife I spoke of it. Please excuse me, I couldn't stay at the hospital. But we had to get over here."

"No problem. Finding anything?"

"Mostly unpaid bills and angry letters against them from collection agencies."

"You can add these to your pile." I handed him their uncollected mail. "Swamped with bills from their son's medical care?"

"Many medical bills. Credit-card bills. Not making their mortgage payments, too."

"Found any life insurance policies yet?"

"Yes." He held up two plastic evidence bags of insurance documents. "They are large ones, too. A million for him and for her. They took these out more than one year ago. I haven't found any late notices from their insurance company yet."

"Looks like Carpenter found a quick fix for his financial troubles, detective."

In law school, my old criminal law professor told us most homicides resulted from "the three Ls"—love, lust, and loot. I dreamed my first homicide would be much more exotic than a mundane life-insurance scheme.

He nodded. "I am agreeing with you."

"What did you mean earlier today about those witness interviews being interesting and strange?"

"Our witnesses are Alice Silva and her grandson, Daniel. Mrs. Silva volunteers at St. Stephen's. Said she was in the basement when the murder occurred. Daniel was in the church when it happened."

"Poor kid. How's he doing?"

"He's not a kid. At least not physically. Daniel's a forty-two-year-old man with Down Syndrome."

"Could he tell you much?"

"The whole thing freaked him out. I tried to settle him down by showing him some of my drawings." Gérard flipped through his interview book with impressive penciled scenes of Boston. "His grandmother told to me that he loves to draw."

"Did he draw any pictures that might help?"

"Not yet. Too upset this morning. I sent them home. Asked him to sketch me some pictures. I'm stopping by tomorrow afternoon to see them. His drawings might give us some clues. Want to go?"

"Absolutely," I said. "Can I help you guys with anything else here?"

"Not much left to do. Better to go to your home. Care for your shoulder." He smiled. "A good hot soak might help."

"Sounds like a plan." A nice bubble bath and scented candles with AngelEyes would cure most gals. But I'd stick to romancing Mr. Epsom Salts and Dr. BenGay tonight.

I left the Carpenters' house as an early January darkness set in. I warmed up the Bomb, my breath floating like smoke in the winter air. It smelled like snow. Driving off, I glanced at that Madonna in her shell-shaped tub in my rear view mirror. To think that Miriam lived and died under her watchful gaze.

CHAPTER 4

I wanted to crash at my apartment, but knew I better go by my family's bakery before going home. My ma must have seen a newscast or got word about my TV debut through Ms. Andrade, my landlady. She headed the Network, a tribe of widowed Portuguese ladies all clad in black who kept a gossip mill going strong in our East Cambridge neighborhood of Portuguese and Brazilian transplants. In the 1940s, my grandfather had sponsored Mrs. Andrade and her family to emigrate from the Azores. After my divorce, I rented an apartment from her in our old neighborhood, wanting to be closer to the office and the vitality of nearby Inman and Harvard Squares. Mrs. Andrade gave me a "nice Portuguese girl" discount on my monthly rent, but thoroughly enjoyed one-upping my mother on my comings and goings.

My head pounded and my shoulder ached as I headed to Monty's Bakery. Hard to believe our family of seven crammed into living quarters above our shop with no air-conditioning and only one bathroom. Over time, most of our relatives escaped to the suburbs for bigger homes and better schools. But my folks stuck it out in the old neighborhood where they grew up and met as teens.

My dad, the baker's son, played an accordion for Jose Furtado, a small-time *fados* singer. Furtado belted out soulful blues songs about star-crossed Portuguese lovers and passions gone wrong at community events and *festas* celebrating holy days. Looking to spice up his act, he auditioned attractive local Portuguese girls as back-up singers. My mother and her sisters won out with their beautiful, harmonizing voices. As Furtado warbled heartfelt *fados* tunes, my dad became smitten with the fashionable youngest sister with her big smile and great legs. They married less than a year later. When they took over his family's bakery, my mother put aside her musical aspirations.

My dad always loved this bakery, rolling dough between his fingers, creating delectable pastries and breathing in heady aromas of *massa sovada*, *biscoitos* and *linguiça* rolls browning in two commercial ovens. My ma tolerated the business, but she loved him so dearly that she toiled by his side for over three decades and kept it running even after he dropped dead while making a delivery one night. I know my dad was disappointed when I picked law school over their bakery and Kiley over friendly delivery driver, Manny DeSantos. In the end, I knew he was proud of his daughter, the prosecutor, even though he didn't understand my choices.

I pulled into a rear alley and banged hard on the back door. My mother opened it a crack and then frowned. I heard her slide a chain lock and she swung it open. Her oversized apron, dotted with splotches of flour and dough, swallowed up her petite four-foot, ten-inch frame.

"You lose your dime?" she asked, hands on her hips.

When we were teens, my parents always asked that question whenever we arrived home past curfew without calling first. I felt like I was back in high school all over again as I trailed her inside.

"I had a lot going on today. I didn't have time to call, Ma."

"Do I have to hear from Mrs. Andrade when she buys my bread that my own daughter is on TV chasing murderers and busting up police cars?"

"It's my first big homicide case. A woman killed in St. Stephen's."

"Be nice to that priest at St. Stephen's. He might be able to help you get an annulment from that bum." She waggled her finger at me.

"Ma, let's not get off on that again. I'm not going to pretend that it never happened. I'm fine with being a happily divorced woman."

"Happily divorced. What kind of crazy talk is that?" Pressing a key for the cash drawer, my mother began to count the day's receipts. "By your age, I already had a wonderful husband, five daughters and a solid business. Two of your sisters have decent husbands and given me three beautiful grandchildren. And Fatima, a school principal, married to the Church. How can you be happy with no one in your life, running around day and night with crooks?"

At that moment, Manny parked a bakery delivery truck and hauled open its rear doors.

"You could do a lot worse than Manny. At least he'd come home every night."

She was never a fan of Kiley and felt betrayed when we impulsively eloped on a weekend trip to Nantucket. Reminding me about Kiley's infidelities was my mother's favorite way to lobby for marrying within the Catholic Church next time, annulment in hand.

"Gimme a break, Ma."

My mother shushed me as Manny hoisted bread racks and made his way to the front door. "*Ficar face*," she whispered.

I rolled my eyes. Portuguese women were experts at *ficar face*—always putting on a happy face in public, no matter what. So what if your husband who beats you? Boast about what a great provider he is for your family. Got a daughter who is knocked up? Keep her out of sight and tell everybody she's visiting wealthy cousins in the Azores. Have a son who drinks up his paycheck? Sigh to your friends about how generous he is, always paying everyone's tab at the Sunset Café. Hey, life is tough for everybody, so accept your troubles in silence and sing a happy, happy tune in public, even if you're dying inside.

I knew *ficar face* kept my mother from confronting our biggest family tragedy, my younger sister Bianca's OxyContin addiction. It started after my dad died, as her way of coping with his sudden loss. Sometimes I overheard my mother tell relatives and neighbors that Bianca was a real go-getter always taking on new, more responsible nursing jobs. In reality, my sister was managing to stay one step ahead of her employers, moving on before they caught her slowly looting their OxyContin supplies. My sisters and I tried to get her help, but Bianca would have none of it and continued to bounce around without forwarding addresses or regular cell phone service.

As Manny wheeled in an empty bread rack, my ma pasted on a broad smile. He wore a puffy olive jacket over his white bakery shop scrubs, his dark curly hair falling over his right eye. The solitary hum of florescent lights in glass display cases filled our silence. Despite my mother's best efforts at *ficar face*, Manny had known us long enough to recognize instantaneously the distinct chill of a family argument. He dumped a stack of newspapers on a pastry display case.

"Hey, it's the next Nancy Grace," he laughed, showing off a front page photo from *The Boston Globe* with me standing in a sea of police cars and Carpenter's truck crunched like an accordion. "Better get her autograph now, Mrs. M., before she starts charging."

I cringed as he gave me a hug that lasted a little too long.

"You okay, Marguerite?"

"I'm fine, Manny. Only a little sore from that accident."

"You oughtta fry that bum for killing his wife in a church."

"He's lucky we don't have a death penalty. But we don't know for sure if he did it. We're still trying to sort out what happened."

"You run like that, you must be guilty," added Manny. "I taped the noon and 5:00 news on your ma's DVR. You looked good on camera. We watched it three or four times. Better than an episode of *Law and Order*."

My mother glared at him and then pretended to be busy counting change from her register.

"I got plenty of papers for your ma to show those ladies at church tomorrow morning. Gonna keep some copies here to give to our regular customers, too."

"Manny, I think you have a few more racks to bring in. And Marguerite needs to get some rest from her busy day."

"Sure thing, Mrs. M. Take care of yourself, Marguerite."

"Thanks, Manny. I will."

My mother turned off several display case lights and began to cover them for the night.

"Want some help?"

"No, I can manage," she said.

"Okay, Ma. You have a good night and I'll see you at Fatima's reception next week."

"Did you forget about singing at our fundraiser?"

"Is it this week?" I asked.

"Yes, Friday night at the soccer club. I told you they moved up the date so they could start to get early bids on roof repairs for the church hall."

"What time?"

My mother threw up her hands in despair. She pulled out a pad of paper to jot down the particulars.

"Just tell me, Ma. I'll put it into my cell phone calendar."

She stubbornly continued to write and handed it to me with a flour-dusted hand.

"I put down those songs people will want to hear and that Mr. Carvallo knows how to play. His grandson is going to stop by and join in with his guitar, too. A trio. Almost like old times."

I smiled and nodded, thinking about our old family trio. My dad on his twelve-string Portuguese guitar, Bianca on an acoustic guitar, and me, singing. A lot had happened since those early days and, like most *fados* music, it was tragic.

"And be on time," she added. "Don't embarrass your family by showing up late."

"Okay. I'll try to be there on time, but I do have a real job that comes first."

"You tell that boss of yours that he needs all the votes he can get. So your singing at a big East Cambridge event might win him this precinct."

"Great idea. I'll bring along some campaign buttons and bumper stickers, too." I doubted that Quinn worried too much about getting this neighborhood's solidly Democratic vote, but I could play *ficar face*, too.

"Here, take a *massa*." She pressed a plastic bag of sweet bread into my hand. "Take care of your shoulder. You be careful with those bums."

"Okay, Ma." I gave her a quick kiss on her cheek as I headed for the back door.

"And don't forget your dime next time."

She always had to get in the last word.

On my short drive home, I couldn't help but wonder why Carpenter had run, too. If he killed his wife, lying to us about being at work all morning would have been easy. Turning on to my street, I drove past a long row of chunky triple-decker houses. With the college crowd still out on winter break, I managed to find a parking space in the same galaxy as my apartment. I skipped trying to reach into my mailbox to pull out bills and junk mail and pushed open a security door. A single, naked bulb suspended from a twisted ceiling wire lit this dim entryway. A barking dog and TV garble echoed in a main foyer. I heard Mrs. Andrade yakking loudly in Portuguese inside her apartment. An aroma of simmering kale soup and marijuana ticked my nose. The soup belonged to Mrs. Andrade and the pot to Autumn, a crystal-gazing grad student on our third floor, still working on her PhD thesis about how to successfully avoid full-time work.

When I unlocked my apartment door, a school bell I'd attached to some inside molding jangled as I shut it behind me. I surveyed my obstacle course of furniture created over these past couple of months as my bouts of sleepwalking became more pronounced and my actual sleep time more elusive. So far, I never made it past my furniture without stubbing my toe and waking up from my dream state. I hoped I never made it to that clanging bell, my last line of defense before strolling out into oncoming traffic. Rubbing my wrist, I picked up fuzzy handcuffs and tossed them in the trash. That novel approach had only bruised my wrist as I wrestled with my sheets all night. Maybe I should've taken that ER doc up on her offer of pain pills, since I could really use a full night's sleep.

My apartment had once been my private haven from the rough and tumble of the DA's office and my family jousts. At my hairdresser's salon, I read a magazine article about the color blue's calming qualities. So I painted my entire living room in peaceful shades of blue and decorated it with little antique treasures I found at garage sales and consignment shops. Lately, between work and restless midnight sojourns to twenty-four-hour joints, I spent little time enjoying my place. I should have cooked dinner, paid some bills, or even wrote my congressman, but I flicked on my TV and collapsed on to my blue couch. Miraculously, I fell dead asleep.

The squad car soars airborne. Shrieks of buckling metal. Smashing into granite steps. Connelly plunges headlong through a windshield. Glass raining over us like hail. Blood gushes out of Connelly's nose, ears and mouth. A tangled seat belt chokes AngelEyes. His cobalt blue eyes burst out of his head and tumble into my lap. My arm rips out of its socket spurting blood all over him. Flames bubble from under Healey's squad car hood. Fire devours the front seat and I can't move. My body freezes in place and black smoke fills the passenger compartment. My chest heaves for air. Can't breathe, can't breathe. Gotta get out. Out.

I jerked awake, locked in that hazy space between sleep and consciousness. Looking around, my TV's screen roared with an infomercial on a wacky kitchen gadget. A brass mantel clock read three a.m. My shoulder had stiffened up and I reached gingerly for a clicker to shut off my TV. I dragged myself up to get a glass of water and pop a couple of aspirins. Only then did I notice a message alert on my cell phone blinking for my attention.

After dialing into voice mail, I put my phone on speaker as I puttered around my kitchen, filling a glass with water while listening to my messages. Three of my sisters called to see if I was all right. My sister, Fatima, the nun, was praying for me. My sister, Delia, a staunch atheist, told me she wasn't praying for me, but was sending positive thoughts my way, and reminded me to renew my website registration. Caridade, a real estate agent, wondered if I'd come speak at her next Rotary Club meeting. Good to see each of my sisters flying their respective flags. A message from my gal pal, Dr. Ronni, offered her services and remarked that I looked great stumbling around all those cute cops on our local news broadcast.

"Hope you got phone numbers from the single ones," she said. Always on the prowl, that Dr. Ronni.

There was a quick message from our office manager, Flora, about a morning meeting with O'Brien and telling me to use a heating pad. And on a less cheery note, my neurologist's office called to remind me about my next appointment. The final message was hard to decipher at first. A man's muffled voice with street sounds in the background.

"Montez, stop persecuting His angels. Fires of damnation will burn your courthouse of injustice to ashes. Stop the persecutions or die."

Nothing but the dial tone followed.

CHAPTER 5

A gentle squall of morning snow skipped around me as I crossed City Square in front of the Charles County courthouse. A smattering of protestors penned in behind blue sawhorses waved signs denouncing same-sex marriages, corrupt judges, and DA Quinn. A couple of bored cops gulped coffee as they watched over these buffer zones around our courthouse entrances. A line for security screening clogged the revolving doors leading inside. I flashed my badge and slid my briefcase onto a moving belt of an x-ray machine and passed through guarded metal detectors.

"Hey, nice job bringing in that loser, Monty," said a security officer who'd seldom acknowledged my existence over these past eight years beyond an indifferent yawn. "Everybody's pretty excited about it."

Strangely, I had transformed overnight into a minor celebrity at our courthouse, an incestuous community that thrived on any bit of juicy buzz.

"Glad he didn't kill us with that wild chase."

"Murdering his wife in a church." She shook her head in disgust. "Nail him good."

"Will do," I said.

Of course, he'd have to wake up before any official nailing could begin. I stuffed my badge back into my case, my shoulder growling in pain. Sore shoulders and death threats tended to work up my appetite, so I headed to Cranky Albert's newsstand for a quick tea and chocolate-chip muffin.

Albert wore dark sunglasses and sat on a tall four-wheeled stool. He whirled around on his stool to serve his customers. A lot of regulars steered clear of Albert Johnson, but I found him pleasantly crabby. No sing-songy "have a nice day." Just strong doses of coffee and straight Celtics talk. He'd lost his sight at age thirteen in a car crash, but he knew the game better than anyone.

"Hi, Albert. How's it going?"

"Well, well. If it isn't our very own action hero. You're the talk of this old place. Cracking open cop cars. And your first homicide," Albert said in a gruff baritone voice. "Monty, you know how to start with a splash."

"Thanks, Albert. Let's hope next time when we catch a murder suspect we don't put him in a coma. Might be nice to ask him a few questions first."

"At least he's not out whacking people over the head."

"Yeah, guess so."

I dropped a tea bag into a Styrofoam cup of hot water and squeezed in some honey. Strictly herbal. I couldn't afford an ounce of caffeine if I wanted to sleep again tonight.

"Listen to last night's game, Monty?"

"No. Too tired."

"Absolutely pitiful. Couldn't find the net all night. I could've done better. That team's never been right since Red passed." Albert punched the air with an authoritative index finger.

"So reading the sports page today is out?"

"Damn straight on that one," he said.

"Check your lottery numbers?"

"My wife did. No early retirement for us yet."

"How about the obituaries for a little amusement, Albert?"

"Nah. My mother-in-law's still alive. That's all I need to know."

I began to hear soft echoes of voices singing. Was it a hymn? Sounded like "Here I Am, Lord," a memory from my old catechism days.

"Do you hear singing?"

"Hearing voices? Maybe you knocked a couple of screws loose in that crash," Albert said.

Yet the singing grew stronger. A neat line of about two dozen men and women came around a corner and filed along a hallway from an overnight lock-up. They shuffled along slowly and sang loudly, mostly off-key. Everyone seemed to stop in their tracks to watch them walk past. Several people clapped.

"Bless all of you!" one woman shouted.

I noticed some familiar faces from past arraignments in district court for trespass and violations of court-ordered buffer zones. The police picked them up outside of their usual targets; strip joints in the Combat Zone, gay bars in the South End, and women's and gay men's health clinics anywhere, all signs—they claimed—of our nation's moral decline. A chubby guy, wearing a huge wooden cross tied around his neck with a leather cord, liked to shove his honking old school camcorder into people's faces. Two nuns carrying rosary beads handed out tiny plastic fetuses at clinic vigils. Another burly man in a white T-shirt with "Leviticus 18:22" printed on it distributed pocket-size green Bibles highlighting this passage and warned that AIDS was God's curse. I wondered if one of them was last night's mystery caller. I'd be damned if I had to change my cell phone number again.

"More protesters?" Albert asked.

"Yeah. It's only going to busier, you know. I heard Edgar Thompson's coming next week."

Edgar Macmillan Thompson, the founder and national chairman of the Center for American Values in Florida, made regular rounds on conservative talk shows and pricey lecture tours. His patrician wife Astrid, daughter of rich and influential financier Norwell Williams, often accompanied him. A tall, handsome man in his early forties, he cut a striking figure with a square jaw, full head of sandy brown hair, and penetrating green eyes. He was always impeccably dressed in Brooks Brothers' attire. A son of wealthy socialite Eleanor Macmillan and former Senator Vincent Thompson, he'd recently announced his Senate run in the Sunshine State with backing from their families' millions. Thompson came to this region annually to pick a few fat pockets of conservative friends and fellow alumni from his old Harvard Law School days.

Paving the way for his visit, his followers filled jail cells to hype his trip and heat up more acrimonious debates in the culture wars. I had faced Thompson twice in court on buffer zone violations when he spoke eloquently about preserving first amendment free speech rights. Otherwise, his organization's well-heeled lawyer, Lillian Harkins, a real ice princess from Harkins, Miller, and Sadler, did the honors.

"What a bunch of self-righteous pests. They're trespassing on private property. And putting a big drain on our system. Keeping cops from catching real crooks," Albert said. "What do you think, Monty?"

"They should be arrested for disturbing the peace with all that terrible singing."

I sipped my cup of tea. Cranky Albert loved a good fight, but like any good lawyer, I saw both sides of these issues. I appreciated the protestors' right to free speech, but also wanted to respect other people's privacy and life choices. Which rights should prevail? I didn't have a clue. But I knew death threats were never the right way to make your point.

Albert shook his head. "Keep playing it close to the vest and they'll put you on the Supreme Court, Monty."

"First, an action hero. Now a Supreme Court justice. I better go before my head gets too big to fit through those elevator doors."

I dug into my purse for some change.

"No, Monty. Keep your money. It's on me today."

I smiled. "Thanks, Albert. See you later."

"Be good now."

I headed for a set of nearby elevators and had to shield my eyes from a flood of TV lights and camera flashes. A gaggle of reporters, clutching microphones and tape recorders, swooped in on their prey. Quinn had tried to sneak in under the radar through a basement. A thunderous chorus of "Franks!" and "Mr. Quinns!" bounced off high ceilings as they yelled out embarrassing questions. Quinn merely smiled like a weary king acknowledging his lowly subjects as he slipped into an employee elevator. An unsatisfied media pack then pounced on one of his political aides, hammering him with pointed questions.

Baldy, one of the court officers, hurried toward me clutching a clipboard, his heavy ring of jailer's keys jangling wildly on his right hip.

"What a circus. Better find a quiet spot," he said.

He pushed me through a swinging door of a men's room and accidentally knocked my cup out of my hands.

"What the hell are you doing?" I asked.

Baldy looked quickly under each stall as droplets of sweat rolled across his smoothly-shaven skull.

"Got that Hernandez file?"

"Baldy, I'm not in district court anymore. You got to talk to that new guy."

"Oh, shit. Some green kid."

"Yeah. What's up?"

"We need to take it off the arraignment list."

"Why?"

"He's dead. Hung himself in protective custody."

"So much for protecting him?"

He shrugged and bailed out of the men's room. I bent over to pick up my squashed cup and felt a quick pinch to my butt. I didn't have to turn around. Six years after our divorce, I easily recognized that awful cologne. Ted Kiley.

"As fluffy as fresh dough," he purred. "You're still my hot little muffin."

Having found crumpled condom wrappers in his dirty laundry during our brief marriage, I knew my muffin wasn't the only one he had tasted. Yet I had to admit that he looked dapper in his European-tailored charcoal gray suit with a scarlet handkerchief sprouting from its pocket. A navy and crimson silk tie accented his white shirt, starched to perfection.

"Got to put this one in the next alumni newsletter, Teddy." I knew he hated to be called Teddy. "Hard to believe that you're slumming it in district, Teddy."

"I know you still miss me, Monty." A Cheshire-cat smile creased across his eternally tanned face. "And I miss all those sweet Portuguese goodies from your mom's bakery."

"Speaking of baked, what's with that tan this time of year, Teddy? Go easy on that electric beach or they'll be calling you prune-face in no time."

Kiley reflexively glanced in the mirror, trying to spy any hint of crow's feet. I grabbed my briefcase and exited with him tailing close behind me.

"Saw you on TV last night. Pretty dramatic stuff for your first homicide. Never too late to come work for me."

A shapely young blonde struggled with an enormous brown leather litigation case in the hallway. "Mr. Kiley. They're calling the list in Superior."

"Okay, Tiffany," he said. "That's my new paralegal. Looks

great sitting next to me at counsel table." Kiley smoothed back his dark hair and straightened his tie. "Lucky I ran into you. I've got a little something for you."

"Gee, and it's not even my birthday," I said. Not that he ever remembered it before.

He handed me a document.

"I've been engaged to represent Patrick Carpenter. Nobody talks to him without going through me. That's my motion to suppress anything and everything your boys took out of the son's home yesterday."

"You bastard." I flipped through his motion papers. "Thanks for wasting more of my time."

"I know you still love me, babe." He gave me a quick peck on my right cheek.

I watched as he stopped and pulled out his Mont Blanc pen to sign an autograph for a young woman who recognized him. Kiley caught me eyeing him.

"Look for me on the six o'clock news, Monty." He disappeared into a stairwell.

I shoved his motion into my briefcase and flinched as a muscle spasm shot through my mangled shoulder. My first case and Kiley planned to dog me. He'd pull out all the stops to embarrass our office, with the added bonus of messing up my mojo. There was no way I was going to let him get the better of me this time.

CHAPTER 6

"Car crashes and threatening phone calls. You are off to a hell of a start, Montez," O'Brien said, finally stringing together two sentences and calling me by my real name.

A dozen malasadas from my family's Portuguese bakery last week only managed to gin up a muffled grumble of thanks from him. Hard to believe that a box of oven-fresh fried dough rolled in sugar couldn't loosen him up, but my potential demise did a better job breaking the ice.

"Notify security and let Judge Newhouse's clerk know about it, too. His Honor will be pissed that someone's violating his injunctions again. Let him put a little fire under Harkins' butt about harassment and contempt of court."

As I walked back to my office, I heard O'Brien grumbling expletives as his nicotine-stained fingers leafed through a copy of Kiley's motion. I didn't need to wait for one of O'Brien's yellow sticky notes to know what to do next. I flipped on my computer and spent several hours plowing through the cases cited in Kiley's motion. I knew how to plant myself for hours in front of a computer screen until my eyes nearly burned out and my back throbbed from leaning over a keyboard. Nothing brilliant from Kiley, mainly pretty standard arguments about a lack of probable cause to search. A dead wife with her head bashed in followed by a merry jaunt through our city streets smelled like plenty of reasonable suspicion to me. I finished my research and hammered out a draft, handing it over to O'Brien for review.

It was time to meet Saint Cyr at Mrs. Silva's home. I made a quick stop in the ladies' room. Didn't want to look like a total mess next to AngelEyes during this interview. As I touched up my lipstick, a fire alarm began to squawk. I collected my stuff and stepped into a hallway filled with emergency strobe lights and honking alarms. Flora waved me over as she held open glass doors for lawyers and staff evacuating our unit. She possessed a million wigs to cover her graying hair. Today's puffy auburn wig sat tilted to the left, blown askew in the howling winds of an incoming nor'easter.

"No elevators," she cautioned, directing people to a stairway fire exit.

"What's happening, Flora?"

"Another bomb threat. They're clearing the courthouse. But O'Brien won't come. Says he's got too much work to do." Her brown eyes looked concerned over the tops of her half-glasses. "Stubborn old goat."

"Where does he stash his extra smokes?"

I figured he'd use this fire drill as a sweet chance to sneak a quick puff with the alarms already triggered.

"Behind some old copies of Imwinkelreid's *Evidentiary Foundations* in the library."

"You go, Flora. I'll get him moving."

I walked back to our small library and discovered two packs of Marlboros secreted behind the texts along with a half-drunk fifth of Red Label. I stood in his open office door while he read my memo.

"If you ever want to see Johnny Walker or the Marlboro man alive again, I suggest you evacuate now," I said.

He looked up. "You put those damn things back where you found them."

"Sorry, as an officer of the court I'm seizing contraband. No smokes and no booze on county property. By the time I hit City Square, they'll be dumped in a trash can or donated to some lucky homeless guy."

"You wouldn't dare."

"Try me." I turned on my heel.

A string of expletives followed. Knowing his beloved addictions and cheapo nature, he was sure to follow. In the plaza, I bumped into Flora chatting amiably with Albert out in the cold with everybody else, while firefighters and police searched our building for a bomb.

"Happy New Year," I said. I handed her O'Brien's Marlboros and booze.

A red-faced O'Brien huffed and puffed his way through the courthouse crowd toward me. An opportune time to head for my appointment with AngelEyes and Mrs. Silva.

Crayons and sketchpads aren't your typical interrogation tools, but I watched AngelEyes using them as he spoke quietly to Daniel Pazo, sitting in his grandmother's kitchen in their duplex apartment. Dozens of sheets of paper were strewn across the kitchen table, mostly pictures of dogs and cats in colors not normally found in nature. Daniel loved the rainbow colors of some of the *suspiros*—the sweet meringue cookies I'd brought with me. He gobbled them down with a glass of milk. His grandmother, Alice Silva, seemed tiny and a little frightened as she sat next to Daniel. Hard to fathom that one day you're dusting a church altar, and then the next you're smack dab in the middle of a murder investigation.

"I love to draw. I love to draw," said Daniel. He smiled broadly at Saint Cyr.

Daniel was a stocky man, with a large balding head, slanted hazel eyes, and squashed facial features.

"The work you do is beautiful, Daniel. *C'est magnifique!*" Saint Cyr finished a likeness of Daniel and handed it to him, to his apparent amusement.

"Any luck?"

"None yet. But we will keep at it," Saint Cyr said.

"Mind if we talk privately for a moment, Mrs. Silva?" I asked.

"Certainly, Ms. Montez," she said. As she stood up from the table, Daniel began to shout. "No, Gammy! No, Gammy!"

He jumped up from his chair and clung to her side. As she tried to soothe Daniel, he backed up into one of the corners of her kitchen and buried his face into his hands, repeating his chant.

"It's all right, Daniel," said Mrs. Silva. "It's all right."

"Don't go. Bad, bad, bad. Don't go, Gammy."

"I won't leave you alone, Daniel. I'll stay here with you."

She whispered to Daniel and gently hugged him as he towered over her. Her reassuring embrace soothed him.

"Daniel, we'll all stay here," said Saint Cyr. "We'll all draw with you, eh?"

"I love to draw. I love to draw," Daniel said, nodding.

In a few moments, Saint Cyr, Daniel and I were all drawing quietly at Mrs. Silva's kitchen table. As Daniel became absorbed in his drawings, Mrs. Silva offered me something to drink and we shared some remaining *suspiros* and spoke quietly in a kitchen corner.

"It's mostly been Daniel and me all these years. My daughter, Susan, had him as a teenager."

"It must've been difficult for her to be a mother so young."

"Yes, it was. Susan married Eddie Pazo, his father. A neighbor boy. He was in high school, too. At first, they thought they could handle it. But being kids, it got to be too much for them. They divorced soon after Daniel was born. Eddie moved away and my daughter never heard from him again. Her friends told her that she should've gotten an abortion. Not ruined her life with a bad marriage and a child." She covered her mouth with her trembling hand as if trying to silence her daughter's antagonists.

"Are you still in contact with your daughter?"

"My daughter was an unlucky woman, Ms. Montez. She died in a car accident two years after Daniel was born. He doesn't really remember her."

"I'm sorry. It must be very hard raising him on your own."

"I've had to make sacrifices, but I'm lucky to have him. He's my constant companion. Without him, I'd have no one. My daughter's gone, my husband dead before that." She stopped for a moment and heaved a weary sigh. "We have fun together. Go to church and the park. Wollaston Beach during summer months. Make pizzas together. Draw pictures. Most grandparents don't get to spend this much time with their grandchildren."

"Does he normally go with you to church in the mornings?" I asked.

"He does on Mondays. Other days he goes to a sheltered workshop at Beacon House. They're helping him with basic job skills. I'm seventy-seven and someday he'll need to transition to a full-time program. Their workshop is a start."

"My friend, Pete, likes to draw, too," said Daniel. "But he's not as good as me. He draws crazy messes, like you." He laughed and pointed at my Crayola masterpiece.

"Now, Daniel, be nice," said Mrs. Silva.

I nodded. "I'm not much of an artist like you or Detective Saint Cyr. Maybe you can draw me some nice pictures. Say, of Beacon House? Or St. Stephen's?"

"I like Beacon House," he said.

"I'd love to see a picture of Beacon House. And then maybe one of St. Stephen's where I came to know you and your grandmother," said Saint Cyr.

Daniel hesitated for a moment, then tore a sheet of paper from a thick drawing pad and drew once more in earnest.

"On Mondays, he helps me with my volunteer work for our altar guild at St. Stephen's."

"What kind of work do you do?" I asked.

"Clean and polish the candle holders. Tidy up pews. Wash sacred vessels. Lay out vestments for the next day's mass. Things like that."

"Do you work with anyone else on Mondays?"

"No. Only Daniel and me."

"How long does it take you to finish your work?" I asked.

"We're usually done within an hour. Then we catch an eleven o'clock bus to the mall for our walking group. And then for a cup of soup or a sandwich at Friendly's."

"Friendly's has yummy sundaes," said Daniel.

"What is your favorite ice cream?" Saint Cyr asked.

"Chocolate's the best." Daniel smacked his lips several times.

"I like very much chocolate," said Saint Cyr. "Maybe next time I visit we'll have some ice cream if your grandmother agrees to it."

Mrs. Silva gave Daniel's arm a gentle squeeze. "That would be nice."

Saint Cyr put down his pencil and joined us. "Did you see anything out of the ordinary in the church yesterday?"

"Nothing much, detective. I noticed that a Eucharistic minister forgot to put away some communion. Fred can sometimes be absent-minded. He left a ciborium on a side altar. So I called over to the rectory for a key."

"A key?" asked Saint Cyr.

"Yes, a key to the tabernacle. But their answering machine was on. Father Mac must've gone out after mass. I left a message and then went downstairs to a basement supply closet for new candles. When I came back, I found Miriam."

She stopped and tears began to glimmer at the corners of her eyes.

"Poor Miriam. And in God's house."

I pulled out a tissue and handed it to her.

"Thank you, dear. Very kind of you." She dabbed her eyes with it.

"Did you ever feel unsafe or uncomfortable in the church, Mrs. Silva?" I asked.

"I never gave it a second thought. I mean, if you can't feel safe in God's house, where can you?"

Fair enough, I thought.

"Did you know Mrs. Carpenter well?" asked Saint Cyr.

"We weren't close friends. But I saw Miriam and her children in church on Sundays. And on holy days, too. Cute little boy and girl. Miriam sang solos for our choir. Beautiful voice. She gave us a ride home a couple of weeks ago after a healing service. Her son's very sick."

"Do you know much about her husband?" he asked.

"I don't see him in church. Don't know him at all." She shook her head.

"Did you see Mrs. Carpenter in church during the week very often?" I asked.

"No. She wasn't part of our regulars. Mostly retired people who go to morning mass. That's why I spotted her praying at Our Lady's chapel."

"When did you head to the basement?"

"It was at ten-twenty."

"This is very important, Mrs. Silva. Are you sure about the time?" asked Saint Cyr.

"It was exactly ten-twenty, detective. I'd just looked at my watch right before I went into the basement. I was worried about missing our usual bus."

"How long were you in the basement, Mrs. Silva?" I asked.

"About twenty minutes. It's two floors beneath our main altar. Our church hall is right under the church, then a basement." She rubbed gnarled knuckles of her right hand. "And with my arthritis, it takes longer than it used to."

"Where was Daniel when you were getting more candles?"

"He was watering plants, detective. Lots of them on our front altar," she said. "A few poinsettias in the chapel."

"Did you hear anything unusual while you were down there?" I asked.

"No. But then, this time of year, that old gas furnace is banging so loudly, I can barely hear myself think."

"So you didn't hear anything up in the church?"

"That's right, Ms. Montez. Not a sound."

"Did you see anyone besides Mrs. Carpenter in church after mass?" I asked.

"No. Only Daniel and Miriam in the church." She paused and looked directly at me. "Daniel wouldn't hurt a fly."

"Don't worry, Mrs. Silva. He's not a suspect," I said. Considering the ferocity of the attack, Daniel would've been drenched in blood when the cops arrived. "Has he said much to you about yesterday?"

"I've asked. But he gets very quiet."

"I saw a ghost," said Daniel. "Oooooo. All in white. Just like Casper." He began to flap a piece of drawing paper in the air.

"A boy ghost or a girl ghost?" I asked.

"A boy, silly."

"Was he a friendly ghost, like Casper?" I asked.

He didn't answer and continued to wave a sheet of paper in his hand.

"Will you draw us a picture of Casper?" I asked.

"Oooooo. All in white," he said once more.

He began to rip up some of his drawings on their table. Daniel rolled one sheet into a ball and tossed it at their refrigerator.

"Daniel, stop that," Mrs. Silva said in a calm, but stern tone. "I'm sorry. He's a creature of habit and he's used to an afternoon nap."

"We should be going anyway, Mrs. Silva. We've taken up enough of your time."

"Thanks for sharing your drawing paper with me," Saint Cyr said to Daniel. "And these are for you." Saint Cyr gave Daniel his portrait and a sketch of St. Stephen's. "Maybe you can draw a picture of me or the church for us next time?" He shook Daniel's hand and gave him a sketch pencil. "See you soon, Daniel."

"Here's my card, Mrs. Silva. If you or Daniel remember anything else, no matter how small, you give us a call. Okay?" I slipped one of my fresh new business cards into her hand.

"Yes, I will. If anything new comes to mind."

"And if you think having him talk to someone professional will help, we can put you in touch with good people," I said.

"Thank you. I may take you up on that," she said, shaking my hand.

"'Bye, Daniel," I said.

"Casper's a friendly ghost." He giggled.

Saint Cyr and I walked outside and braced ourselves against a gust of cold January air.

"What means this Casper?" asked Saint Cyr.

"A chubby cartoon character who was a friendly ghost. An old TV show you can still find on cable."

"He thinks he saw a friendly boy ghost, eh?" he said rolling his eyes.

"I don't know. But at least we can rule out all of those girl ghosts," I shrugged with a laugh.

"He is our only eyewitness. Let's hope he starts drawing something besides Casper."

"I think it's time we talk with Father MacNamara, Gérard."

"He already spoke his statement to me yesterday afternoon. He was out on his morning walk after mass. Then went to visit the sick at area hospitals. Says he didn't see anything."

"The pastor may not know anything about her murder, but he said he's known Miriam since childhood. He should be able to shed a lot more light on the state of the Carpenter marriage."

CHAPTER 7

"Please call me Father Mac," said the pastor, greeting us in the rectory lobby.

He led Saint Cyr and me into his private parish office, tastefully decorated with crown moldings lining the off-white walls. An enormous Bible was propped open on a wooden lectern, next to tall bookcases filled with volumes of spiritual and inspirational materials. A round conference table laden with church brochures and copies of *The Catholic Sentinel* sat under a bow window. Heavy brocaded curtains were pulled back neatly on each side with maroon rope ties, revealing a hidden contemplation garden connected in the rear of the church.

His housekeeper brought us cups of coffee as we sat in stiff-backed chairs. He thanked her and then sat down in a leather chair behind a large mahogany desk. "My mother admired St. Francis Xavier. My parents named my older sister, Frances, so that left me with Xavier. As a kid, I got nicknamed Mac. And, thankfully, it stuck."

The pastor was a good-looking man and I wondered if his handsome features might easily lead some female faithful astray. He reminded me a bit of Father Steve, this gorgeous young priest who'd arrived at St. Anthony's, my childhood parish, when I turned fifteen. Father Steve wore tight jeans and college sweatshirts over his collar. Every girl in the parish went wild over him. Some girls openly flirted with him, but my youthful shyness and my strict parents wouldn't allow such behavior. Although, one time, I did make an extra trip to a confessional box to swoon over his sexy voice in the darkness.

"This is a terrible tragedy for the Carpenter family and our church community."

Father Mac's voice quavered and his blue eyes moistened. He caught himself and cleared his throat to continue. "I hope you can resolve this matter quickly. There have been enough tragedies for the Church in recent years."

Mostly self-inflicted, I thought, and easy to avoid if pedophiles had been bounced out rather than coddled. But I knew to censor my quick tongue. Kid gloves. We didn't need any more dust-ups with local Church officials.

"We're sorry about the loss of your parishioner and your friend," I said. "We appreciate the statement that you gave our officers yesterday. Please excuse our directness in asking follow-up questions about Mrs. Carpenter and her family this afternoon."

"Yes, I understand. I hope you recognize that I may not be able to answer some of your questions because of my obligations to my parishioners," he shot back, leaning forward in his chair.

"Of course, Father Mac. In light of priest-penitent privilege, we hope you will be as candid as possible with us," I said.

"Your statement indicated that Mrs. Carpenter and her family were good friends to you. How long ago did you meet them?" asked Saint Cyr.

"I've known them all of my life. Miriam and I grew up as next-door neighbors in Watertown. I had five brothers. Miriam was like a younger sister to me. Her parents were wonderful people. Hard-working, solid folks. They're both deceased. Spared this terrible tragedy."

"Do you know if her sister is back in town?" I asked. "We'd like to speak with her, too."

"I don't know. It's unlikely that Rachel would contact me. She's always been her own person. I've rarely seen her over the years."

"I noticed some recent photos of you with the Carpenter family in their home. Were they active parishioners?" I asked.

"Miriam and their children were. I was fortunate to become pastor of the church I'd grown up in. So many good friends, like Miriam, in our parish. She sang at my installation as pastor and regularly in our choir. Their children attend our parish school."

"And Patrick Carpenter?"

"He's not a regular parishioner. He keeps mostly to himself."

"But haven't you known him a long time through Miriam?" I asked.

"I first met him when he started to date Miriam in high school. They married quite young. Right after Miriam's first year at college."

"Did you perform the ceremony?" asked Saint Cyr, scribbling a few notes.

"No, I wasn't a priest yet. I'd kicked around for a few years after high school without much direction. Went off to Boston College later. Followed all of my high school buddies. Then in my last year, I received my call to the priesthood. One of my professors, Dr. Wakefield, encouraged me to go to seminary. Even helped me with my tuition. Miriam was already married and a young mother by then."

He pointed over at his diplomas hanging next to pictures of the pope and cardinal.

"Being Miriam's friend, did you approve of her marrying so young?" I asked.

"It wasn't my place to approve or disapprove."

His evasiveness would make him great at a deposition, forcing us to ask him just the right question to get any meaningful answer. "But as a close friend, did you have an opinion?" I asked.

"Miriam was a very intelligent, caring woman, Ms. Montez. She always dreamed of becoming a doctor. Earned a full scholarship to Harvard. Yet marrying and starting a family so young meant she sacrificed her dream. She would have been a great doctor. So smart, so compassionate."

"Do you think she could've done better than Patrick Carpenter?" I asked.

"One marries for better or for worse, Ms. Montez."

Unfortunately, from personal experience, I knew a great deal more about the worse than the better.

"Miriam took her vows quite seriously. A truly devoted wife and mother."

"Did Patrick show a similar dedication to his vows?" I asked.

"I believe he worked very hard to try to provide for his family. But he got caught up with running his business. Tended to neglect his family responsibilities at times."

"How so?"

"He missed many of their children's events. Parents' Night. Christmas concert. Church picnic. Things of that nature. His business seemed to dominate his life."

"Did Miriam or Patrick ever discuss the state of his business with you?" I asked.

"No, not directly."

Father Mac was beginning to turn into quite an artful dodger.

"How about indirectly, through your own observations?"

"I knew they struggled, Ms. Montez. Their children are on scholarship at our school. And we organized a bone marrow screening and family fundraiser in November to help with Joey's medical costs. I'm sure Joey's illness put a tremendous strain on them, both emotionally and financially."

"Were you aware of any other problems in their marriage?"

"Every family has its challenges."

"Could you be more specific?" I asked.

He paused and ran his fingers through his hair.

"Not that I can discuss."

I knew he was about to pull the priest-penitent privilege, but I asked anyway. "Since Patrick wasn't much of a churchgoer, did Miriam tell you anything that might help us with our investigation?"

"The sacrament of confession and pastoral counseling prohibit me from saying anything more."

"Did you think he might do violence against his family?" asked Saint Cyr.

"We're all capable of violence, but we don't all act on it, detective."

"Did you think Patrick was the type to act on it?" I asked.

"I don't know. I pray not, for their children's sake." He might as well have painted a target on Patrick's back.

"Any other thoughts or observations about their family life that could aid our investigation?" I asked, although I already knew his answer.

"No. It would be privileged. But I can tell you that this morning we discovered several sacred vessels and candlesticks missing from our church. And one of my hooded vestments, too. Perhaps Miriam surprised an intruder."

Saint Cyr jotted down this additional information. Before anyone could say a quick Hail Mary, Father Mac whisked us out of St. Stephen's rectory. He told us he had to leave for his usual rounds visiting sick parishioners, including Patrick Carpenter at Boston Memorial Hospital. When he put on his coat, I recognized an angel pin on his lapel, like the one found in St. Stephen's. "That's a lovely angel pin, Father Mac."

"Yes. A gift from a friend. A reminder of my guardian angel."

Where had Miriam's heavenly protector been yesterday morning? Probably chatting up Ginny's guardian angel about Lucifer's shortcomings.

As we picked our way around slippery ice patches toward our cars, Father Mac drove by us in a large black sedan.

"Not exactly a ringing endorsement for Patrick Carpenter," said Saint Cyr.

"He pretty much threw Carpenter under the bus. Seems pretty strange that he doesn't know much about a guy who's been married to his dear friend for nearly fifteen years. Except that his business and their marriage were in trouble. And that Miriam could've done better."

"Looks like he even thinks Carpenter is our man. That bit about the marriage vows made me wonder if Patrick had an extramarital rendezvous."

"Sisters talk. Miriam might've told her sister something. We gotta talk to her when she lands back in town," I said.

Only a few steps away from the Bomb, I felt a now-familiar tingling, then numbness in my legs and my vision blurred. I realized I was about to take an involuntary tumble. Instinctively, I seized hold of Saint Cyr's arm as my knees crumpled under me. He stopped me from falling hard on the slick pavement as I landed on my butt. He helped me over to my car and I leaned against the driver's side door.

"Are you okay? You looked like you were going to pass out, eh?"

"I'm fine. Probably some lingering effects from our car crash."

"I think I should give you a ride back to your office, Marguerite."

"No, I'm fine. Got dizzy for a second. It didn't help that I missed lunch today. All better now. I promise."

"Actually, I'd feel too much better if you let me give you a ride."

I smiled at his sporadic grammar-mangling. "Gérard, I'm okay. Nothing a cup of tea won't cure. Besides I'm heading for a doctor's appointment only about ten minutes away."

In reality, it was more like twenty-five minutes, but I didn't want AngelEyes to press the issue. I even entered it in my office calendar as a gynecological appointment knowing that no man, especially O'Brien, wanted any details about potential female problems.

"What if I follow you to make sure you get in safety there?"

"Then I'd have to report you as a stalker. I'm okay. I swear."

Saint Cyr didn't look convinced.

"Scout's honor," I said, holding up three fingers. So what if I'd never made it past the lowly rank of a Brownie?

"Scout?" He looked puzzled. "Ah, yes. Girl guides."

I could tell he was reluctant to let me drive off in the Bomb under my own steam, but I promised to call his cell phone if I got loopy. I didn't intend to give AngelEyes or anybody else in the DA's office a medical briefing on my Machado-Joseph's Disease, a rare genetic condition similar to Parkinson's with a Portuguese pedigree. Any hint of it would have deep-sixed my promotion to homicide.

So far the illness hadn't progressed beyond occasional unsteadiness, sporadic vision problems, and many sleepless nights lurking around my neighborhood's all-night coffee houses, bowling alleys and Laundromats. My neurologist wanted to run more tests to be sure, but it didn't look promising for me. I hadn't even told my family yet and I wasn't ready to weather the inevitable family drama that would unfold in its wake. Only Dr. Ronni knew.

In my neurologist's office, I leafed through stale magazines, trying not to dwell on this afternoon's battery of tests. I looked around at my fellow losers in life's neurological lottery. The preternaturally cheerful staff fought to counterbalance a waiting room full of moody patients who knew they were in varying stages of slipping away. Like any degenerative disease, no one could tell me how slowly or rapidly it would overcome me, only that someday, with deadly certainty, it would. Pulling on a hospital gown, I tried to concentrate on our interview and connecting the dots instead of the pungent smell of antiseptic and a cold tile floor under my bare feet. Thin tissue paper crinkled as I hopped on to a CT scan bed.

"You need to stay very still. So do your best not to move at all," advised a female technician in a glass booth.

I closed my eyes and took a deep breath. The motor whirred as the bed slowly moved into the center of a giant metal circle.

"Just remain as still as you can," she said. "It'll be all over before you know it."

That's what worried me. It would all be over before I barely got started. I couldn't be shaking or stumbling in front of judges and juries. And once my speech faltered, I knew my days as a prosecutor were numbered. But then everybody's days were numbered. I tried not to think about it as the machine clicked and hummed. Better to focus on those things I could control, like finding and prosecuting Miriam's killer. His days were numbered, too.

CHAPTER 8

I got into our office early the next morning, but not early enough. O'Brien already left a yellow sticky on my office door. "Sleeping Beauty woke up. Boston Mem."

When I arrived at the hospital, AngelEyes was speaking with a clean-shaven guy in cargo pants and a blue sweatshirt. As I got closer, I noticed a stethoscope around his neck and a brown ponytail tucked into the collar of his scrubs.

"I present you Marguerite Montez. She's also working on the case. This is Craig Ross, Mr. Carpenter's ICU nurse."

"Nice to meet you," I said.

Ponytail Craig. No white starched uniform for *this* nurse.

"You folks have more people working to lock this guy up than we have trying to keep him alive," he said.

"Murder has a way getting people's attention," I said.

"Like I told those other two guys, I appreciate your concerns. But this man's just awoken from a comatose state."

"We only want to ask him a couple of questions," said Gérard.

"He's still in critical condition and we don't want to risk his health."

"We'll be out of here once he tells us his side of the story," I said.

"He's been in a coma, so I doubt he can tell you much right now. Besides, only family members in ICU. Everybody else needs permission from his doctor or family."

"Is his family here?" I asked.

"Yeah, the grandmother and his kids. Along with Father Mac," said Ponytail Craig.

"Where can we find his doctor?" I asked.

"Connelly is already in his office talking to him," said Gérard. "And O'Brien's talks on his phone to Carpenter's lawyer now."

Kiley. He'd be dedicated to jamming things up even more.

"Mr. Ross, are you his primary caregiver here?" I asked.

"Yup."

"Do you mind answering a few questions?"

"Patient confidentiality. I can't tell you anything about his medical condition." He gave his ponytail a quick tug.

"No, not any medical stuff. More like your general observations."

He seemed agitated, but curious. "I'm about to take a smoke break."

A ponytail and a smoker, to boot.

"Mind if I tag along?"

"I guess. Why not? If you don't mind the cold. But nothing confidential."

"No problem. Be back soon," I said to Gérard.

Outside a rear hospital exit, a half dozen medical staff smoked in the freezing cold. An odd choice for people who probably witnessed cancer's deadly ravages on a routine basis. Ponytail Craig offered me a smoke, but I declined. I didn't smoke, except for my annual Garcia y Vega cigar on my dad's birthday, his favorite brand.

"Anybody else try to see him besides his family and Father Mac?"

Ponytail Craig took a quick puff on his cigarette. "Well, a sister-in-law blew into town late last night. She's a hoot."

"How so?"

"A real man-eater. Three husbands and tons of money and vacation homes around the world to show for it. She smokes these cool Italian cigarettes."

"Did she have anything to say about her sister's murder?"

"Not much. Said it all hadn't sunk in yet."

"What does she think about her brother-in-law?"

Ponytail Craig raised his hand in the shape of an "L" to his forehead. "Doesn't think too highly of him or the rest of his Carpenter clan for that matter. Thinks her sister really missed the boat in life marrying that guy."

"Does she think he's a killer?"

"You'll have to ask her. I was more interested in her foreign smokes and hearing about her villa in southern France."

"Anybody else stop by?"

"Some reporters were snooping around. Security kicked them out. And both of his lawyers visited a couple of times."

"He's got more than one?"

"Yeah. One guy who smiles like a lizard and wears way too much cologne." Ponytail Craig tilted his head back to blow out a cloud of white smoke. "And an anorexic blond woman."

Pretty odd for Carpenter to have two lawyers, but not two nickels to rub together.

"Was her name Tiffany?" I asked, thinking he might be talking about Kiley's paralegal.

"No, not a Tiffany. Lois or Louise, something like that."

"Did she say what firm?"

"Can't remember. She came by once really late. That walking Polo ad's been here the most."

"When he was comatose, did Mr. Carpenter ever cry out or say anything?"

"You mean like, 'I killed my wife'?" he asked with a snort.

"That would be nice. But any interesting ramblings?"

"He sometimes blurted out little bits of prayers."

"Prayers?"

"Stuff like, 'Hail Mary full of grace' or 'forgive us our trespasses.' Stuff like that."

For a person who wasn't much of a churchgoer, Patrick still murmured Catholic prayers.

"Did that seem unusual to you?"

"People say lots of things when they're out of it. One old guy, dying of colon cancer, yelled out the same dozen or so knock-knock jokes for two weeks solid in his sleep. Annoying as hell. Hate to sound cruel, but our whole staff was pretty glad when he finally bought it."

I smiled. "No angry words or outbursts about anything?"

"Not from him. But his mom and sister-in-law had some words out in the hallway."

"Did you hear what they argued about?"

"Not really arguing. More like trading petty insults and barbs. Pretty clear no love lost between them."

Ponytail Craig stamped out his cigarette and we headed back up to ICU. When we arrived, Connelly, O'Brien, and Saint Cyr were commiserating off in a corner. I thanked Ponytail Craig for his help, handed him my card, and then joined their sewing circle. A stiff white bandage remained taped over stitches on Connelly's forehead.

"How's your head?" I asked.

"Sore. But I'll live. How's your shoulder?"

"Still attached."

"Get anything out of the nurse?" asked Connelly.

"A little. Miriam's sister hates Carpenter. There's lots of tension between her and Carpenter's mother and family."

"Anyone question her sister yet?" asked O'Brien.

"Yeah," Connelly said. "I spoke to her briefly by phone. She came in from overseas last night. Offered to talk to us in more detail this afternoon."

"I want to be in on that one," said O'Brien.

"What about Carpenter's doctor?" Saint Cyr asked.

"Like most doctors, he's not in," said Connelly.

"I called Kiley's office to avoid any trouble on that end," said O'Brien. "Lucky for us he's not in either. We can give Carpenter's family a shot. Maybe they'll give us some info without Kiley butting in."

Around a corner, a fireplug of a woman with unkempt white hair and a red face that looked as if it had been scrubbed with a washboard marched directly toward us, looking ready to spit nails. "So you're the ones that nearly killed my boy," she said in a thick Irish brogue.

"Mrs. Carpenter?" asked Connelly. He put out his hand to shake hers.

She ignored his outstretched hand.

"Don't 'Mrs. Carpenter' me. You almost killed my son."

"Ma'am, we're doing our job," said Connelly. "Investigating a homicide."

"Investigatin' or causin' one?" she asked.

"Actually, your son almost killed us." Connelly pointed to his bandaged forehead.

"You're not in intensive care, now, are ya?" She waved a boney index finger in Connelly's face.

"Innocent men don't lead police on a high-speed chase."

"I doubt my boy was runnin' away from anyone. He's done nothin' wrong, I tell ya."

"Then you won't mind asking him to consider answering a few of our questions," said O'Brien.

"Questions? He barely knows his own name. Doesn't even recognize his own children. Thanks to you."

"No one wants to cause you or his children any more pain. We're looking for any information that might help us uncover your daughter-in-law's killer, Mrs. Carpenter," I said. "Answering a few questions might help rule your son out as a suspect."

She glowered at me as the wheels must have been grinding in her head. If she said no, she'd be admitting that her son was a killer. If she said yes, he might say something damaging.

"Okay. I'll answer your questions. But you'll have to wait until me and his kids are done with our visit. And we won't rush for you, neither." She turned on her heel and headed back into ICU.

One tough old bird, Mrs. Carpenter remained true to her word. She didn't hurry up for us and kept us waiting for over an hour. Long enough for Kiley to get there before we could talk to his family alone. As the elevator doors opened, Kiley chatted amiably with two tittering teenage candy stripers, fighting to keep its doors open for him. He walked slowly, relishing a chance to eat up more of our time.

"My, my. Three of law enforcement's finest here to question a comatose man. Hardly seems like a fair fight to me." Without taking a breath he extended his hand to Saint Cyr. "Ted Kiley. Attorney for Mr. Carpenter. You wouldn't happen to be a reporter for *America's Most Wanted?*"

"Don't go looking for your close-up quite yet," said O'Brien. His voice dripped with sarcasm. I knew he still smarted over losing that high-profile Beacon Hill Strangler case to Kiley last year.

"Gérard Saint Cyr, Québec City Homicide," said Saint Cyr.

"Calling in the Mounties? Seems a bit extreme."

"No, I'm here to learn more good police techniques," he said.

"I doubt you'll learn much of value from this group. Although there's still some hope for Ms. Montez." He flashed a sly smile at me. "Detective Saint Cyr, I'm sure we'll all get to know each other better in these coming weeks. But for now I'm off to see my client." He strolled into Carpenter's hospital room.

"That bastard. We'll never get to talk to his family today," said O'Brien.

Yet less than a minute later, Kiley came out of ICU with Carpenter's mother, who stood there for a moment collecting her thoughts. "I got nothin' to say to ya. You can come in once his kids finish sayin' goodbye to their daddy. But only for a couple of minutes. Mr. Kiley will be there to keep ya honest."

About ten minutes later a boy and a girl emerged from ICU clinging to Father Mac. Although about fourteen years old, the boy appeared much younger in his frail frame. Two deep brown eyes, sunken into his pale face, peered out at us. He kept pulling at a hem of a blue knit hat covering most of his bald head. His sister, with fiery red hair and red freckles, looked to be about ten or eleven. She clutched her brother's left hand and glared at us. Father Mac nodded and escorted the children and their grandmother to an elevator. They waited by its doors for several uncomfortable moments. I felt bad for his children, particularly Joey. It must be frightening and confusing for them to be in the middle of a murder investigation. I knew what that felt like.

I can still remember a nightstick rapping against our upstairs apartment door, surprising us all as we watched an episode of *Cheers.* I was petrified when a police officer asked my parents to speak with me about Ginny. He seemed like an enormous blue giant with a scary black gun in a leather holster. I remember nervously fiddling with my pajama shirtsleeve as he asked if Ginny told me about any trouble with her parents at home. Did she talk about any plans to run away from home? How did Ginny feel about school? Was anyone touching her in a bad way at home or school?

When he made no progress, the officer asked me to describe what way we came home from school every day. My heart practically burst out of my chest. I gave him what I thought my parents wanted to hear: Ginny and I always came straight home from school by walking down Cambridge Street, a busy roadway cutting through our neighborhood. But the officer sensed I was hiding something, so he asked if there were any special routes we took home from time to time. My parents glared at me. I could feel my face burn hot and tears rolled down my cheeks as I finally gave up our secret shortcut through some deserted mill buildings near the Charles River. My folks were clearly very upset with me, but said nothing in front of the police officer. *Ficar face*. We never spoke about that night again.

As an elevator light pinged down, Mrs. Carpenter and Father Mac guided Carpenter's children inside and its doors slid shut behind them.

"You can see Mr. Carpenter now," said Kiley. "Be sure to note his voluntary cooperation in your investigation."

"Cooperation, my ass," said O'Brien under his breath.

If Kiley let us talk to Carpenter, his client must have nothing of value to tell us. When we entered his room, the bleary-eyed man gazed into space and didn't register our existence. He lay buried in a white mound of blankets and pillows. Tentacles of tubes and wires crisscrossed his bed connected to three beeping monitors.

"Patrick, Patrick," whispered Kiley. "Patrick." On his third try, he tapped Carpenter's shoulder.

The man looked up at Kiley, his eyes glazed.

"Do you know who these people are?" asked Kiley.

He stared at us and then looked back at Kiley. Carpenter shook his head no.

"They're from the police and DA's office. Do your best to answer their questions, Patrick, okay?"

"Okay," he said.

"Do you know your name, sir?" asked Connelly.

"Patrick," he said, in a halting voice. "Patrick, right?" he stammered.

"Your last name, sir?"

He glanced at us and strained to remember, then shrugged his shoulders.

"I dunno."

For about fifteen minutes, things pretty much went this same way. Connelly and O'Brien asked him numerous simple questions, including basic facts about his life, family, and work. He couldn't answer any of them. We got absolutely nowhere in record time. It seemed damn convenient for him to lose his memory once he became our prime suspect. We decided to call it quits, but warned Kiley that we'd be back once Carpenter recovered more fully.

"Do you think he is faking a memory loss?" asked Saint Cyr as we stood in a hospital parking lot.

"Maybe," Connelly said. "We'll have to wait to see if this is a snow job."

"He's got motive and opportunity. Now you guys gotta find that murder weapon so we can tie this case up with a big shiny bow," said O'Brien.

"We'll talk to his dear mother and scour their house and yard again," said Connelly, pointing to Gérard and himself.

"What about his sister-in-law?" I asked.

"She's at some swanky downtown digs. Much more up your alley, O'Brien," Connelly said with a wink.

As he flipped through his battered blue notebook for her hotel address, a mischievous grin spread across Connelly's face. "Her name is Rachel Childs. O'Brien, I suggest you bring Monty to add some class to your team." He raised the pinky of his right hand. "She's staying at the Ritz."

"If only my mother could see me now," said O'Brien.

CHAPTER 9

Rachel Rogers Devereux Mazziotti Childs paced back and forth in a penthouse apartment suite, on loan from a dear friend wintering in Anguilla. Twice as large as Carpenter's home, velvet window treatments, gleaming crystal chandeliers, original oil paintings, and ornate Louis XVI furniture decorated this residence.

Definitely the kind of place that put you on your best behavior. I smiled politely and O'Brien squirmed in a stiff burgundy wing-backed chair.

"How grateful should you be to the man you lost your virginity to?" Mrs. Childs sighed and stared out a large palladium window with a magnificent view of Boston Public Garden. "She should've left Patrick a long time ago."

Her words sounded pretty harsh considering she spoke of her murdered twin sister. No weepy tears or swollen red eyes for this lean lady wearing an elegant black silk pantsuit. She wore the color of grief well, but appeared more annoyed than saddened by her sister's death.

"Marrying him was bad enough, if understandable at that time. Sticking with him all these years was absurd."

She smoothed her blond hair, swept back from her face in a perfect French braid. Sitting on an ivory settee, Mrs. Childs flicked off her expensive designer shoes. As she struck a match, she paused and watched it burn between her fingers before lighting up a long brown cigarette. An amethyst bracelet and an enormous diamond ring twinkled from her left hand.

She looked much younger than her twin, but then Mrs. Childs hadn't been burdened with any stresses of a sick boy, a shaky marriage and a doomed business. Her weighty problems likely revolved around finding exclusive designers for her spring wardrobe or redecorating her Aspen house in time for ski season.

"I know it's a bad habit. But I got hooked on 120s when I lived in Milan with my second husband, Maurizio. Santos Dumont. And St. Moritz, of course. My favorite."

Blowing out the match, she took a slow drag from her slim cigarette. It smelled like a dirty sock to me. I was certain that O'Brien sweated out not being able to light up one of his own ciggies.

"Any particular reason why you don't get along with your brother-in-law, Mrs. Childs?" asked O'Brien.

"Oh, please. He's an idiot. Although a handsome fool in his day. I'd hoped Miriam would have put him far behind her when she got into college. A much better life lay within her grasp."

Mrs. Childs knew she'd done much better than her twin, with two profitable divorces and her most recent widowhood from a wealthy shipping magnate. She'd managed to place a canyon's distance between her past life and her present social status. Her sister's murder must have threatened that comfortable expanse.

"Did you both go to the same college?" O'Brien asked.

"No. My sister had a very high IQ. I was the artistic one. She got a four-year scholarship to Harvard. I went to the Museum school to study painting on scholarship. We were from a poor family." She lifted her chin toward the ceiling and blew out a white ring of smoke. "I met my first husband, Henri, there. One of his paintings hangs in the Louvre. He introduced me to a more refined life. Too bad Miriam didn't go to Yale, outside of Patrick's orbit. My twin was book smart, but never very wise about men."

Hmm. On that score, Miriam and I had more in common than I thought. Mrs. Childs stood up again and walked back and forth in her suite.

"After a break-up with some college boy, she consoled herself with Patrick at the end of her freshman year. He got her pregnant. She dropped out and married him. Sacrificed her scholarship and her hopes for a bright future. I think the world of my niece and nephew, but Miriam could have terminated that unplanned pregnancy and stayed in school to become a doctor. Associating with a higher quality of person than Patrick Carpenter."

"Were you aware of trouble in their marriage?" I asked.

"From day one. They struggled at every turn. No marriage can survive under that constant pressure, "she said, taking another puff on her cigarette. "*L'amour fait beaucoup, l'argent tout.*"

"Excuse me?"

"It's an old French proverb. Love does much, money does everything. In my sister's case, she deserved more of both."

"Was there any physical abuse in their marriage?" I asked. "Father Mac suggested that Patrick might be capable of violence."

"Ha! Father Mac." She tossed back her head. "That ambitious little hypocrite. I'm surprised he took time out from his march toward becoming pope to speak with you. I wouldn't trust anything he'd say about Patrick."

"Why do you believe that?" I asked.

"He hated Patrick. Always had a thing for Miriam ever since we were kids. Ran off to become a priest when it became clear she'd never leave Patrick."

Father Mac in an old love triangle with the Carpenters? That sure helped to explain why he'd thrown so much mud at Patrick in our interview yesterday.

"There was no physical abuse to my knowledge. But I think Patrick liked to play boss. He held very old-fashioned views about men and women."

"Did you know that his business was failing?"

"It has been failing for years, Ms. Montez. I've wired them money numerous times." She plopped on to her couch once more.

"Do they owe you a lot of money?" O'Brien asked.

"She was my twin sister, Mr. O'Brien. Miriam didn't owe me." Mrs. Childs angrily crushed out her cigarette in a porcelain ashtray. She immediately lit up another. "We're family."

Alternating waves of agitation and sorrow seemed to wash over her as she fell silent. Maybe she was beginning to realize that her only living sibling was dead, brutally murdered and not merely wintering in Anguilla. Mrs. Childs got up and began pacing barefoot again.

"I gave them a great deal of money. I'm not sure why they're still having financial difficulties."

"Do you think Patrick had a drug or drinking problem? Or perhaps gambling or another woman that could have drained them financially?" I asked.

"Patrick's a lousy husband and a poor businessman, but he's no druggie or high roller. I'm doubtful about another woman. With his business in turmoil and Joey's illness, he wouldn't have much time for that."

"Any chances that your sister had someone else in her life?" asked O'Brien.

"Absolutely not! My sister spent all of her energies on her children and helping that dolt of a husband keep his business afloat. Joey's illness devastated her. Made her a bit crazy. Even desperate at times."

"What do you mean by desperate?" I asked.

"We'd all been tested. Her church even held a community bone marrow drive. But there were no donor matches. She was so afraid, frantic that time was running out for Joey. Even thought of having another child in hopes of creating a match. Right before Christmas, she even asked me if I would consider having a child with Patrick."

She paused and squashed another cigarette in an ashtray.

"Artificially, of course," she said, arching her right eyebrow.

"Did you agree to do that?" I asked.

"Although I couldn't stand Patrick, I love my nephew. I told her I'd think about it. We spoke a couple of weeks later and she told me to forget about it. Said she thought she found a donor, but didn't want to get her hopes up yet."

"Did she tell you who the donor was?" I asked.

"No. She didn't want to jinx things. Miriam was supposed to call me this week if there was a match."

Suddenly, Mrs. Childs stopped pacing and looked out a suite window as wispy snowflakes blew around outside.

"When did you last wire them money?" O'Brien asked.

"For his business?"

"Were there other monetary gifts?" I asked.

"I was helping them with Joey's medical expenses, too. Lining up some of the best specialists at Dana-Farber."

"Did you retain cancelled checks, Mts. Childs?" I asked.

"I have business managers that handle all my finances." Frowning, she picked up her smartphone and punched its buttons. "I've emailed them your numbers. They'll be in touch with those details."

"When did you make your most recent gift?" I asked.

"About three months ago for the business while they waited on some overdue reimbursements from a state subway project. I sent them $30,000. I would have been willing to give them more. Maybe Miriam was too embarrassed to ask, particularly since I was handling Joey's medical bills."

"Were there any other issues in their marriage?"

She spun around and glared at O'Brien. "Surely, Mr. O'Brien, a bankrupt business and a sick child are more than enough obstacles for any couple."

"True, but were there any other problems we should know about?"

"None that I know about. But then there's probably a great deal I don't know about my sister. We've lived very different lives."

"This may be hard to answer, but do you think your brother-in-law killed your sister?" O'Brien asked.

"I can't believe he'd do such a thing. Yet I never thought my sister would be murdered either. Stress can do terrible things to people. Maybe their troubles took their toll and he simply snapped."

She took another long drag on her cigarette and then looked squarely at us. "I keep asking myself, if he's innocent, then why did he run from the police?" she asked. "Why run?"

It was a damn good question, and neither O'Brien nor I had a good answer for her.

When we stepped outside the Ritz, piercing winds rolled off the green space of Boston Public Garden and rush hour traffic began jamming up on Arlington Street. O'Brien fumbled for his Marlboros and lit one up.

"She's a piece of work," he said, sucking in a deep haul.

"But she's credible and bolstering our case against Patrick. A bad marriage and financial troubles all cured in one fell swoop," I said.

"With all those loans, we gotta nail down reasons for his financial mess. Maybe some minor, but consistent, withdrawals to pay off a bookie or to tide over a girlfriend," O'Brien said. "I gotta go with Connelly to brief the deputy mayor. This case is generating a lot of political heat."

"I'll go back to the office and double-check his financials. See if I can figure out where all those loans went."

"Can't bear that dry stuff anyway. You dive right in and let me know what you find," said O'Brien, happy to unload any grunt work on me.

We agreed to split up as I could walk faster to Park Street station than O'Brien's car could thread through this traffic. I crossed the street and hurried along a gray asphalt walk wending through the gardens. As George Washington kept watch astride his granite stallion, the public garden slept beneath a wintry stillness, devoid of all its dazzling spring blooms and abundant foliage. Patches of brown grass curved around a frozen reflecting pool, summer home of the swan boats as I hurried across a stone footbridge.

My mind jangled with facts and figures as I rushed through the gardens to grittier Boston Common. I made it past a gauntlet of panhandlers and descended into the grimy bowels of Park Street's subway station. Why did Carpenter run if he was innocent? Why was his business still sinking after all of those loans? I knew the real story remained buried somewhere in those financials.

CHAPTER 10

I slid my card key through rear courthouse entrance slot and signed in at a security guard's desk. It was 5:30 p.m. and our normally jammed lobby was dead quiet. I headed up to my office, unlocked its front glass door, and flipped on a light switch. Every office door was shut tight. The place felt a little spooky as a copier softly hummed and a water cooler let loose an occasional burble. I unlocked my office door, dropped my bag and fell into my chair. I leafed through my phone messages. Nothing major. Without any interruptions, I figured I could work for a good two or three hours.

After two hours of rummaging through Carpenter's invoices to customers and purchase orders to his suppliers, I struggled to cobble together his messy paperwork. It didn't take an MBA to figure out why his business continued to fail: lots of expenses without much action on the account receivables side. Carpenter's customers weren't paying him on his invoices and, in turn, he wasn't paying his suppliers.

But what about all those hefty checks Miriam's sister sent to bail him out? Bank deposits into his business account were few and far between, too. Where did those wired funds end up? Mrs. Childs was already footing Joey's medical expenses and the Carpenters hardly lived a lavish lifestyle. Maybe I didn't have all of his financial data, or perhaps there were other accounts we didn't know about for his business. I called Saint Cyr and left him a voice mail message. Maybe he'd dug up more records from Carpenter's home or from his files at Hockings Construction's trailer.

I then reviewed their personal bank account information,

starting back about three years ago. That's when I noticed some substantial deposits and wire transfers into their joint account, possibly money Mrs. Childs sent them. O'Brien was right about consistent withdrawals. Every three or four months, wire transfers were made from his account to another account. All of the amounts were cleverly under $10,000.00 to avoid bank-reporting obligations. Over the past two years, these wire transfers totaled about $60,000.00. I needed to find out where they'd ended up. Maybe they were paying off some debts or trying to shield money elsewhere in case of bankruptcy. I called O'Brien and told him I'd follow up with Carpenter's bank and Childs' business managers about these transfers.

I looked at my watch, almost seven-thirty, time to go home. I rubbed my eyes and wasn't sure if my vision was blurry from reading those tiny numbers on all these records or a flash of Machado-Joseph's. Dr. Ronni warned me not to stress my nervous system so much with overwork. But I had a lot to do in life and not a whole lot of time to do it in.

Grimacing with soreness, I buttoned up my winter coat and stuffed a copy of *Lawyers Monthly* and some notes into my briefcase. Tonight, I was determined to finally get a warm bubble bath with a glass of wine. As I turned off my desk light, my office phone rang. I should've let it go, but it might be news on Carpenter's case.

When I picked it up, a harried voice said, "Oh sorry, I need to put you on hold for a minute. I gotta take this call."

It was my old law school pal, Susan. I never understood why people would call you and then put you on hold. It was rude, so I hung up. My phone rang again a few seconds later.

"Did you hang up on me?"

"How can I hang up on you when you're not even on the line with me, Susan?"

"You didn't forget about tonight, did you?"

I flipped through my desk calendar and groaned. Charles County Bar Association, 8:00 p.m., was scribbled on today's page. I remembered scrawling it into my datebook several months ago, hoping for a horrific snowstorm to cancel this event. I dreaded these deadly dull affairs and had more important things to do, like soaking in my bathtub.

"Is it too late to call the governor for a reprieve?"

"Don't back out now, Monty."

"Susan, you know how much I hate these things."

"You'll hate it even more when you can't pay your rent or have to bag loaves of bread at your mother's bakery. I read this morning's papers. Your man Quinn is twenty points behind in this week's poll. It's best to start networking now and not next fall when it is too late."

I knew Susan was right. But I couldn't bear all that aimless chitchat. Susan loved it and belonged to every legal organization under the sun. She sat on tons of boards, committees, and panels with important-sounding names that provided endless opportunities to exchange more business cards to pacify the insatiable god of networking.

"My shoulder is still killing me from that accident."

"Good. Go with that as an opening line. Then you can tell them all about your police chase, your car crash and being on TV. That'll generate some good buzz. You gotta strike while the iron is hot, Monty."

As soon as I promised to meet her at eight o'clock, my shoulder throbbed again. I trudged up Park Street like a prisoner heading for the gallows, disappointed to see the building for our county bar association still standing. Yet I needed to bite the bullet and go in.

In its main lobby, several bubbly bar association staffers greeted newcomers. Smiling young lawyers who looked like they were still running for student council. One grinning bar association gal behind a counter took my black coat and briefcase. I noticed an angel pin on her suit lapel that looked like the one we'd found near Miriam's body. "Excuse me. That's an interesting pin. It's an angel, right?"

"Oh, yes. I wear it every day."

"Does it have some special meaning?" I asked.

"Yes, it's to support a friend battling cancer. Although I know some people wear it for domestic violence and other causes like that."

"That's thoughtful of you," I said. "Where did you buy it in town?"

"They gave them away at a fundraiser. A local company

donated them."

"Do you know the company's name?"

"I can't remember it. But if you call Greater Boston Cancer Society they might know."

"Thanks so much. I'll give them a call."

It was a long shot, but maybe their customer list might help our investigation. She directed me to a table filled with "Hello My Name Is" tags. I wasn't big on them, but I promised Susan to play along with this silly ritual. I slapped a name tag onto my jacket lapel and went downstairs to a large function room. I glanced at a poster board on an easel announcing tonight's featured bar association speaker, a beaming photo of Kiley with a caption, "Winning Cases Through Broadcast Media." Nice going, Susan. I could've throttled her.

This place was packed with more than a hundred people milling around in a sea of blue and gray suits. Partners from stodgy Boston firms, polyestered politicos, and anxious associates were huddled together in groups of three and four. They balanced munchies on tiny cocktail napkins and sipped table wine or spring water from plastic cups. I watched Boston's legal movers, shakers, and rainmakers making small talk and circulating around in this stiff networking dance. Nobody was having an ounce of fun.

Susan coached me that networking is not meant to be fun. It's serious business. As a pianist played in a corner, I scanned the room looking for Susan, but she was nowhere in sight.

A speaker's rostrum was placed on the right side, so I bolted far left toward a food and beverage table. Round metal trays were filled with undistinguished arrays of ripple-cut cheese, dry crackers, and sliced raw vegetables encircling white globs of dip. It made me wonder what those expensive bar association dues were being spent on.

I fidgeted with my brand new card case, making certain to have some business cards at the ready. I amused myself briefly by seeing how fast I could pull it out of my pantsuit pocket, like a quick-drawing gunslinger in an old-time Western movie. On one last try, my card case slid out of my hand and burst open, my business cards flying out like a sprayed deck of playing cards. I frantically stooped over to gather them up. My face burned and my scalp tingled with embarrassment. A rotund attorney with wild curly hair waddled over to help me. His shirt buttons strained against the pressure of his ballooning belly. As he bent over to help me retrieve my business cards, his thick glasses slipped off his nose. I caught them before they smacked the tile floor.

"Oh, thanks. I think I'm all set." I quickly handed his glasses to him and picked up the last few cards.

"Slippery little devils," he remarked. As he adjusted his glasses, he stuck out his thick, sweaty hand and I reluctantly shook it.

"Harvey George," he said with a nod.

I wasn't sure if his first name was Harvey or George. I glanced at his name tag. It read "Herbert George."

Pointing to my name tag, he said, "My mother's name is Margaret, too."

"No, it's Marguerite, not Margaret. You can call me Monty."

He didn't seem to hear me. "Always loved the name Margaret. It comes from the Latin word for pearl." Barely taking a breath, he continued. "Few people recognize early linguistic roots of their names. Similar to many legal terms, Latin is the source for most names. Like Margaret."

"I think we have a bit of confusion here," I said.

"Oh, I know people have a hard time keeping up with me," he chuckled. "My love for nomenclature."

He waved a cautioning finger at me. "Remember, my dear, that words are every lawyer's building blocks. The raw materials of our profession. Upon which to build a strong foundation. Just as studs and screws are essential for carpenters."

I wasn't sure how to respond to a stud-and-screw analogy, so I simply nodded my head and prayed for Susan to appear. Dead silence followed, yet he filled the void in a flash. "My sister is also named Margaret. After our mother and our mother's mother. She recently went in for gall bladder surgery. Totally botched by her surgical team. Those idiots over at Memorial. A real malpractice lawsuit in the offing for Margaret," he confided.

"I hope your sister recovers soon."

Not my most creative response, but at least it beat saying I'm not Margaret.

"She'd better recover or those doctors will be sorry. I do medical malpractice. I'm a tough bastard in court. My firm blows away all that charitable immunity, nonprofit crap. Got all the best financial and medical experts at my fingertips. Here's my card." He handed me his business card, giving my hand a firm shake. "Very nice talking to you, Margaret."

I didn't have a chance to give him one of mine as he moved off to another group of unsuspecting lawyers.

"Harvey George," I heard him say again. "Edmund, now that's my brother-in-law's name. It is derived from a king and Christian martyr. Born around 869 AD..."

His voice trailed off. Harvey must have memorized a boatload of Trivial Pursuit cards. NameGame Harvey looked harmless, but he knew how to do the dance. He'd found an innocuous, all-purpose topic to start any conversation. A few minutes with each person on that name thing, then letting them know about his medmal and nonprofit specialties and his cadre of financial and medical experts, before ending with a critical business card hand-off. And then swing your partner, do-si-do. Excellent technique, Harvey.

I lingered at a drinks table, wondering if Susan would ever show up and hoping Kiley wouldn't. I looked up and saw the smiling face of Scarecrow Don. Don Bailey, Charles County's civil counsel, handled all of our county's civil lawsuits, everything from slip-and-falls to police brutality. Over the years, we'd met to discuss criminal matters that had overlapped into civil litigation.

"Hi, Monty. Quite a surprise to see you here tonight."

"Hey, Don. How's it going?"

"Great. I've been meaning to call you to congratulate you on your new job. Nice bump up to homicide. Good going."

"Thanks, Don."

I had to reach up to shake his hand, as Scarecrow Don stood over seven feet tall. In his early fifties, he looked like a modern day Ichabod Crane, all knobby knees and elbows. His shoulders were hunched over like a self-conscious teenager trying to compensate for his gawky size. "I see you're already drumming up some business for us. That car chase will end up costing the county a few bucks," he said.

"Don't tell me we've already been sued over that crash?"

"No, not yet. But give it a couple more days. Everybody and his brother will claim you guys sideswiped them."

I laughed. He dipped a couple of carrot sticks into a lumpy glob of dip. "I suppose you're here to get a closer look at Boston's most eligible bachelor lawyer, Monty."

"No, I've already seen Kiley at close range. He's better appreciated from a distance." Scarecrow Don looked a bit puzzled. Like many people, he wasn't aware of our short union. "Guess what? I saw you on video last week," he said, between crunches on carrot sticks.

"Me, on video?"

"Yeah, in a civil rights case."

"Which case?"

"The Center for Family Values versus everybody in Charles County. Some protesters claimed cops roughed them up outside the courthouse. They were taping themselves and you happened to be going inside in several frames."

"Those protesters outside our courthouse are taping themselves?"

"Oh sure. They tape themselves all the time at their protests. At the courthouse. Buffer zones at clinics, strip joints, gay bars. You name it, they've filmed it. Still using mountains of old VHS tape. Took us a week to dig up an ancient VCR to play a bunch of them."

"All that taping so they can make a civil rights lawsuit against our county?"

"Sure. Helps build their police brutality cases. Sometimes they use them to defend themselves in trespass or disorderly cases. And partly to piss off the government. They lose most times, but they keep appealing on First Amendment grounds."

"Who's taping them?"

"That fat guy with the big cross around his neck. I can't remember his name. But he's their big video freak here. They've got others, too. Different people in other parts of the country."

"Can't imagine where they're stashing all this stuff."

"Probably in some private bunker with their videos of Elvis and alien abductions," he said.

"Who are you up against in the case?"

"Ice Queen, of course. Harkins' firm is looking for big fat attorney's fees, too. Gave us a stack of bills during discovery. The Center's gotta be one of her best clients. Thompson's coming here next month to give a deposition in one of their cases. He's planning to speak to the bar and attend a bunch of other fundraisers."

Someone blew loudly into a microphone. "Thank you, ladies and gentlemen, for coming to our monthly bar association meeting."

Don glanced at his watch. "Monty, that's my cue to get outta here. My wife will go ballistic if I get home after nine." He grabbed several some crackers and carrot sticks.

"Drive safe."

"You, too. See you in court." Don squeezed through the pack, his head bobbing high above this crowd.

A knot of lawyers finally disgorged Susan, her standard forty minutes late.

"Where have you been?"

"Sorry. Clients love to talk my ear off. Why are you hiding over here? You'll never meet anybody this way, Monty."

"And this would be a bad thing?"

"You gotta be out there. Never know who you'll meet here. I bumped into a really interesting medmal guy already."

"Not Harvey George, by any chance?" I asked, laughing.

"No, I think his name was Herbert," she said. "Did you know that my name, Susan, is derived from a heroine in the Book of Daniel? She was falsely accused of screwing around and they cut off her breasts or something."

"Sounds like a solid medmal case to me." I rolled my eyes. "Susan, I'm out of here. My shoulder is killing me."

"Not to mention that Kiley is about to speak tonight," she said. "Sorry about that. I didn't know he was our guest speaker. You should stay to show him who's the bigger person."

"I'd rather show him who's the better lawyer in the courtroom. See you soon." I gave Susan a quick hug.

"Call me next week," she said.

I worked my way toward the lobby. As I reached a foyer entry, Kiley made his grand entrance with dear Tiffany in tow. His eyes lit up. "Fancy meeting you here," he said.

"So nice to see you again, Tiffany." I shook her hand and squeezed Harvey George's card into her palm.

"I'm about to deliver my speech. You don't want to leave

now, Monty."

"Sure I do. Besides I got some breaking news on Carpenter's case. Gotta go," I said, moving past him.

There weren't any new developments, but I enjoyed letting Kiley stew on that while he spoke to the bar association. My big plans involved a nice hot bubble bath and that glass of Merlot with my name on it.

But the parking gods were going to make me work for that hot soak. When I got home, a parking space about five blocks away from my place was my best option. As I started my walk home, I saw a familiar skeletal figure trudging toward me, lugging a bulging plastic grocery bag in each hand. Her plaid coat hung loosely over her slight frame and a brown woolen scarf was tied tightly under her chin.

"Mrs. Viera. It's me. Marguerite."

She looked up at me with weary eyes set deep in sunken cheeks. A chill tingled down my spine. Her uncle, Serafim, had set her up in one of his triple-decker buildings after Ginny's death and her husband's abandonment left her shattered and alone. Always a shy, nervous person, her twin tragedies pushed her into the shadows of existence.

"Marguerite," she said, barely above a whisper. A wan smile crossed her lips.

"Let me help you with your bags."

She briefly protested, but I wrested them from her hands. "Where's your gloves?" I asked. "Too cold to be out here without them.

Her bony, cold fingers brushed my cheek. "Always such a good girl."

We walked together quietly. I felt an urge to fill up the silence of shared loss that hung heavy between us.

"How are you doing?" I asked.

She shook her head and shrugged.

"Is Seraphim and his family doing well?"

"Okay, I guess." she said softly.

"I heard your nieces are both doing great in college. Dean's List."

"Sure. Smart girls."

"Glad that everyone's doing fine." What a dumb response. "Are you going to that church fundraiser on Friday?" I knew she seldom left her home, but I couldn't stop myself from saying stupid things.

Mrs. Viera shrugged again. Her apartment was less than a block away from my car, but it seemed like an excruciatingly long walk that night. As we approached her building, she pulled her keys out of her pocket, her hand trembling slightly. Unsteadily, she climbed her front steps and had trouble sticking her keys into her entryway lock.

"Can I help you bring these bags inside?"

"No, it's okay," she replied.

As she opened her door, I reached over and put her bags inside a main hallway.

"Thank you." She patted my shoulder.

As she was about to disappear behind her door, I said, "I still wear it."

Reaching down beneath my scarf and blouse, I pulled out a miraculous medal of St. Anthony, the patron saint of Portugal. Ginny wore it when we received our First Holy Communion together. I remember Ginny in her lacy white dress with a tulle veil and white stockings, clacking the heels of her shiny white patent leather shoes. After Ginny's funeral, Mrs. Viera gave it to me as a keepsake.

Her slender fingers reached out to touch Ginny's medal. Pressing it to her cheek, she closed her eyes for a few wrenching moments. She opened them and then gently draped Ginny's medal back over my scarf.

Once more, she stroked my cheek with her icy fingertips. "Always such a good girl." She gently closed her front door.

Unfortunately, I wasn't a good enough girl the day Ginny disappeared. I'd stayed home from school, pretending to be sick to avoid a really tough math test. I wasn't there to walk Ginny home from her school dance rehearsal, like I usually did. When Ginny didn't come home, Mrs. Viera knocked on everyone's door looking for her. No one had seen Ginny, and I was too afraid to tell her about our special shortcut.

That night, the police came knocking, too, and ultimately found one of her dance shoes and torn material from her backpack in one of those decrepit structures. Perhaps if I had gone to school she would never have been abducted? Maybe if I had walked her home, we could have fought off an attacker together? Or if I had spoken up earlier, Ginny might still have been rescued alive?

With each step back to my apartment, I continued to bludgeon myself with an endless stream of "what ifs." I knew I could play this game with myself all night long. And my biggest fear was that I would.

CHAPTER 11

Morning brought another yellow sticky scribbled in O'Brien's handwriting. It read, "Score one for the good guys." I pulled it off a court memorandum sitting on my desk and glanced through it to the last page. Denied. Oh, such sweet words. Denied. Denied. Judge Walters denied Kiley's motion to suppress the stuff we had hauled out of Carpenter's home. Score one for the ex-wife, too.

O'Brien went kicking and screaming to the three-day regional prosecutor's meeting in Worcester, so I decided to follow up on Carpenter's financials. Working from a list of twenty companies listed on his purchase orders and invoices, I started making calls or paying visits to his vendors, from office supplies to equipment rentals and explosives.

His angry suppliers wished Carpenter, and not his wife, had been killed. They couldn't shed any light on his personal life, but his mounting financial troubles continued to provide a million good reasons to kill his wife.

After two days, only Riddell Brothers Demolition, which sold explosives and detonators to Carpenter, remained on the list. I didn't know much about explosives, except that Wiley Coyote tried to blow up the Roadrunner with ACME explosives every episode. We played telephone tag, and the owner eventually left me a voice message to come by their offices in the afternoon.

On the way over, I stopped at Mrs. Silva's home. Nobody home, so I stuck my business card in her screen door and went looking for the Riddell Brothers in Charlestown. I hoped the Riddells could educate me about Carpenter's purchases of dynamite and the discrepancies in his paperwork.

It wasn't easy to find 1010 Egan Way—no street sign, no number on the building, no markers to suggest that anybody even used the building anymore. I pulled into a gravel parking lot between 1008 and 1012 Egan Way. Rocks pinged off the Blue Bomb's hubcaps and rear fender.

I looked up at a tumbledown five-story brick warehouse near the Charlestown docks with rows of window arches boarded up with wooden planks. On one side, chipped white paint read Worthingstone Textiles—in a region where the textile industry had died or headed overseas decades ago. The gray mortar crumbled from its worn walls with tons of graffiti scrawled over the old warehouse at street level. It could be mistaken for your friendly neighborhood crack house.

I guess it made sense to store explosives in a building that already looked like it had been bombed.

As I pulled around the back, I noticed a metal door adjacent to a loading dock, its skirting dented and scraped from years of sloppy truck deliveries. A couple of video monitors whirred quietly above the door and the loading dock. I rang the doorbell beside the steel door under a hand-written company sign attached with duct tape. No one came to the door for at least a minute, but I got the eerie sense of being watched through a tiny peephole.

"Yeah?" The voice boomed out over a crackling intercom to the left of the door.

"I'm Marguerite Montez from the Charles County District Attorney's office. You left me a message earlier today about your dealings with Patrick Carpenter."

"Badge?"

I pulled out my badge, the kind most ADAs used to get out of traffic tickets.

"Higher."

I raised the badge high over my head. An anemic buzzer sounded and I pushed open the steel door. Right in front of me, a short nebbish with thinning red hair and Coke-bottle eyeglasses stood wearing a rumpled tan shirt with khaki pants that were too long on him, his arms folded across his paunch. The inside of the building seemed surprisingly clean, with only a hint of the musty smell of mildew. Endless rows of neatly stacked boxes about 15 or 16 feet high surrounded a glass-enclosed office.

"Warrant?"

"No."

"No warrant, no luck."

"I'm working on the Carpenter homicide, Mr. Riddell. Trying to run down some information on Mr. Carpenter's business practices. I thought you might prefer to handle this more informally. Avoid any bad publicity."

"It's not Rye-dell, it's Rid-dell. Like the farmer in the dell. Doug Riddell."

Okay, Dynamite Doug.

"Sorry about that, Mr. Riddell," I said, making sure I pronounced it correctly. "Our office needs your help to find a local mother's killer. Make sure we have the right man, and not leave a murderer running loose in the community."

He scratched his head, and then stuck his hands in his pockets. I smelled the wood burning as Dynamite Doug mulled over how to respond. "Carpenter didn't blow up his wife so I guess I got nuttin' to hide. But make it quick 'cuz I got a ton of computer work to do."

"No problem. Just a couple of questions."

He led me into his office and he settled into a lumpy brown chair while I sat on a beige plastic one. Dynamite Doug looked even more slight when he sank into his. I pulled a dozen unpaid invoices for explosives from Carpenter's records out of my briefcase.

"Patrick Carpenter listed your firm as the supplier of dynamite and detonator caps on these invoices to the subway project. Can you confirm the purchases?"

He examined the invoices for a minute, pushing the steel frame of his glasses up on his nose once or twice. Then Dynamite Doug separated the invoices into two stacks. "These five, maybe, but not these other ones."

"Are you sure?"

He glared at me for a moment. "I'm sure. We only do dry and these ones are for wet."

"Dry? Wet?" I asked.

"Explosives."

Dynamite Doug rolled his eyes and sighed. "Two basic kinds. Dry and wet. We only sell dry. That's all Carpenter can order from us. And the detonator caps ya need to explode the stuff."

"And what about the wet?"

"Don't carry it. Too unstable. Ya keep it too long, it starts to break down and ya can blow yourself up if ya knock it over. And I like havin' all my limbs."

Dynamite Doug wiggled the fingers of his left hand. I couldn't argue with him on that point.

"Do you know who he might get the wet stuff from?"

"Not too many guys gotta license to sell it. I'm sure ya can run it down."

"Can you confirm if he ordered any dry dynamite from you?"

"Read out his purchase order numbers and I'll check my files."

I read out each number and only one of them turned up in Riddell's files. Perhaps Carpenter had been shopping around for his explosives and mixed up his suppliers' names.

"Do you or your brothers know who else he might order the dry stuff from?"

"I'm an only child, miss."

"Then who are the Riddell Brothers?"

"Made it up. People like to do business with a family-owned place. Decent service at decent prices from decent family people."

Hard to believe that anybody might need to feel warm and fuzzy about dealing with a family that helped people blow stuff up. "Any thoughts on who might have sold him the stuff?"

"No idea. But it kinda surprises me. Most guys stick with one wholesaler for discounts. Carpenter coulda gotten a bigger discount if he ordered more through me. But who knows?" he added with a shrug.

"Was he a good customer?"

"Good enough. Always paid on time. Never made fun of my ties," Dynamite Doug said. He flapped the end of his tie, decorated with two electric green palm trees.

"So he didn't owe you any money?"

"Nope. Not a dime."

Riddell may've been one of the only suppliers Carpenter didn't owe money to on the planet. "If we checked his inventory, could we figure out who might've sold him that dynamite?"

"Maybe. But not all dynamite has a tracer. Lots of manufacturers use a chemical signature that's a bit different in each batch, which might let ya know who the source is."

"And manufacturers can tell us what wholesalers they sold it to?"

"Unlikely. Their batches get sent all over the place, so it'd be tough to know exactly what batch went to which wholesalers. Should be able to figure out who made that stuff, but it'll be tougher to figure out who sold it to him."

"Do you think he could get his hands on dynamite illegally?"

"I got no idea. I don't operate that way." Dynamite Doug straightened up in his chair.

"I'm sure you don't, Mr. Riddell. But you've been around this industry for a while, haven't you?"

"Twenty-seven years."

"You look like a man in the know to me," I said. It didn't hurt to stroke his ego if it meant finding a killer.

He relaxed back into his chair. "I'm definitely a guy in the know."

"You must've seen a lot. Heard a lot from other people?"

"I know all the ins and outs of this business."

"How else might Carpenter get some dynamite that would be tough for us to track down?"

He sat quietly for a moment, and pushed his glasses up the bridge of his nose. "Hypothetically speaking, Carpenter might know some guys who found some stuff in an unlocked truck or came upon a couple of boxes that fell off a loading dock or somethin' like that. These guys might sell it to him for a cut-rate price since they found it and all. And then Carpenter decides to charge his customer, like the subway project, full freight." He had a knowing smile. "Or maybe Carpenter plays middle man and when he gets his discounted stuff he sells it illegally to some unsavory types at a premium. And he might dummy up some purchase orders for these explosives and invoices to his customers to make it all look legit."

Perhaps dealing in stolen explosives and drawing up fake invoices or ripping off the subway project might explain why Carpenter ran from us.

"Do you think he might be successful enough in his legitimate business that he could afford to pay for his dynamite orders without being reimbursed immediately by the state or his other customers?"

Riddell let out a snort. "Maybe you're not familiar with business. Ya go broke if ya don't collect on your customer invoices."

None of this added up as I tried to sort it all out on my way back to the office. Carpenter should have been rolling in the dough. He wasn't paying most of his bills, except Riddell's, and likely overcharging the state thousands of dollars or selling hot goods at sky-high prices. Plus he's draining his rich sister-in-law of wheelbarrows full of money.

Where did all that money go?

I went back to the office and cranked out the day's events in a detailed memo for O'Brien. Perhaps Harvey or Herbert George might be willing to have his experts do some *pro bono* work for the DA's office.

I spent more time poring over Carpenter's business records and then remembered that I hadn't heard back from Saint Cyr about any remaining business or financial records. I checked my watch, awfully late, but I needed to nail down that information. I dialed his number. "Hey, where are my business records?" I asked when he picked up his line at the homicide unit.

"Hello. I'm fine, thank you. And how are you, too?"

I wasn't in the mood to joke. "Fine. Find any additional business records? I'm trying to catch a murderer here and I'm not getting much help from the police."

"I spent all day napping on my grandma's Chesterfield while you were enjoying reading invoices and purchase orders."

"A Chesterfield?"

"I mean a couch. And I am only poking fun. We, the police, were freezing our butts off questioning the whole lovely church people, searching Carpenter's home once more, and beating those bushes for a murder weapon."

"Any luck on our murder weapon?"

"No, but those bushes said to tell you *bon jour*."

I laughed. AngelEyes had a sweet sense of humor to go with those gorgeous baby blues. And he knew how to say my name right.

"We did find one strange thing. A key hidden under that

Virgin Mary in their backyard."

"Any chance it's a spare house key?" I asked.

"No, it didn't fit any of their door locks or any file cabinet in their home office. Our lab's running it through some databases right now."

"How about Hockings' trailer?"

"Didn't have a chance to go back there yet."

"Any interest in meeting me for a dark, secluded rendezvous?"

"Sounds intriguing."

"It is. How about going to your property office, and grabbing those spare key to Hockings' trailer to make sure we cleaned out all of Carpenter's business files?"

"It's seven o'clock, woman. Don't you ever rest?"

"I'll rest once I know we've got all of his records in our custody."

"We removed his file drawer from that trailer already, Marguerite."

"I've still got gaps in Carpenter's paperwork and maybe those files got accidentally mixed in with some of Hockings' legit files.

"Ah, Marguerite."

"And to sweeten my offer, I'll even buy you a lovely dinner beneath the Golden Arches. Bet you haven't eaten dinner yet."

"Can't it wait 'til tomorrow?" he moaned. "I'm drowning in paperwork."

"If you're too busy tonight, I'll go to an unlit scary place all by myself and then they'll find my body in a shallow grave. Think of all that paperwork."

He sighed. "Okay, but you're driving and you're buying."

On our ride over to Hockings' trailer, I filled Saint Cyr in on my visit with Riddell. I drove up a rutted road to the trailer and parked near a concrete stanchion. Saint Cyr suddenly reached over and turned off my car lights. "Shut off your car," he whispered.

"What's wrong?" I asked, switching it off.

"I thought I saw a flash of light up ahead."

We sat for a minute in my car peering in the trailer's direction.

"Look. I think somebody's inside that trailer," he said.

I scanned the dark and saw a narrow beam of light bouncing off the trailer's inner walls. Somebody prowled inside with a flashlight. Maybe one of those shady guys Riddell mentioned to me, trying to cover his tracks.

"Best for me first to look, eh? Stay here," said Saint Cyr. "Call for help if trouble shows up."

Saint Cyr opened the car door and stepped out into a bitterly cold night. The wind howled as it whipped down from a rusty steel overpasses. Roaring traffic on the overpass above us grew deafening. Saint Cyr crept up to an anchor fence and pulled its shackled gates far enough apart to squeeze through them.

As Saint Cyr neared the trailer, I noticed another flicker of light coming from the construction tunnel a couple hundred yards behind the trailer. I pulled my cell phone out of my purse and started to press 911. The phone blinked on and off. No service. Oh, great. I couldn't stop Saint Cyr as he neared the foot of the trailer. As it looked like I'd be Saint Cyr's only backup, I had to grab something, some kind of weapon. I flicked on a tiny pen light at the end of my key ring and slipped out of the car.

My Blue Bomb's trunk creaked as I opened it. I pulled up its felt pad and struggled to free a tire iron from the well. It wouldn't budge, frozen into place. A souvenir wooden bat from a Red Sox game was the only other loose item in my trunk. It would have to do. I crept up to the gates and squeezed through them, scraping my right cheek. I hid behind a Bobcat about twenty feet from Hockings' trailer as I watched Saint Cyr make his way up a front set of trailer steps. Before I could warn Saint Cyr about this second intruder, he kicked in the trailer door.

"Police, freeze!"

I heard yelling and several loud crashes coming from inside. I dashed to the opposite end of the trailer and stuffed my pen light into my jacket pocket. A body flew out of the door and over a front railing. I squinted around a corner into the darkness, trying to make out a figure moaning in pain on the ground. A flashlight in the tunnel clicked off and I heard the second intruder's running footsteps. As they grew closer, I raised my arms high above my head. I had to time this right.

When he ran around the trailer corner, I stuck out my foot and he fell hard. I whacked him over his head several times with my miniature bat, using every ounce of my strength. He groaned and fell silent. I nudged him to his side, and a backpack rolled off his shoulder to the ground. I pulled the ski mask off of his face. He was bleeding, but still breathing.

Suddenly I heard the trailer door squeak shut. I fell tight against an outside trailer wall with my heart charging and my breathing clipping along at a furious pace. I didn't move as I listened to someone saunter down the trailer's metal steps. As he rounded a corner of the trailer, I lunged out like a wild animal and nearly cracked Saint Cyr's head with my bat. He caught my swinging bat with his hand as I crashed into him. We both tumbled to the ground together with a thud. I couldn't tell if we were laughing or crying in relief as tears rolled down our cheeks.

CHAPTER 12

It must have been a comical sight for anybody walking past Connelly's office.

We all sat in one line on a long bench, like kids outside a principal's office waiting for detention for brawling during recess. I thought of Ginny and me sitting outside the principal's office, sentenced to a humiliating week on our school's detention bench for hitting classroom windows with snowballs.

I had a feeling striking a federal officer came with a tougher punishment.

On one end, Saint Cyr had his head back, holding a wet cloth to sop up a bloody nose. On the other end, one of the Feds juggled a lopsided ice pack on the back of his head—where I had smacked him with my souvenir Red Sox bat. And another agent had taped up his badly cut knee, courtesy of Saint Cyr flipping him over Hockings' trailer stairs. I got away pretty lightly with a minor scrape on my cheek from that gate, but I assumed O'Brien was going to kill me tomorrow for causing this entire ruckus.

Connelly had been beeped about a half-hour before and came lumbering into the homicide unit looking a little disheveled and a whole lot pissed. He walked over and stood in front of us and surveyed our sorry situation with his hands on his hips. "What the hell were you doing at Hockings' trailer?"

Before Saint Cyr or I could mumble an apologetic reply, I realized that he was barking at those ATF guys. They looked at each other and said nothing.

"Are you guys deaf?"

Again, neither of them answered.

"Well, you sure as hell can't read. What part of that yellow crime tape didn't you understand?"

They said nothing.

"You guys are really pissing me off. Maybe if we put you in one of our holding cells with tonight's collection of riffraff until we can verify your ATF IDs, which might be some time next week, then maybe you'll have something to tell us."

Connelly motioned angrily to two duty cops to come over to them. "Cuff these idiots. Book 'em for tampering with a crime scene and obstruction of justice."

The Fed with the cut-up knee finally piped up. "You can't be serious."

"I'm dead serious, asshole." Connelly pointed his index finger right into this ATF agent's charcoaled face. "Throw 'em in the most crowded holding cell we got until their memory returns or until their owner comes to pick them up."

He wasn't screaming at me, but the anger in his voice made me nervous. I'd never seen Connelly like this, and I was glad he was on our side.

"Their owner is here," a voice said from across the room. "And they know better than to speak without my permission."

Connelly turned around and his eyes locked on a tall man in his early fifties. His close-cropped black hair sharpened his pale, angular features. He must have been a military man at some point: he stood ramrod straight in his crisp white shirt and black suit. He held a slim leather portfolio in his right hand. For a moment, I felt as if I should snap to attention and salute. He pulled his badge out of his coat pocket and showed it to Connelly. "Stephen Nolan. ATF. New England bureau chief."

Connelly snatched the badge out of his hand, but didn't look at it. "So you're the moron who's got his people trampling all over my crime tape."

"Trampling? No. Protecting? Yes."

"Don't play cute with me," Connelly shot back. He tossed Nolan's badge back to him. "What were your people doing crawling all over that construction trailer?"

Nolan caught his badge and took his time placing it back into his vest pocket. "Perhaps you have a place where we can speak privately?"

"Yeah, yeah," said Connelly. He pointed toward his office behind us.

Connelly slammed his door so hard that its paper-thin walls shook against the backs of our benches. While those ATF guys glowered at us, I tried to hear the conversation inside Connelly's office. I caught fragments of Connelly's angry words, but strained to pick up this ATF chief's softer tones with no luck.

About fifteen minutes later, Nolan walked out of Connelly's office and signaled to his men. "Get up. We're leaving."

One agent limped slowly behind Nolan. The other one groaned as he got up, still holding a soggy ice pack to his head. As they reached the edge of the homicide unit, this guy turned and threw his melting ice pack at me.

I ducked and it struck a wall behind me and fell dripping onto the floor.

"Watch out who you hit with bats, bitch."

"Maudit bâtard!" yelled Saint Cyr. He bolted up to chase that guy down, but I grabbed his arm and stopped him. "Hey, ignore him."

"That bastard tried to hit you."

"He's just trying to scare me. It's okay."

"No, it's not. I should tear off his head."

"It's fine. He missed. Don't worry."

I tugged at his jacket to get him to sit down again. Who said chivalry is dead? At least the kind that focused on yanking off a jerk's head still bumped around.

"It's no problem. Really," I said.

Saint Cyr eased up for a moment. "You sure, eh?"

"Yeah. Besides, I still got in my best shots."

Saint Cyr looked at me and broke into a gorgeous smile. That smile, AngelEyes. Too bad I'd sworn off any more men in this lifetime. "How's your nose?" I asked.

"I think it has run dry."

He dabbed some stray drops of blood from under his nose. "Thanks for your tea towel. I will repay you for saving my head from a bullet."

"Anytime."

"Too bad she didn't help you duck that punch." Connelly stood outside his office door with his arms folded across his chest.

"Looks like Monty's the only one in the bunch who knows how to bob and weave."

"Guess all that law school training finally paid off."

"Guess so," he said, waving us into his office.

I thought for sure that he would instantly chew us out. But he had returned to his old calm self again, asking us about what had led us back to Hockings' trailer. I told him about the inconsistencies in Carpenter's paperwork that I'd found, and my visit to Riddell Brothers. I said I wanted to go back to see if we missed anything in our first sweep and that Saint Cyr offered to go there with me for protection.

"Monty, when were you going to tell me about all this?" asked Connelly.

"I didn't want to say anything until I had something more solid from the financials."

"And she must be finding things or else we would never run into those ATF guys," said Saint Cyr, backing me up.

"Yeah. But they're not interested in our little murder. They've supposedly had a number of subway project sites under surveillance for nearly six months as part of Homeland Security. Nolan said they picked up some tidbits from informants and wiretaps suggesting that terrorists might try to steal explosives from several construction sites. So they've been snooping around in hopes of catching bad guys."

"Maybe Carpenter's explosives weren't being stolen. Could be that Carpenter was illegally selling them. Miriam may've paid the price for his shady dealings," I said.

"Nolan claims that Carpenter's clean, Monty. Said those thieves targeted Carpenter's business as a small demolition company. But we'll follow up to be sure."

Connelly looked at a wall clock hanging in the homicide unit, running its usual ten minutes slow. "It's getting late. Why don't you go home?" he asked.

Saint Cyr and I stood up to leave.

"You and I still have something to talk about," said Connelly, motioning to Saint Cyr. "Why don't you grab a cup of coffee while I say good night to Monty?"

As Saint Cyr left the room, Connelly quietly closed his door and sat down next to me.

"You got good instincts, kiddo. But what you did tonight was dangerous, very dangerous. Not just for you, but for Saint Cyr, too."

"I'm sorry. I was just trying to chase down every lead. Close every loop."

"That's our job," he said, pointing to himself. "Not yours. Don't start confusing your role with being a police detective. You're not trained for it."

"I hope you don't blame Saint Cyr, I asked him to do it."

"There's plenty of blame to go around. He should have followed proper procedure, too." He shook his head and let out a slow deep exhale. "You know, they don't all turn out like your friend's case. We can solve this one."

I looked down into my hands in my lap. "I know," I said softly.

"This isn't your murder investigation. We may ask for your help from time to time. But you're not calling the shots. I am. Got that?"

"Got it," I said.

"Now get out of here," he said.

My ears and face burned red with embarrassment. I felt awful about putting AngelEyes into hot water with Connelly. I trudged through the squad room toward an exit, knowing I'd managed to make complete asses out of both of us.

"Monty?"

I turned around and saw Connelly standing in his office doorway.

"Be sure to go straight home and get some rest. I don't want to be looking for what's left of you in some remote landfill."

"Thanks for the advice. Good night."

What's left of me? A remote landfill? Not exactly the stuff of a good night's sleep.

CHAPTER 13

I did go straight home but couldn't keep my eyes shut for very long. Insomnia has always been a problem for me, even as a kid. Since my diagnosis, it seemed that my sleeplessness was back with a vengeance. Sometimes in the early-morning hours, I'd show up and sing a few modern *fados* songs to a samba beat at underground Brazilian bars springing up in Inman Square. The first generations of Portuguese immigrants were dying off, but a new influx of vibrant Brazilians were helping revive East Cambridge's local restaurant and nightclub scene.

But tonight I didn't feel much like singing about death, betrayal and tragedy. I had enough of that in my day job. So I threw on my sweats and winter coat and drove over to Lucky Lanes. In recent months, I'd experienced too many sunrises at this all-night hangout.

I sat at the snack bar and sipped caffeine-free diet sodas, trying to leaf through recent cases on criminal procedure. After eleven o'clock, the bowling alley turned into a night club with blinking multi-colored flashing strobe lights glinting off multiple disco balls hung from a low ceiling. The building reverberated with throbbing beats of techno music, the rolling thunder of bowling balls, and hollow smacks of thin candlepins. A bunch of drunk college students tossed gutter balls and jumped around to blaring techno music.

Syd, a sixty-something ex-Marine with a smoothly shaved head, owned Lucky Lanes and didn't mind me sticking around all night. He enjoyed having a sober person to talk to at 2:00. Too busy for a wife or kids, he'd bought this bowling alley with accumulated winnings from gambling to stay active in his retirement. His pale face turned red with excitement when he talked animatedly about his two favorite subjects, politics and blackjack.

"So your man going to get his ass kicked or what this fall, Monty?" he asked, sorting through a pile of rental bowling shoes.

"There's a long way to go before the fat lady sings."

"She's warming up for sure."

He warbled a few notes of a fake aria.

"Careful now, you might shatter my glass." I pointed to my beverage.

"This church murder is getting people pretty upset. Never had a murder at Lucky Lanes. What's the world coming to when a bowling alley is safer than a church?"

"No sane person is going to mess with an ex-Marine."

"Uh-rah. Damn straight there, Monty." Syd adjusted twisted shoestrings on every pair of bowling shoes and sprayed disinfectant inside before placing them in their proper cubbyholes. "I'm betting on her husband. Spouse is usually the one that does it. Part of the reason why I never got married. You're basically sleeping with the enemy."

I laughed. "Syd, you're a hopeless romantic. But don't worry. I'm sure we'll wrap it up well before November. Besides, I doubt this county is suddenly going to go Republican."

"That's what they thought about Kennedy's senate seat, too." He waggled his finger in the air. "Anything can happen when John Q. Public is riled up."

"I hope you're wrong. I need this job."

"And your health insurance, by the look of ya." He motioned toward my cheek. "You're getting some kind of swelling going on there."

I dragged myself into a restroom and glanced into a grimy mirror. My small scrape had ballooned into an ugly reddish purple welt sore to my touch. Crap. I left Lucky Lanes for my apartment as dawn peeked over the city. When I arrived home around 4:00, I placed an ice pack over my cheek and popped two aspirins for my bumps and bruises, the price I paid for being an action hero.

With only three hours of shut-eye, I slept through my morning alarm. As I trudged into my bathroom, my face looked bruised in the mirror, but not as puffy as last night. I hurriedly got ready for work and dabbed on some concealer to help hide my unsightly abrasion. By the time I got it together, I was two hours late so I skipped my usual visit to Cranky Albert's.

When I hobbled into the office, Flora jumped up from behind her desk, her face framed by a chin-length frosted blond wig.

"Oh, my God! What happened to your face?" She put on her glasses, dangling from a chain, to take a closer look.

"A misunderstanding."

"Looks like you're trying to cover up a big hickey to me."

Just my luck, sporting a fat hickey on my face without enjoying any of the fun of getting a real one. "A bit of a dust-up with some federal agents."

Flora look puzzled.

"I'll explain it later."

"Mr. O'Brien left these files for you to look at while he's away at that prosecutor's conference. He'll be back on Monday." Flora handed me a short stack of files blanketed with yellow sticky notes. "And you had a very handsome visitor this morning."

In my current state, I prayed she wasn't talking about Kiley.

"Who?"

"Detective Saint Cyr. And *mais oui*, that sexy French accent. If I wasn't twice his age, I'd give him my telephone number."

I ignored that remark, since I assumed Flora was fishing to see if I'd given him mine already. "Did he leave a message?"

"I think he left something for you on your desk." Flora smiled like a cat that's swallowed a canary. "I left a fax in there for you, too."

I sauntered into my office and found a box of decaf Earl Grey tea resting on one of his sketches, my face drawn on Wonder Woman's body. I hurled a bat in one hand over two scrawny figures pleading for mercy with tea bags attached to my belt in place of her lasso of truth. A cartoon bubble over my head read, "Troublesome Feds ain't my cup of tea!" It was pretty funny and showed an amazing artistic talent. I reached for my phone to call and thank him, but then I put the receiver down. I shouldn't be encouraging this—quite the opposite, under the circumstances.

A bank fax brought more odd news. Carpenter's wire transfers landed in an account for Archangel Investment Trust, an offshore entity in the Grand Caymans. This guy was going broke, but managed to ship off $60,000 over time to some Caribbean outfit. I winced as I pushed aside Carpenter's financial files and scrunched my face as my scrape tingled and burned. I hoped Susan had kept Harvey or Herbert George's business card. I couldn't share any confidential bank information with him, but I wanted his take on Carpenter's financial records.

Flora buzzed me.

"Yes?"

"You have two more visitors."

"Who?"

"Mrs. Silva and Father Mac."

Mrs. Silva hadn't responded to my follow-up calls, and now she suddenly showed up in person with Father Mac? This visit must be serious. She stood in my office doorway, twisting a pair of black gloves in her hands. Father Mac, by her side, looked anxious, too.

"Good morning, Mrs. Silva," I said.

She dropped one of her gloves trying to shake my hand and Father Mac picked it up.

"Hello, Father Mac. Good to see you both again."

"Are you all right, Ms. Montez?" Mrs. Silva pointed to my bruised face.

"Only a little scrape. I'm okay."

I escorted Father Mac and Mrs. Silva into a conference room.

"I'm sure you're very busy, Ms. Montez. I'm sorry we came here without calling first," said Father Mac.

"No problem," I said. "Please take a seat."

They both sat quietly, and then Father Mac gave an encouraging smile to Mrs. Silva. "Go ahead, Alice."

She reached inside her canvas tote bag and pulled out several drawings. "Daniel drew these. They're quite upsetting. I showed them to Father Mac this morning. He was good enough to drive me here."

I scanned each drawing. One picture showed a man in a white sheet with a hood holding a club in his hand with blood squirting out of it. A second one displayed a woman in a pool of red blood with the same white-sheeted figure above it with the words, "Judis,

Judis!" inside a cartoon bubble. A third drawing offered scribbles of another man in torn clothes next to a shopping cart.

"What did Daniel say about these drawings?" I asked.

"Not very much. He kept repeating that this Casper wasn't a friendly ghost. He was a mean one."

"Did Daniel tell you anything about this white sheet on the man?"

"No, he didn't."

Father Mac stirred and said, "I thought it might be a church vestment. We're missing one from our sacristy. A white one with a hood."

"Could be," I said.

"What about these words, 'Judis'? Do you think he was referring to Judas?" asked Mrs. Silva.

I wondered if Carpenter might have felt betrayed by his wife in some way.

"I'm not sure," said Mrs. Silva. "There's something else you need to know." She began twisting her gloves again.

"What else, Mrs. Silva?"

"Daniel told me he let someone else into the church when I was in the basement."

"Who?"

"The professor."

"Professor who?"

"I don't know his last name. Everyone calls him the professor," she said.

"I think he worked as a teacher once. Maybe even in a college. Taught Shakespeare," added Father Mac.

Oh good, a literate killer.

"Do you know where he lives?"

"He's a homeless man. A very gentle soul," said Father Mac. "Comes to our afternoon soup kitchen nearly every day."

"The professor must've gotten there early. Such a cold day and starting to snow again. Daniel couldn't bear to see him freezing outside with that old shopping cart. Let him into the foyer near a side entrance to warm up." Mrs. Silva's voice trailed off as she pointed to a third picture.

"So Daniel let the professor inside on the morning of the murder?"

"Not actually inside our church. In an outer lobby. The professor probably wanted to keep his eye on his shopping cart. Always parks it near our church's dumpster."

"Did Daniel tell you if the professor entered into the main church, Mrs. Silva?"

"No, I couldn't get him to tell me much more."

"How long were you down in the basement, again?" I asked.

"About twenty minutes or so."

Plenty of time for the professor to whack Mrs. Carpenter over her head, steal her purse, and grab a few church valuables on his way out.

"And when you returned the professor was gone, and that's when you found Mrs. Carpenter's body?"

"Yes." She brushed a tear away.

Father Mac put his arm around her shoulders to console her. He handed her his handkerchief and told her that everything would be all right. She wiped her tears and blew her nose loudly.

I asked, "Have you seen the professor since then?"

"No. I'm very concerned. The weather's been so terribly cold. I hope he's still okay," Mrs. Silva said.

At this point, I hoped he wasn't roaming around town bashing in somebody else's head. "Did he know Mrs. Carpenter?"

"I don't know. I don't think so."

"What do you think, Father Mac?"

"She may have seen him around town. But Miriam didn't volunteer at the soup kitchen, only our church choir. I doubt they'd know each other," he said.

"Has he ever caused any problems at the church?"

"He's always been quite docile, Ms. Montez. From time to time, he's done some odd jobs around the church. He never gave anyone any trouble," said Father Mac.

A strange remark, considering he thought his dear friend's husband quite capable of violence, yet not a homeless stranger. Still pointing his finger at Patrick.

"I don't think he'd harm anybody. He may look scary to some people because of his shabby clothes, but he's quite sweet," said Mrs. Silva.

"This is very important information. I appreciate you coming to us so quickly. I think it may be important for Daniel to speak with a forensic child psychologist. They may be able to coax him into opening up more about that morning."

"I'd hate to disrupt his routine. Is there any way they can come to our home? Or Beacon House?"

"I'll see what I can do," I said.

For the next couple of hours, she sipped my Earl Grey tea and leafed through mug shots, trying to identify the professor. Once Mrs. Silva picked him out, it took local police less than three hours to track him down. Beat cops saw him around quite a bit. They'd shoo him out of bathrooms at a local mall or try to convince him to move from metal street grates to a county shelter on cold nights. He'd been arrested several times for loitering, but nothing serious.

Officers found the professor inside a battered tent in woods near a city parkway. He lay passed out with an empty bottle of no-name booze in one hand and a golden chalice stolen from St. Stephen's gripped in the other. Two heavy church candlesticks were propped up in snow mounds inside his tent, including one stained with blood. They were rushed to a lab for analysis. A trash bag in the professor's shopping cart held Mrs. Carpenter's purse, an empty ciborium, and other church vessels.

Sitting in an interview room, you would never have guessed that fourteen years ago, Robert Huntington had taught English literature at local colleges before life's struggles and the bottle took hold of him. His once-brilliant mind eroded, floating somewhere between fantasy and reality. For over a decade he roamed around with his shopping cart full of bottles, cans, clothes and trash, spouting snippets of Shakespeare to passersby. Year round, he wore several layers of dirty sweaters, jackets, and pants. His blackened fingers peeked through holes in two unmatched gloves. No hat covered his thin strands of gray hair. A scraggly salt-and-pepper beard half-hid deep wrinkles creasing his face. Aged by years of drinking and life on the streets, he looked at least ten years older than his actual 56 years.

"Mr. Huntington, do you understand the rights I just read to you?" asked Connelly.

"Professor Huntington, young man. Shakespeare 210," he said.

"Okay, Professor Huntington. We're not in class right now. We're in a police station. Do you know you're in a police station?"

asked Connelly.

"Cassius, Bait not me: I'll not endure it: you forget yourself," the professor said.

"No baiting here, Professor. Do you understand that you're in a police station under arrest for stealing? Maybe even murder?" asked Connelly.

"Murder?" he mumbled. "Murder most foul, as in the best it is, but this most foul, strange, and unnatural." He threw his head back and belched aloud. His burp stank of whiskey.

"Perhaps we'll have better luck when he sobers up," I said.

"Take him back to a holding cell until he sleeps it off," said Connelly.

As one patrol officer tried to help him stand, the professor lost his balance and fell toward me. I helped to steady him as another officer pulled him away. He didn't appear to possess enough strength or balance to sneak up on anybody, let alone crack someone's head open.

"O, speak again, bright angel. For thou art as glorious to this night, being o'er my head, as is a winged messenger of heaven," he boomed.

He continued to babble as two officers hustled him out of an interrogation room.

"O'Brien's gonna love this. First a comatose husband. Then a mentally challenged eyewitness. Now a deranged homeless guy spouting poetry." Connelly shook his head in disgust. "When does O'Brien get back from his conference, Monty?"

"Tomorrow morning. I've already left him voice mail."

"Julius Caesar. Hamlet. Romeo and Juliet. He certainly has a taste for Shakespearean tragedy, eh?" said Saint Cyr.

"I don't know much about Shakespeare, but our lab results are likely gonna spell one big tragedy for the professor," said Connelly.

"Do you think he's even physically capable of it, Connelly?" I asked.

"Who knows?"

"Carpenter might still be our killer. Maybe he dumped these things in the professor's cart on his escape from the church," Saint Cyr said.

"It's possible. Let's hope those lab finds something useful."

I knew that anything short of Carpenter's fingerprints on those items would hand Kiley enough reasonable doubt to drive a truck through our case. I tapped in Susan's number on my cell phone. Harvey George might prove useful after all. His financial smarts might glean critical information from Carpenter's records to shore up our case against him.

And it needed serious shoring up at this point.

CHAPTER 14

At the San Miguel Sports Club, the only sport that really counted was soccer. This all-male bastion only opened its doors to the neighborhood for certain community events, like this fundraiser to fix a leaky roof at St. Anthony's church hall.

I could already hear a couple of wheezing accordions and a solitary snare drum beating time as rancho dancers stamped their feet on a makeshift stage. I dutifully spread out some campaign brochures, buttons, and bumper stickers from the office on rear tables near two exits. Peeking into the main hall with its low drop ceiling and dated wood paneling, I saw about one hundred mostly elderly people, sitting on card chairs at five long cafeteria tables.

Some guests sporadically shouted out their support to five teenaged dance couples while dunking crusty hunks of bread into large bowls of steaming kale soup. Platters of half-eaten stewed beef and linguiça sandwiches and wicker baskets with dwindling slabs of bread were scattered across white plastic table coverings.

Walking along a narrow side corridor, I passed a small kitchen where bubbling pots rested on a gas stovetop. As rancho dancers pounded their heels, I reached a rear space where club members likely gambled over games of cribbage or dominos after work. Tonight, this room was strewn with empty musical instrument cases and dancers' garment bags. A tabletop vanity mirror sat on a wooden table with two mismatched metal chairs. Squeezing my winter coat on an overstuffed coat rack, I couldn't see any other Quinn re-election buttons. Maybe my mother was right. Even in working-class East Cambridge, Quinn's voting base needed propping up.

I took off my suit jacket and draped it over my winter coat. As I freed my hair from its constricting bun, my dark curls fell loosely around my shoulders. I popped a couple of extra buttons on my collared shirt and freshened up my blush. Glancing into the mirror, I applied dark red lipstick. Singing *fados* music was not a buttoned-up affair. I could sense my mother's irritated glare boring a hole into the side of my head.

"Glad you could make it." Her voice was drenched in annoyance. "You are on in about ten minutes."

"Plenty of time." I dabbed more concealer over my bruised cheek.

"What's wrong with your face?"

"I took a little tumble. I'll be fine, Ma."

My mother frowned and handed me the same list of four songs she'd written down the other night. Old-time favorites from the late queen of *fados*, Amália Rodrigues. *Abril em Portugal,* a poetic favorite, followed by two tear-jerkers, *Solidão* and *Triste Sina,* with a rare upbeat tune, *Uma Casa Portugesa,* a rousing finale where participants joined in on its refrain.

"Mr. Carvallo and his grandson are finishing up their soup. You'll be in a trio. Just like the old days."

With my dad gone, and Bianca a lost soul, it had been a long time since I'd sung in a trio. I missed those shared family moments over music. And now with my disease, my *fados* singing, along with everything else, would soon be a distant echo.

"Wear this, too." She pulled out a black widow's shawl from a plastic shopping bag. Hipsters at Cambridge's Brazilian nightclubs would laugh themselves silly at this old-school touch.

"You gotta be kidding?"

Scowling, my mother put her hands on her hips. "You wear a suit to work to be a lawyer, right?"

"Yes." I said, shaking my head. "And?"

"Because that's what your judge and jury expect. So you wear a shawl when you're a *fadista*. Because that's what your audience expects."

I sighed and threw it over my shoulders. "Happy now?"

My mother didn't reply, but fidgeted with the shawl, smoothing it around my shoulders and tying its ends low beneath my chest. As the dance came to an end, spectators roared their approval.

"See, even they agree with me," she said. My mother always has to get in that last jab.

A stream of buzzing dancers jostled past us to take off their traditional costumes. My mother headed back to her table to rejoin her friends in the Network. Mr. Carvallo, a lively eighty-something, dragged a couple of microphone stands on stage with help from his nephew, Jimmy. A friend handed up their guitars and a couple of folding chairs.

Doubling as master of ceremonies, Mr. Carvallo spoke a bit too loudly into a microphone with his lilting Portuguese accent. "We have a special treat tonight for our church fundraiser. Mrs. Montez not only brought us wonderful fresh bread from her bakery, but she brought along her daughter, Marguerite. Who I think a lot of you read about in the papers this week..." A brief smattering of applause followed. "Yes, she is quite a crime fighter, like a Batman!" A couple of people laughed. "And single, too, her mother tells me." Thanks, Ma, I thought. "But tonight she is going to sing *fados* for us."

The onlookers erupted in enthusiastic cheers.

"For every tear you cry, you put at least a dollar into the church hall fund," he added mischievously.

The musicians tuned their guitars briefly, then Mr. Carvallo pointed to Jimmy to dim the house lights. The tinny mandolin-like sound of a Portuguese guitar and the bass notes of an acoustic guitar soon filled this hall. After a few notes, listeners clapped their recognition of this familiar tune. Unexpectedly, I felt a rush of emotion as I stepped on stage. Memories of my dad and Bianca, and thoughts of Ginny and her dancing, swirled suddenly in my head. As I began to sing at the center microphone, tears welled up in my eyes and streamed down my face for my second and third songs. I pulled it together for my finale, cheerfully leading a sing-along as people stomped their feet.

Mr. Carvallo bowed and kissed my hand at the end of my brief set. "She sings from her heart and soul like a true *fadista,*" he called out over his microphone. "Now you give from your heart and soul for our church fund. Put your donations in the envelopes on your table and write your dollar amount with those little pencils, too. Then enjoy some hot coffee, nice desserts, and good conversation with your friends and neighbors."

Suddenly I felt dizzy and thought I was going to fall down. As I quickly exited the stage, I took off my mother's shawl and felt everything reeling around me. My vision became blurry and my knees and hands started to tremble. I stumbled out the side door into a service alley. The narrow passageway seemed to spin out of control around me, faster and faster.

Leaning against a brick wall, I closed my eyes and took several long, deep breaths, trying to center myself. I felt myself sliding down as each corner of an uneven brick jabbed my back. In an instant, I was shivering and sitting on cracked pavement next to a smelly dumpster. Slowly opening my eyes, I found my vision had cleared and my hands and knees no longer shook.

Like a violent passing storm, my Machado moment was over. It scared the crap out of me, but at least I didn't pass out on stage. Not enough sleep, I thought. I'd better go home before I took a swan dive on to a dessert table. Reaching for a dumpster grab bar, I pulled myself up and brushed dirt off my shirtsleeves and skirt. In the cold evening air, I watched my breath for several more slow inhales and exhales before going back inside.

Throwing on my suit jacket and winter coat, I tugged my gloves out of my pockets. A neatly creased donation envelope fell out and fluttered to the floor. I picked it up and unfolded it. Someone with an unsteady hand wrote in pencil on an outside flap.

"A sick killer lives while Ginny and Luisa sleep in heaven. *El Galo.*"

El Galo was no stranger in a Portuguese home, a small hand-painted clay rooster, displayed in a kitchen, including my own. A token of good luck, his legendary crowing saved an innocent man from the gallows and pointed to a true culprit. Someone wanted to tip me off to a connection, but I had no idea who Luisa was.

Maybe I wasn't going to leave just yet.

Stuffing the note into my skirt pocket, I took off my winter coat and put on my best *ficar face.* Wading into the crowd, I exchanged pleasantries with a host of old family friends and neighbors. I had known most of these folks since I was a kid, and puzzled over why one of them had never stepped forward earlier. Yet most of them were immigrants from another generation who thought speaking up only got you in trouble, and keeping your head down and your mouth shut helped you get by in a strange new land. But with one of their own in our county's homicide unit, this person may have decided the time was right.

Dead tired, I stayed anyway; chancing another Machado moment and hoping someone might squeeze my hand a bit too long or give me a knowing glance as a sign. Nothing out of the ordinary happened.

After the event, I helped my mother wrap up leftovers and asked her if she remembered a missing girl named Luisa in her childhood. She didn't. At evening's end, I waited outside the deserted club, wondering if a lone straggler might pull me aside to talk.

But no one did.

CHAPTER 15

A clanging school bell woke me up. I discovered myself about to sleep-walk right out my front door. Glad I'd put that door chain on last night before zonking out, or else a squeal of bus tires might have been my Saturday wake-up call.

I put on hot water for tea and fired up my laptop. Logging into our county's police database, I plugged in the name Luisa and found there were about a hundred and fifty hits. Most of the Luisas were either witnesses or defendants in a bunch of domestics, petty thefts, and other criminal cases, but no homicides. Yet our online database only went back about thirty-five years, and most of last night's crowd had longer memories than that. Any earlier case files were boxed up in a dank police warehouse basement in Chelsea where mold spores would kill me long before I'd ever find my Luisa.

Besides, I didn't need any whiny file clerks complaining to Connelly about my mucking around their ancient homicide records. I'd have to find another way to discover her identity.

Sipping on my tea, I ran an Internet search on Luisa homicides and came up with only two cases. One unsolved Luisa murder appeared in an online police portal looking for cold case tips in San Antonio, Texas. That case involved a 1990 robbery-homicide at a seventy-year-old victim's home. More recently, another Luisa homicide dealt with a college student in Miami last year. Her boyfriend was charged and remained in custody without bail in that case.

Neither seemed connected to our old neighborhood.

Once more, I picked up last night's envelope. Turning it over, I scanned a list of individual and business donors to the church hall fund, stopping at Gomes Funeral Home. This family-run business had expertly handled my father's funeral and pretty much owned the Portuguese market since the 1930s. If Luisa's family lived nearby, the Gomes family probably handled her funeral arrangements, and might even be continuing to post anniversary notices in St. Anthony's church bulletin.

Luckily, my mother had a cozy relationship with Mrs. Gomes, another widowed member of the Network. Despite her best efforts to wheedle more details out of me, I simply told her that I was working on a cold case that needed her utmost confidentiality. She put me in touch with Mrs. Gomes son, Tomaz, the founder's great-grandson.

His weekend calendar was packed with two funerals and three wakes, but he could squeeze me in Sunday between a mid-morning funeral and afternoon calling hours. A connection in the Network and the promise of a box of fresh *sonhos*, doughy pastry puffs rolled in sugar, could open a lot of doors in my neighborhood.

I dreaded any visit to a funeral home, not merely because of those dead bodies, but also my human awkwardness in expressing condolences to bereaved family members. A few mumbled words and a hug or handshake seemed woefully insufficient to ease a loved one's pain and grief. It always struck me as odd that anyone would choose to be a funeral director, considering all of the sadness and weird backroom preparations required for that role. So I guess it made sense that family members, used to growing up around the dead, would be more comfortable following in their grandparents' and parents' footsteps.

Like any good funeral director, Tomaz greeted me with a warm handshake and a soft-spoken tone in a low-lit lobby, painted in muted tones. His neatly tailored black suit, subdued gray tie, and crisp white shirt bespoke quiet refinement in this forty-something man. Not a single dark hair stood out of place and there was only a subtle hint of aftershave on his clean-shaven round face. Piped-in classical music floated faintly in the air. Tastefully decorated, the unobtrusive dark blue drapes and restrained traditional furnishings further nurtured a calm environment. Thick wall-to-wall carpeting ensured that we padded discreetly past the closed mahogany doors of four viewing suites and a couple of neatly furnished offices for client meetings.

Unlike the rest of his family's funeral home, Tomaz's back office was a light, bright space. Colorful superhero and sci-fi movie posters were splashed across its cheerful yellow walls and action figurines were displayed on built-in bookshelves. Two large computer monitors glowed on a modern teak desk. He could read my bemused reaction.

"I know. Not what you expect," he said, with a smile. "Nobody comes back here, except my wife and me. We met at a *Star Wars* convention. Even we need a fun spot at the end of our day to handle business details." He hung up his jacket on a coat rack and loosened his tie.

"Thanks, Tomaz, for making time in your busy day."

"No problem. Your mom said it was important and I can't resist her *sonhos*. Thanks for bringing them." Tomaz pointed eagerly at the bakery box. "Do you mind?"

"Go for it." I said.

He quickly untied the box's twine and savored a first bite as a gentle spray of powdered sugar fell on to his desk. "Still warm. I love 'em. Now, how can I help?"

"I'm looking to see if your family handled a funeral for a deceased person with a first name of Luisa."

"Do you have a last name?"

"No. And I don't have a specific date, either. Only that she died more than thirty-five years ago. I hope your records go back that far."

"Luckily, Granddad's obsession was keeping perfect client records. He always wanted to get the family connections right in his obituaries, including predeceased family members here and in the old country. Even beloved pets. He wanted to make sure month's mind and anniversary mass notices were accurate in church bulletins, too. Those genes run deep in our family." Tomaz punched a few keys, logging on to his computer. "My dad was pretty smart. Made sure everything got scanned in and computerized back in the 1980s, so we could serve families for generations to come."

"You're way ahead of us. Aside from criminal conviction records, most of our pre-1980s cases are still stored in paper files.

Makes it nearly impossible to do efficient cold case research."

"We've had to stay ahead of the times to compete." He squinted into his monitor as a flood of text filled its screen. "I've got a hundred and eight funerals where a deceased's name is Luisa. It was a pretty popular name back then. Any way you can narrow it down for me?"

"The only other thing I know is that she was probably a young girl or early teen."

"That helps. We usually special order white coffins and arrange a Mass of the Angels at St. Anthony's for children's funerals. I can reformat my search looking for those two data elements."

He clicked away on his keyboard. "That brings it down to twenty-three. Some of their vital records information is confidential, but I'll print out their published obituaries for you."

As his laser printer spat out copies, we munched on *sonhos* and discussed our favorite sci-fi characters. I left Gomes Funeral Home with twenty-three new Luisa leads and a better understanding of Boba Fett's pivotal role in the original *Star Wars* trilogy.

I jumped the Red Line to Harvard Square and warmed myself up in a crowded coffee shop. I found a solo stool by a window that looked out over this lively square. While most customers slurped coffee and chatted animatedly about their Saturday-night partying, I drank my tea and read through my obituary printouts. Anybody peering over my shoulder probably thought I was a ghoulish creep.

Most of these notices were short blurbs, only a few lines long. The per-word costs of newspaper obituaries may have limited some young parents' ability to spend their scarce resources on a lengthy farewell to their unfortunate child. A handful of them offered more detailed accounts of a child's special interests and talents.

As I read through each girl's notice, I made certain assumptions to try to thin my list. Four decedents were toddlers who died from pneumonia or flu, so I removed them from further consideration. Two death notices were about infant girls only a couple of days old. Although I knew I might be wrong, I figured they likely died from natural causes rather than homicides. In three other instances, I ruled out a Luisa because her announcement indicated that she'd died after a serious illness.

That left me with fourteen potential Luisas, assuming that my victim was amongst the children in Gomes's records. I'd need to do more tedious newspaper research at the nearby main library.

A block away, the Cambridge Public Library was a grand place to spend the rest of my Sunday trying to find my Luisa. This Romanesque gem with its spiraling central tower, textured granite and sandstone masonry, and burnt red roof sat majestically on a historic green pasture. A librarian directed me to its newspaper archives in a gorgeous contemporary glass and steel addition. Brilliant sunlight streamed in every floor-to-ceiling window in stark contrast to my somber research.

The local newspaper, *The Cambridge Daily*, was only available on microfilm so I knew that approach would be a time-consuming slog. I hoped that a murder and rape of a local girl might merit at least a few lines in *The Boston Globe*, which offered a searchable online database. With this main branch closing in three hours, I decided to go year-by-year through these announcements. I plugged in each deceased girl's name along with such unsavory search terms as "murder," "homicide," "strangle," and "rape." Sadly, it turned out that hundreds of people died or were badly injured under these gruesome circumstances.

Not one of them was named Luisa.

CHAPTER 16

When I made it to the office on Monday morning, I discovered another yellow sticky note on my telephone. "See me!!"

Two exclamation points aren't ever a good sign.

I walked down to O'Brien's office fully prepared to be chewed out royally for the dust-up with the ATF. I popped my head into his office doorway. O'Brien rubbed his swollen left cheek, moaning as he read some court document. A torn package from a messenger service lay on his desk. "Jesus, Mary and Joseph!" he cried out.

"What's wrong?" I asked.

O'Brien spat an ice chip out of his mouth into a paper cup on his desk. "My goddamn wisdom teeth are killing me. And that ass Kiley's filed a motion to reconsider. Demanding that we return evidence seized from Carpenter's home now that this homeless guy's been picked up."

"The professor."

"Yeah, the professor. Kiley's claiming that we've got no cause to keep Carpenter's stuff anymore."

O'Brien kept flipping through pages of a document and massaging his left cheek. "Flora, you gotta get me some more ice chips. I'm dying in here."

"Do you think the professor actually committed the crime?"

"Flora, for the love of God!" bellowed O'Brien, not hearing a word I said. "And now this goddamn gift from Kiley. A motion for its immediate return and looking for an expedited hearing date. *Flora!*"

A moment later Flora came in with two cups, one of ice and the other with water. She pulled two aspirins from the pocket of her sweater vest. She was wearing an interesting bob cut wig today.

O'Brien stared into her cup of water. "Nothing stronger?

"Drink up and behave. Sounds like you're in labor, having a baby in here," Flora said.

"Yes, Mommy." O'Brien grimaced as he downed two pills with a swig of water.

"Good boy. Now if you're going to make that dental appointment you'd better go now. Unless you want them to get infected. Then you're talking real pain."

She handed him his coat and scarf. As he began to pull his coat on, he barked out a few orders. "Go up to Judge Walters's ASAP and try to push it off if you can. Let 'em know I'm sick. Make a copy of his motion, check out his cited cases and get a draft response to me by this afternoon. Send it to my home by messenger. And write something up for me about those explosives you're tracking down and those Feds you beat up."

"Get moving." Flora guided O'Brien out of his office.

As O'Brien started to exit, he turned to me at the last minute and said, "Glad to see somebody in town still knows how to swing a bat."

He gave me a nod and left. Progress, I thought.

I skimmed over Kiley's motion and called Judge Walters's chambers. His clerk asked me to come up to discuss a hearing date, considering the judge's packed schedule. As I stood at the elevator bank, a short, rotund woman came out of one elevator. She almost knocked me over in her heavy down parka, carrying a beat-up green canvas bag overflowing with papers and files. She puffed hard as she pushed back thick black curls on the left side of her head, her large chunky earrings clinking against her hand.

"Just the gal I'm looking for," she said, thrusting her hand into mine. "Nan Pinkowski. Director. Women's Health Clinic. Nashua, New Hampshire."

Her accent sounded decidedly New York, not Cow Hampshire. She followed me right back into the opening elevator doors. As they slammed shut behind us, she hit a down button, while I wanted to go up.

"Marguerite Montez. Homicide," I said. "I'm not working on the clinic trespass cases anymore, but let me direct you to a new

ADA in district court."

She cut me off. "I didn't come all this way to talk trespass. I'm here to talk murder."

"Murder?"

"Yup. That Carpenter murder. You're the one I saw on TV the other day. I get all the Boston stations. We're not all rubes and bumpkins up there."

"What about that murder?"

She looked around. "I'd feel better discussing this in a more private place. You gotta office?"

"I'm about to go to the judge's chambers. Can we set up an appointment?"

"Yeah, right. While we wait for you folks to squeeze me in, we lose a few more of our people to these whack jobs. Or they blow our clinic or a gay bar to kingdom come. I already put myself at risk coming here. They're probably videotaping. I don't want them to know that I'm on to them. Gives them time to destroy any evidence."

"Who are you talking about?"

She stuffed her business card into my hand.

"I don't feel good talking about this in an elevator. They're probably bugging the joint, too. Meet me at that diner across the street after you make nice with that judge."

"Hang on a minute. If you have any information, you should contact the police." I knew Connelly wouldn't like me talking to her on my own.

"More like the Keystone cops. We've been dealing with the FBI for more than a year now. And they haven't done squat. Meet me over at that greasy spoon in twenty minutes. Otherwise, I'll hand all this stuff over to defense counsel. Let them make hay with it." She pointed toward the contents of her canvas bag.

The elevator doors opened and she hustled out without looking back. I glanced down at her business card. It looked legit, but then anyone could gin up an ID card with a computer and a color printer. She might really be a director of a women's health clinic. Or a crazy publicity seeker who claimed to know who killed everybody from JFK to Jon Benet. Every time it looked like we were about to wrap up this case, it kept getting blown open. I better check this out, since we couldn't afford to leave any loose ends for

Kiley to pick up.

Judge Walters was embroiled in a kidnapping trial dragging into an unexpected second week. His clerk marked up Kiley's motion for a hearing next Monday. Remembering Connelly's earlier warning about investigating on my own, I headed back to my office to call him. He'd left for a doctor's appointment to remove his forehead stitches. I asked for Saint Cyr, but he'd gone to a hospital for x-rays of his nose to see if it was broken. Our whole team was falling apart physically, and now this Pinkowski woman. I left voice mail for Saint Cyr and Connelly to meet me at the Fifth Amendment Diner across from the courthouse when they got back.

I grabbed my briefcase and headed across City Square to the diner. As I entered, it was abuzz with its breakfast crowd of local cops and lawyers. If Pinkowski turned out to be some kind of whacko, at least there would be armed help at my disposal. Waitresses raced around with pots of coffee. Busboys lugged huge round trays of dirty dishes off to the kitchen. Counter cooks called out orders as they hit a hotel-style bell. Demetri, its owner, as always seemed angry with his entire staff for not moving fast enough. I noticed Pinkowski sitting in a back booth digging into one of Demetri's enormous deluxe omelets specials and a mound of home fries.

"I hope you're not one of those food Nazis who's going to tell me all about that cholesterol crap," she said as I joined her.

"Nope. I like a good artery-clogging every now and then, too."

She wiped a spot of ketchup from her chin with her napkin.

"What do you want to tell me about, Ms. Pinkowski?" I pulled a yellow legal pad out of my briefcase.

"Please call me Nan. Hate all that formal crap."

"Okay, Nan. What do you want to talk about?"

"The Carpenter murder."

"Yes, you said that before. What about it?"

"Our clinic's been getting threatening phone calls, letters and emails for more than a year. Even calling staff and volunteers at their homes. Vandalizing their cars. Bastards even poisoned a dog belonging to one of our volunteers."

She stopped and took a bite of her omelet as a waitress inter-rupted to ask me for my order. I ordered a bagel and a large Irish

Breakfast tea, hoping caffeine might help me wrap my head around Pinkowski's claims. "I'm aware of violence against clinics, but that's a matter for the U.S. Attorney's office in New Hampshire. What does any of this have to do with Miriam Carpenter?"

"She didn't show last week. Comes every other Saturday to volunteer as a clinic escort. And then I see a news broadcast showing pictures of some homeless man that supposedly killed her. I couldn't believe it when they flashed a photo of Rachel."

"Rachel?"

"Yes, I knew her as Rachel."

"I think you must have the wrong person. Our victim name is Miriam Carpenter. Not Rachel."

"She went by the name Rachel when I knew her. She's been a volunteer escort at our clinic for over eight months. Sacrificed many Saturday mornings to help us out."

"You must be mistaken. Mrs. Carpenter was a practicing Catholic, killed in a Catholic church. Not a likely candidate to be an escort at your abortion clinic."

I began to think that I should have ordered my breakfast to go.

"It's a health clinic. We do more than abortions. Besides, haven't you ever heard of Catholics for Choice? Lots of them support a women's right to choose. Rachel did excellent escort work. Always stayed so calm. Even when they got right in her face."

"Are you sure you just haven't confused our victim with your volunteer?"

"Nope. Here's her application. Same face. Same date of birth."

Pinkowski opened a file showing me a copy of an application with Miriam's photo, her face more weathered than her twin, Rachel Childs, whose name appeared on the form. She included an address in Bar Harbor, Maine, probably one of her sister's swanky summer places. I wondered why she didn't use her own name. Perhaps she feared disapproval from her church friends, like Father Mac? Hard to believe that she'd be courageous in the face of protesters, but too afraid to share her convictions with her own circle of friends.

"Like I told you, it's the same gal. Those creeps videotaped her when she entered and left our clinic. Once they get your license plate number, they just go online or to the Registry of Motor

Vehicles to find out your name and address. Then their harassment tactics begin. And now a murder."

"Ms. Pinkowski."

"Nan, Nan."

"Nan, I think you're getting a bit ahead of yourself here. Certainly videotaping can be disturbing, but it's often a legitimate exercise of free speech. Besides there's a big difference between poisoning a dog and killing a person."

"Yeah? Seems like the same cruel mentality to me. If you've dealt with them as long as me, you'd know these fanatics will stop at nothing. And the powers that be haven't done much to curb them. "

"Had Rachel received any specific death threats?"

"Yup. I've got copies here for you. A small fraction of the ones we get all the time at the clinic."

She handed me a wad with copies of nearly a dozen threatening letters or e-mails sent to clinic that mentioned Rachel. I glanced through them. They were all typed letters or printed emails, so no signatures or handwriting to analyze. No specific group claimed responsibility. But each one threatened harm to Rachel and her family in this life, and eternal damnation in the next, if she didn't stop her work as an escort.

"Did she report the threats to local police or FBI?"

"Our clinic's got very strict security policies. We report any threats to our local FBI office and they've got the originals of these reports. Any bomb threats, the FBI coordinates with the ATF. We've been getting more of those recently. Those dolts scratched down a lot of notes, but did nothing. Rachel's death might finally bring this whole mess to light, for all to see." Her green eyes flared with rage and her face turned red. She stopped and took a sip of her coffee, seeking to regain her composure.

"Who were you working with in New Hampshire?"

"We've been trying to work with Tom Prentiss, FBI. He claims he's been coordinating with big cheeses at ATF. Some guy named Steve Nolan."

As I jotted down Prentiss' name, I realized that Nolan had been holding out on us about these clinic bomb threats. Perhaps with explosives courtesy of illegal dealings between Patrick Carpenter and some extremist groups. Nolan might know more about Miriam's death than he had let on. "Any idea who might be behind these threats?"

She frowned and dipped her home fries into a puddle of ketchup. "I don't have an individual's name, but maybe a group that's behind this."

"A group?"

She stopped short as the waitress left my order, waiting for her to walk away before continuing to speak. "Yup." She leaned forward. "The bastards call themselves St. Michael's Messengers, but they're no angels. Nothing but a bunch of thugs. When they're not busy making death threats, they're bombing health clinics, strip joints or gay bars. Ask those Feds. They gotta have a thick file on those kooks."

"None of these letters or emails claims to be from this group. How can you be sure that it's the Messengers?"

"They're nuts, but they're not stupid. They've picked methods that are hard to trace to one person. But we network with other clinics and we compare their threats. The Messengers use a lot of the same language in their calls and emails. Always up putting Revelation 12:7-9 in the cc: line of their emails."

I looked through some of the email threats and Rev. 12:7-9 in tiny font was found in cc: lines of each of these emails. "I haven't been to Sunday school in a long time. What's the passage all about?"

"Talks about the big battle at the end of the world between good and evil. And about St. Michael fighting off the dragon trying to swallow up the Virgin's child. Sort of their group's battle cry."

"Do you have any audiotapes of their threats?" I asked.

"Yes, back in our office, we've got copies of several messages left on the clinic's answering machine. FBI has them, too."

"What about Miriam, or Rachel? Did she receive any other threats besides these written ones?"

"She was contacted a couple of times at home. Several months ago, she told us that her young daughter picked up their home phone and a caller threatened their family. Really shook her little girl up. She stayed home from school the next day. But we got nothing on tape."

"Did your clinic recommend any special security measures or other protection for its volunteers?"

"We've got a number of safety measures that we keep private for security reasons. We also give tips in our volunteer training, like not opening unfamiliar packages or driving different routes to our clinic, stuff like that."

"Do you recommend that they take on any financial precautions, like disability or life insurance, in case they're injured due to their clinic activities?"

"Our clinic maintains some liability insurance, but we leave it up to our volunteers to decide what to do regarding personal life insurance policies."

Maybe her escort work explained that huge life insurance policy on Miriam.

"I'm not sure how well you know your volunteers, but did you know if Rachel—well, Miriam—had any personal problems at home or work? Family business and such?"

I wasn't ready to let Patrick Carpenter off the hook yet.

She paused for a moment to think about my question. "I know she had a son who'd been pretty sick recently. It weighed heavily on her. She said her work at the clinic helped. Kept her from becoming too down about her own troubles."

"Did you know much about her marriage? Was she having any marital difficulties?

"I'm no Ann Landers. It's hard enough to get decent volunteers. We try not to pry into their personal lives."

I nodded. We sat quietly for a moment, sipping our drinks.

"Can I keep this application folder and these threatening emails and letters?"

"Yeah. As long as you promise to actually do something with them."

I didn't make her any promises. But I told her that I'd talk with Connelly at the homicide unit to see about following up on her claims. I knew she didn't like that response, but then I didn't like getting sucked into somebody else's political battle. We needed hard evidence, not shadowy conspiracy theories to make our case.

CHAPTER 17

I considered myself lucky to have a gal pal like Dr. Ronni, a crack physician who knew how to diagnose her patients' ills and my personal troubles at lightning speed.

Dr. Ronni had heard all about Kiley's sexscapades in our short-lived participation in a divorced women's support group about six years ago. Neither of us loved the group sharing thing, so we bolted those gripe sessions and remained close friends. This evening when we got together, she gave me soothing antibiotic cream for my icky scrape, handed me extra strength ibuprofen for my aching shoulder, and took me out to dinner at Vincenzo's in the North End.

"Can't believe that jerk Kiley is haunting you in your first murder case." Dr. Ronni dipped some bread into a green pool of olive oil floating on a white plate. "Geez, I shouldn't be eating all these carbs this late in the day. Looks like at least one extra hour on the treadmill tomorrow."

"Hey, pal, enjoy it," I said, running my eyes down my menu. "Besides, you look great."

And Dr. Ronni always did. I admired how pulled together she looked whenever we went out. Tonight she dressed in a chic black pantsuit with subtle touches of Tiffany silver jewelry, her light brushes of make-up applied flawlessly and her nails perfectly manicured. I never had the knack for that polished appearance, particularly on an assistant district attorney's salary. She primped her short, dark brown hair as she munched on an oil-soaked piece of bread.

"It's an occupational hazard. I can't tell my patients to eat right and then stuff myself with all these fatty foods. Maybe I'd better order a salad." She glanced down at her menu.

"It's the North End, Ronni. You'll insult their cook if you don't order some pasta."

"Okay. But no creamy sauces. No Alfredo."

She looked at her menu once more, and then tapped her index finger on the table. "Hey, missy, weren't we talking about your occupational hazard? I heard on a news report that a homeless guy was arrested, caught with stolen church stuff. I'm no legal genius, but doesn't that mean that Kiley's client is going to wriggle out of this one?"

"Not quite yet. We're still waiting on forensic tests. Do you mind if I ask you something medical?"

I didn't like to pester Dr. Ronni with medical questions after hours. But the professor seemed too weak from years of marinating himself in booze to have killed Miriam with repeated, forceful blows, and then possessed the presence of mind to steal her purse and church vessels, too. I still put my money on her fleeing husband.

"What kind of medical questions?" she asked, leaning in. "You're feeling okay? No new MJD symptoms?"

"No, I'm feeling about the same on that score," I said.

I hadn't told her about my recent nosedives or my nocturnal sleep-walking jaunts. Besides they were likely some dumb side effects from my new meds.

"It's about the homeless guy we brought in." I stopped mid-sentence when our waiter came over to take our order.

Dr. Ronni loved to flirt and turned on her charm. She ended up ordering mixed greens and some naked pasta to keep her size-six figure. Stressing about my case, I went full tilt, Caesar with anchovies, homemade lasagna, and a slice of cheesecake for dessert. Probably worth about three days on Dr. Ronni's treadmill, but what the hell.

"He's been a chronic alcoholic for years, Ronni. He seems pretty feeble. Shaking and unsteady on his feet. Confused about where is he is. Doesn't look like he'd be physically able to bludgeon someone to death."

"If he's shaking, he may be going through acute alcohol withdrawal. If he's a habitual alcoholic who's suddenly stopped drinking or hasn't been able to get his hands on alcohol, he can exhibit symptoms of delirium tremens."

"His shaking is the DTs, right?"

"Yes, it can be one symptom. But there are others, too."

"Like what?" I asked.

"He can have all kinds of hallucinations, memory disturbances, elevated pulse rate, difficulty sleeping, and things like that."

"What kind of hallucinations?"

"They can be auditory, visual, or tactile. He might hear or see people or things that don't exist. Or think he's touched someone or something that never existed."

"These hallucinations might be scary to him, Ronni. But could he be dangerous to others?"

"Absolutely. Sometimes a patient with this syndrome can become very agitated and prone to violent outbreaks. He may look feeble, but he might be capable of great strength and violence, Monty."

"He looked so pathetic, but I guess he could be a killer."

She leaned in a bit further and whispered, "Why, do you think someone else did it?"

"In my gut, I just don't think it's him. I still think it's her husband."

"Said like a true divorcee."

"I can't get out of my mind that her husband tried to run away. That's not usually a sign of an innocent man."

"Maybe he's got a guilty conscience about something else. Is he still in a coma?"

"No, he's been out of the coma for about a week, which leads me to my next question."

"Hey, keep this up and I'll have to charge for an office visit, Monty."

"How about I grab this check?"

She laughed. "No, I'm only kidding. This stuff is much more interesting than hearing my patients complain about their bowel movements."

"Okay, her husband seems to be suffering from selective memory loss. A day or so ago, we find out from his sister-in-law that he's starting to recognize his family, knows his name and remembers certain things about his work. But he's still claiming that he can't remember anything that happened the morning his wife died or that wild ride he took us on. Could he really be suffering memory loss or is he really faking it?"

"Yes, to both. A trauma to the head followed by a period of coma or unconsciousness can cause a host of mental and physical problems, including memory loss. But there's no set formula for memory disturbances. He might suffer short-term memory loss, while still retaining more long-term memories, such as his family, friends or work life."

"Or he could be feigning the whole thing to cover his tracks?" I asked.

"Yes, he could be."

"No way to test that in any definitive way?"

"Not really. The brain and memory processes are still great medical mysteries."

"Damn it."

I'd hoped she'd bolster our case against Carpenter, but she confirmed my concerns about what medical expert testimony at a trial. Kiley would end up making Carpenter look more like a victim than his dead wife. Unfortunately, the professor might have done it, and Carpenter might be telling us the truth about his memory problems. So why did he run? Maybe Riddell pegged him right for illegal activities with his demolition business.

"Sorry to have bugged you with this medical talk. No more shop talk."

"Hey, not so fast. What about that cute detective from Canada?"

AngelEyes. I'm sure he was disappointed that I didn't thank him for his sketch and tea gifts, but I didn't want to encourage his attention. "What about him?"

"Is he single?"

"Yup. Never been married, Ronni."

"Does he have a girlfriend back home?"

"I don't know."

"How long is he here for?"

"I think it's a year-long program," I said.

"A lonely guy in a strange town. Makes him ripe for something new. And why shouldn't it be you?"

"I think he's married to the job right now."

"At least you two have that in common," she said. "You'll be spending a lot of time together on this case. Day and night. Night and day. Night after night." She raised her eyebrows suggestively.

"Office romances are never a good idea."

"How else do you expect to meet anyone since all you do is work?"

"I'm not really looking to meet anyone right now," I said, only half-believing the words coming out of my mouth

"Monty, I hate to be a nag. But you've really got to get more serious about getting out there again."

"I'm busy. Besides I've been out there."

"When?"

"What about that singles cruise in Boston Harbor you dragged me to last year, Ronni?"

The Love Boat from hell. Ten minutes after it left dock with three hundred desperate women and about ten very excited bachelors, I wondered if I could swim back to shore.

"That was two years ago."

"What about that blind date last fall?" I asked.

"The guy your sister Caridade set you up with from work with a pituitary gland problem? He was forty-one and hadn't even completed puberty yet. That doesn't count."

"Doesn't exactly sound like I'm missing out on a lot of quality options out there."

"So why not try to get to know that Canadian detective better?"

"At least he looks like he's made it through puberty already," I said. "I don't know. Timing's wrong."

"For crying out loud. The dating gods are dropping a cutie in your lap. Don't be ungrateful. Go for it. Remember, you let Kiley win if you give up on finding love."

"You got me in love with this guy already?"

"No, but a little lust might do you some good," she said.

"Oh, the lusting part is easy. It's the acting on it that's so hard."

"Give it a try anyway," Ronni said. "That's doctor's orders. Okay?"

"Yeah, I'll think about it."

"Promise?" she asked, touching my shoulder.

"I promise to think about it."

I definitely thought about AngelEyes. He looked like the total package; smart, handsome, artistic and nice to be around. Yet I knew I'd never make any real move. Why would any guy like that want a thirty-seven-year-old sleepwalking divorcée with horrible work hours, lousy pay, and a tragic MJD future? Wiser to stay focused on this case and make my mark in homicide than to blunder my way through a workplace romance with a guy who'll be gone in a year.

That cheesecake dessert ended up being the sweetest thing I allowed myself tonight.

CHAPTER 18

Driving to Nashua didn't take as long as I'd expected, so I got to the Dunkin's before Saint Cyr arrived.

I'd turned down his offer to drive up together, since I needed to make some stops on the way. I dropped off copies of Carpenter's financials with Harvey George and got a short list of licensed dealers for wet explosives working on the subway project from staff at our state transportation authority. I probably should have done those tasks with Saint Cyr, but I was working on distancing myself from him.

I sat near a window, looking out at a gray sky as cars swooshed by and pedestrians hopscotched their way along slushy streets. I sipped my tea and leafed through a few pages of a newspaper somebody had left on the table. I glanced at my horoscope for guidance, sort of a guilty pleasure for me, like my home subscription to *People* magazine. I knew I should be reading slip opinions from our Supreme Court or recent developments in criminal procedure, but a little brain candy never hurt anybody. As I flipped through the paper, I suddenly saw AngelEyes out of a corner of my eye.

"Hi. Sorry to be late." He stood next to my booth. "I had a difficulty to find parking."

"No problem."

"How is your nose? Not broken, I hope."

"It's fine."

His chilly tone meant that I was succeeding in pushing him away. Keeping my distance from AngelEyes made sense, even if it felt lousy.

"I see you have your precious tea. I'm going to get a coffee."

My cell phone buzzed with an alert and I glanced at a new public posting on Ginny's website. It was short and to the point. "A sinner blasphemed our Holy Ghost stealing our innocents. Seek justice. *El Galo*." Another puzzling blurb with little additional information for me to investigate. Yet moving from a hand-written note to website posting led me to believe that more than one person might be reaching out to me.

I put away my phone as Saint Cyr brought his coffee over to my table. He tried to cool it with several quick breaths. "No Tim Horton's, for sure."

I thought he might be expecting me to mention or thank him for his gifts. A few seconds of uncomfortable silence ticked by. I fought my desire to fill up this quiet with silly jokes or aimless remarks.

"What do you think about this Messengers stuff?" I asked, breaking the silence with a safe subject.

"Not much help, eh? Husband trying to run away from us, insurance policy, failing business. Those things to me add up. The only value of investigating this is to fight reasonable doubt."

"Did you have a chance to check out a copy of Pinkowski's file?"

"Yeah." He nodded. "I see she used the name of her sister. It looks like harassment, but nothing serious enough to suggest murder," he said, drinking his coffee. "She is quite a paradox, this Miriam. Married, church-going Catholic with two kids, volunteering to be a clinic escort. Sounds like grounds for excommunication."

"I don't know, Gérard. Perhaps some personal situation shaped her beliefs. Maybe a friend or sister who suffered in some way due to an illegal abortion. Or could be she wanted others to have more choices than she did." I glanced at my watch. "Hey, we'd better get going. Hate to keep Agent Prentiss waiting."

"Yes. You're right."

"One car or two?" I asked.

"Let's take two cars. I need to make a call."

"Sure. That's fine," I said, pasting on a smile.

It was only about ten minutes to the federal building in Nashua, a standard government-issue granite building looking even more somber on this cloudy morning. When we asked for Tom Prentiss at security, an officer told us that Prentiss had been reassigned to another office.

"To me he just spoke yesterday," said Saint Cyr, in disbelief.

The security guard shrugged his shoulders.

"It's a regular revolving door in that office. They're sending Agent Vasquez down to meet with you."

Five minutes later, a short Latino stepped out of an elevator. "Hi. I'm Armand Vasquez. I've taken over Prentiss's caseload for now."

"For now?" I asked.

"Yeah. Everybody's got to do their time in the doghouse."

"Doghouse?" I asked.

"Yeah. This office doesn't get much action. And this clinic stuff's not major on our radar screen. Especially if you're looking to move up in the Bureau. Not exactly global terrorism."

"Where is Agent Prentiss?" asked Saint Cyr.

"Got reassigned to Bangor. On his retirement track. Plenty of time for his grandkids and fishing up there," he said, escorting us to an elevator.

Once we got to the third floor, Vasquez led us down a hall to a cramped office full of files in green and white rectangular storage boxes. An empty black metal desk stood next to two lonely blue plastic chairs. "Here you go." He pointed to three untidy boxes overflowing with manila files and loose sheets of paper.

"What?" AngelEyes and I exclaimed in unison.

"Here are his files going back three years on this clinic stuff. That's why you're here, right? To look over his files?"

"We came up to talk to Agent Prentiss about a murder in Boston that may be linked to harassment at a women's health clinic here. We wanted to talk to him about his investigation," I said.

"Prentiss *investigating?*" Vasquez laughed out loud. "He clocked in every day, but he didn't investigate much of anything at this point in his career."

"What about their alleged threats? Their harassment claims?" I asked.

"He took a few pictures at protests. Scribbled down some

notes. Passed on his info to DC."

"So no real investigation of these threats, eh?" Saint Cyr asked.

"They got their own security. Local cops deal with the vandalism, stuff like that. The threat data goes to DC. They look for national trends. Decide if they want to go for federal charges. Hardly anything for us to get too worked up about on a day-to-day basis."

"So all you've got for us is files?" I asked, in exasperation.

"Yup. Files are better than nothing."

Probably worth nothing, I thought. Whenever the Feds let you look at their files, you can be sure it's useless junk. If it had any real value, they wouldn't be sharing it with us.

"Thanks," Saint Cyr said, in a sarcastic tone.

"Copier's in room 303. Vending machines at the end of the hall. I'm in 308 if you need anything else." Vasquez closed a door behind him.

Saint Cyr and I looked at each other in amazement. Now I was beginning to understand Pinkowski's frustrations.

"*Sacréfisse, sacréfisse!*" said Saint Cyr. "Can you believe this bullshit?"

"Yeah. I think Pinkowski knew these guys would screw things up. So she came to us directly. Let's hope we find something of value in this mess."

Saint Cyr pulled two boxes on to a desktop.

"What do you want I do?"

I thought for a moment. "Pinkowski said Miriam volunteered for the past eight months. Might as well look at the past year for any problems."

We tried to make ourselves comfortable in the plastic chairs and began to read stacks of dull reports. Saint Cyr soon grew bored of this task, getting up several times to stretch, to check his cell for messages, or to go to the men's room. I had heaps of patience and self-discipline to dredge through minutiae for days on end, and moved systematically through the files. In each manila folder, a parade of different agents had scribbled in a series of minor cruelties experienced by clinic staff over the past year.

I read a litany of issues. Staff member followed home by unknown person. Protester brushed up against clinic staff escorting patient. Protester pushed video camera into face of clinic staff. Unknown person found snooping around dumpster at clinic. Staff member's car vandalized by person or persons unknown. Death threats left on clinic answering machine. That one sounded familiar. Each file gave little more detail than Pinkowski's summaries to me. Nothing specific in the files about Miriam, masquerading as Rachel. But then Prentiss had been too busy baiting hooks to waste time on writing detailed reports. I hoped those ATF guys did a better job keeping track of incidents involving bomb threats. Yet it seemed unlikely that Stephen Nolan would give us much of anything.

After several hours, AngelEyes got up from his chair for a zillionth time. "How do you sit without moving? Like a statue, you are?"

"I've got bags full of self-discipline."

"Discipline I admire, Marguerite. But I need to move to keep my brain going."

"Blame it on law school. The only way to get through reading tons of cases every day. I'd totally immerse myself or else I'd never get that job done. And I like getting jobs done."

"Me, too. But I like to follow leads and question witnesses. All these ancient files are death to me."

"I don't love plowing through records. But I know I need to do it. So I drill down and power through them."

"Finding anything too good?"

"Not much, Gérard. Few leads to follow."

"Like what?"

"The file notes say that these protesters made videos of their rallies. A lawyer pal told me as much a couple of nights ago. If we could get our hands on those videos they might show us if someone stalked or targeted Miriam."

"It is a needle in a haystack. There might be hundreds of hours of video to swim in."

"Close enough. Endless weeks of wading through home movies."

"Yes, wading," he said.

"Sounds like fun, doesn't it?" I was tempted to echo his Canadian "eh?"

Saint Cyr smirked. "I leave it to you disciplined types."

"No, thanks. I prefer sci-fi films. You discovering anything?" I asked.

"Nothing too special. Except bizarre stuff, like this website, vengeancesword.org. Includes a most-wanted list of names of clinic staff. See, this site crosses off their names once they have been driven out or killed, eh?"

"Doesn't sound very pro-life."

"That group is really militant. It supports killing clinic doctors and staff as justifiable homicide."

"We should check to see if Miriam's name ever appeared on their list, Gérard."

He was frowning. "Those people are not pro-life. They are extremists. I have a family friend in a pro-life group. They help pregnant women access social services or tap into adoption agencies in Québec. Her group promotes dialogue, not threatening or killing people who disagree with her," said Saint Cyr.

"I guess that's because Canadians are so decent," I said. "It's too bad it's become such a toxic subject here."

I opened a cover of a third storage box. "These might be more interesting than those lame reports."

I handed Saint Cyr one stack of black-and-white photos held together by a rubber band. Lots of crooked shots of people protesting outside Pinkowski's clinic. Plenty of out-of-focus ones, too, that hardly seemed worth developing. "Doesn't look like Prentiss made much of a photographer." I held up a blurry shot.

"Yes, but a brilliant fisherman."

I scanned a few more, hoping to catch a glimpse of Miriam. I stopped suddenly at one photo, a profile shot of a white guy with dark hair resting a bulky beast of a video camera on his shoulder. He stood behind Edgar Thompson, Mr. Family Values. A huge wooden cross on a leather cord around his neck caught my eye.

"Hey, Gérard, I've seen this guy before. In district court. Part of a regular group of violators of buffer zones at clinics, gay bars, and strip clubs."

I flipped through a few more black-and-whites. "Here he is again," I said. I pointed to a shot taken at a Thompson rally with this same guy in the background with his video camera again. On the back of the photo someone had jotted down, "Link to Messengers?"

"Looks like somebody here thought he might be one of those Messengers," I said. "I'd better get a copy of these photos and run down his name with my pals in district court. He might know where they store their video cassettes."

"Being one of the Messengers, or taking their videos, this doesn't mean he caused Miriam's death."

"No. But as a famous detective once told me, it's good to check this stuff out, just to fight reasonable doubt." I grinned at him. The famous detective rolled his eyes.

After more than an hour of slogging through these photos, even my eyes begged me to stop. Saint Cyr paced around the room, dying to get out of this cramped space.

"What do you think about paying a visit to Pinkowski? These files don't reveal much, but she might be able to tell us something about their videos and web site," I said. "Besides, we could both use some fresh air."

CHAPTER 19

We got directions to Pinkowski's clinic on Oak Street and took my Blue Bomb. As I turned on Oak, we saw the narrow street blocked by orange cones with local police directing traffic away from Pinkowski's clinic. People packed sidewalks lining the street and crowded on grounds of an adjacent public park. Loads of protesters waved signs denouncing abortion while others knelt quietly in prayer with rosary beads hanging from their fingertips.

AngelEyes brought down his window and showed his badge to a local cop. He pulled a cone away to let us through to the clinic.

"Keep your heads down," the patrol officer said.

It made me glad we took my Blue Bomb, since she doubled as a Sherman tank. As we drove towards Pinkowski's clinic, we noticed a long black limousine parked on the opposite side bordering a recreational area. I could make out someone in the distance speaking over a bouquet of microphones from a tiny bandstand at this rally.

I rolled down my window part way and recognized Edgar Thompson's voice. He exhorted his audience to fight the nation's moral downfall. "Our society has lost its ethical compass. Legalization of same-sex marriages. Obscenity broadcast over TV and the Internet. And women killing their unborn babies. We must fight to take back our society from these decadent forces."

His voice trailed off as we drove further along Oak Street toward an isolated strip mall housing Pinkowski's clinic. Local cops struggled to keep protestors 500 feet away from the clinic's entrance. As we started to turn into its parking lot, several protesters bolted out of a crowd and pressed up against my car doors. A young woman wearing a Choose Life aprons banged on my window. "Don't kill your baby. Don't kill your baby," she pleaded, flapping a bloody rubber doll in her hand.

It startled both of us and my heart began to pound. An officer pulled her away and several other cops corralled protesters back behind wooden sawhorses.

"Liking this fresh air?"

"Only in the States, Marguerite."

As we turned into the parking lot, a clinic security guard waved us around to one side of the building. Another security guard stood sentry at the bottom of a set of steps leading to a back entrance. When we parked and stepped out, protestors continued to scream at us, begging us not to kill our child.

The first security guard approached us. "Did you make an appointment?" he asked.

"No. We're here to speak with Ms. Pinkowski about a murder of one of your escorts." Saint Cyr flashed his police badge.

"Rachel. Such a nice lady. She deserved better," he said.

I nodded in agreement.

"Are either of you armed?" Lyle asked.

"Yes, I'm armed," said Saint Cyr.

"Only armed with a legal pad," I said, trying to add some levity to this heavy atmosphere.

The guard smiled. "Sir, you'll have to lock it in your car or surrender it to me before we go inside."

"In her glove compartment, I'll lock it."

I popped open my glove box as Saint Cyr pulled his gun out of its holster and slipped it inside. I reached over to lock it with my key.

"Just follow me once Sam unlocks this back door and gives us an all clear signal." He gave the okay sign to his partner who strode up several concrete steps and unlocked an entryway. Sam waved us forward and his partner escorted us to that door. We walked through a narrow corridor leading to a metal detector and x-ray machine. Lyle walked through the detector and an alarm beeped.

"Please put your purse and other belongings on this belt and step through the detector," he said.

I placed my purse and briefcase on the belt and walked

through the detector. Saint Cyr followed me and set off their alarm. He went back and Sam watched him dump his change and take off his watch, placing it in a plastic basket. Saint Cyr walked through a second time without any trouble. Sam handed him his change and watch. When we turned the corner toward a lobby area, we saw a receptionist behind a thick glass partition.

"Is it bullet-proof?" I asked.

"Yes, ma'am. Can't be careful enough these days."

The receptionist spoke into a microphone. "Hi. Can I help you?"

She pointed to a telephone to the right of us, like ones in the visitor's center at the state prison. I picked up a receiver under the guards' watchful eyes. "I'm Marguerite Montez, Charles County DA's office, and this is Detective Gérard Saint Cyr. We wanted to speak with Ms. Pinkowski about the Carpenter case."

"Can I see your badges?" She pushed out a sealed metal drawer that resembled a bank drive-up window.

I pulled mine out of my purse and Saint Cyr grabbed his from his wallet. We put them in the drawer and she pulled it back over to her side. She puzzled over them for a moment. "You'll have to hang on. I want to clear this with Nan first."

She disappeared through a back door. When she returned, Pinkowski followed her, looking peeved in a rumpled brown sweater dress.

"Your timing really sucks," she said. "But come on in."

Always a pleasure, Nan, I thought. The receptionist unlocked her door to the waiting area and we entered the clinic's inner sanctum.

"I see you've brought reinforcements today," she said, pointing to Saint Cyr. "You'll need an armed escort to get out of this town in one piece today."

I introduced them to each other.

"Your security measures are certainly thorough," said Saint Cyr.

"We're under siege today. Normally we only have to deal with a handful of protestors. But when Thompson comes to town, lots of outside troublemakers come into our neighborhood."

"No clients today?" I asked, as we walked through an empty waiting area.

"None. We cancelled most of our appointments because we knew they would be out in full force. Referred our emergency cases to other clinics in Massachusetts. They'll do the same next month when that vulture swoops down there."

Her words were thick with the same venom Thompson spewed from that bandstand. Unlike Saint Cyr's friend, I doubted any dialogue group would spring up between them anytime soon. She led us to a windowless conference room and we sat around an oval conference room table.

"Well, what can I do you for?" she asked, lightly tapping her pen.

"We just spent some time looking over the FBI files. We've got a few questions for you about Miriam's work here," I said.

"Like what?"

All graciousness from Nan as usual.

"You told me earlier that Miriam received threatening emails and phone calls starting about eight months ago."

"That's right."

"And that you reported these incidents to the FBI," I said.

"Yup. We did."

"But we don't see any specific references to Rachel Childs in their files."

"That's hardly a surprise. We weren't exactly a top priority for them." She frowned.

"Did you notice anyone videotaping Miriam when she volunteered?" I asked.

"Like I told you, they constantly tape us. She's bound to be in their films."

"Any idea about who normally does their taping?"

"Yeah. I see a few regular video geeks here all the time."

"Who?" asked Saint Cyr.

"Mostly Fetus de Milo and Simple Simon."

"Who?" he asked again.

"A couple of nut jobs who get off shoving their cameras into people's faces."

"Know their real names?" I asked.

"No. But you can't miss them on any given Saturday. Fetus de Milo's a Hispanic gal who wears a baseball cap with a miniature bloody plastic fetus with no arms glued to its brim. And Simple

Simon's this roly-poly nerd wearing a huge wooden cross around his neck."

I pulled a copy of a black-and-white photo from the FBI files. "Is this the man?"

She glanced at it. "Yup. That's Simple Simon."

"Any ideas where they store their videos?" I asked.

"Not a clue. I'm hardly part of their inner circle. Anything else?"

"Yeah. Can we talk to your staff about Miriam? See if they noticed anything?" I asked.

"Sure. No problem. But I want to warn you that they're still pretty upset about all this, so be nice."

"I can do nice," I said.

Pinkowski eased up for a moment. "You know. I may not seem grateful, but I do appreciate your follow-up. But I've been down this road before. I just hope you won't drop the ball, too."

"We'll do our best to find Miriam's killer," I said.

I didn't want to disappoint her like the Feds had done. But I couldn't guarantee that we'd please her, either. Most of our evidence still stacked up against the professor and Miriam's husband, not any extremist group.

Saint Cyr and I spent the next hour or so talking to security guards and office staff. No one could tell us much about Miriam's personal life or her potential enemies. Everybody kept saying what a good person she was, dedicated to this work, so sensitive to their patients. One of the guards noticed that she seemed anxious about security, particularly after she received those threats at home. He tried to reassure her and spent a great deal of time explaining all their safety precautions being taken at the clinic to protect patients, staff and the property. Unfortunately, no measures could keep her safe in her own church.

As we left Pinkowski's clinic and walked over to my car, something whistled through the air and struck the back of my head. Ouch! It felt like a rock and it really hurt. Before long rotten eggs rained down on us thrown by a knot of protesters from a hill in the park. Eggs glanced off Saint Cyr's shoulders and a few smashed at my feet. Lots of eggs slammed against my Blue Bomb. Exploding yolk and shells splattered all over us. I fumbled wildly for my car keys.

"*Merde!*" yelled Saint Cyr. "Assholes!"

I jumped into the driver's seat and reached over to pop up a passenger button for AngelEyes. He slammed his door shut. "Are you okay?" he asked.

"Yeah, I'm pissed, but fine. Where the hell are those cops who're supposed to be keeping the peace?" I asked.

"Probably out fishing with that idiot Prentiss."

Saint Cyr whipped out a handkerchief from his pocket and brushed broken eggshells from the back of my head. It was a kind gesture in an otherwise mean-spirited attack.

CHAPTER 20

My mother's right. Always wear a hat in the winter.

Since I didn't follow her advice, gooey egg yolk and crunchy shell fragments had embedded themselves in numerous tangles in my hair. It took some doing to get them out of my curls in a hot shower.

You wouldn't think it, but eggshells can really travel. I found tiny bits inside my briefcase, panty hose, shoes, and even my bra cups. I'd have to drop off my dress winter coat at the cleaners before I headed back to the office tomorrow morning. I hated having to wear my other winter coat to work, a puffy hunter-don't-shoot-me red parka. It made me look like the Michelin tire man. That parka was only intended for use when I'm taking out trash barrels or shoveling out my parking space in the dead of winter. After midnight. Not exactly proper lady lawyer wear, but the weather was too cold for me to be a slave to fashion at that moment. Who knows? Maybe AngelEyes liked the Nanook of the North look.

As I shook out my briefcase, I glanced once more at a photo of Simple Simon. Tracking him down should be pretty straightforward since he was already in our court database. I'd also contact my district court pals who likely had escorted him into a courtroom from holding cells a number of times. Maybe all those years in district court dungeon might finally pay off now in my first big homicide case. Carpenter was still our man, but we needed to sweep away any doubts about extremists.

When my teapot whistled for attention, I poured hot water into a thick mug and warmed my hands on its side. My apartment building seemed quiet tonight. After a long day, it felt good to be back in familiar surroundings among my own things. With no messages on my answering machine or posting alerts from Ginny's website, I decided to turn off the ringer, mute my cell phone, and enjoy some rare quiet time. I scuffed into my living room taking sips of tea and flipped on my favorite digital music station. I expected to be awake into the wee morning hours. For the next few hours, I plopped on to my blue velour couch sifting through mail, straightening up my place, and responding to personal emails from friends.

Sometime after midnight, the irritating horn beeps of another useless car alarm went off under my apartment window, rousing me. I shambled back to my kitchen and microwaved a cup of chamomile tea followed by my favorite late-night snack, popcorn. Not exactly the healthiest meal, but at least a high-fiber one.

I cuddled up in an afghan on my couch and flicked on my TV, clicking through numerous stations. A bunch of infomercials. Home shopping junk. Some really strange music videos. A replay of the eleven o'clock news seemed like my best bet. Between slurps of tea, I watched clips of terrorist activity in Europe, a growing tax scandal for our state governor, and a blazing fire in Medford. The microwave beeped and I headed back into my kitchen for my popcorn.

As I dumped it into a plastic bowl, I thought I heard Pinkowski's voice on my TV. What the...? I raced back into my living room and there she was, Nancy Pinkowski, speaking to news reporters covering the clinic rally with muffled chanting in the background.

"These protestors are a dangerous threat to a woman's right to choose. They claim to be pro-life, except when it comes to the lives of our patients and staff. These extremists are currently under suspicion in the murder of one of our escorts."

The reporters leapt on that remark like hungry dogs. They pushed their way toward Pinkowski, sticking their microphones under her nose.

"Just ask Marguerite Montez at the Charles County District Attorney's office," she said. "They're investigating the killing of one of our escorts and some pro-life fanatics are prime suspects. I wouldn't be surprised if they're members of groups rallying here today, like Edgar Thompson's Center for Family Values."

What the hell? The broadcast then jumped to video of Edgar Thompson, meticulously dressed and surrounded by a group of supporters, with the Ice Queen visible near his right shoulder. "That charge is ludicrous," he said. "How sad that Ms. Pinkowski should try to capitalize on a murder of this poor woman. It's just an attempt to smear our organization with outrageous claims. Although we may not approve of this victim's volunteer work, we don't condone killing of anyone, including clinic escorts. Sadly, Ms. Pinkowski's merely diverting attention from millions of innocent lives her industry takes every year for profit. Imagine those who perpetrate this national genocide on children trying to paint us as killers."

The camera returned to a newscaster's smiling face. "We contacted Charles County's District Attorney's office, but they did not return our calls before our broadcast. And in a moment, our latest Bruins highlights..."

Holy shit. Damn that Pinkowski! I couldn't believe she'd make this overblown charge, trying to drag us into her political quicksand. Didn't she realize that her remarks might compromise our investigation into Miriam's death? But then, she had a different agenda from mine. She already believed extremists killed Miriam and she wanted it out there, front and center. And it didn't hurt to galvanize her troops while Thompson incited his own forces in the region.

I grabbed my cell phone and had forgotten my ringer was on silent. Checking my voice mail, I couldn't believe that I'd missed so many calls from Saint Cyr, Dr. Ronni, my mother, Susan, and other assorted family members, all telling me to turn on my TV to watch the eleven o'clock news. Saint Cyr left a second urgent message asking me to call him before I left for work in the morning. His call came right before one from O'Brien, who sounded mighty angry.

"Hey, Montez. What the hell did you tell that Pinkowski gal? This is sure to cause a shit storm. Be in my office at eight-thirty tomorrow morning. We've got a meeting with Mr. Quinn at eleven on this case and he's gonna expect some answers."

I really wanted to call Saint Cyr to talk strategy, or to phone my sisters or gal pals to complain about the situation, but not at this hour. It had to wait until morning, even though I knew I wouldn't get much sleep before then. I lay awake in my bed until I called Saint Cyr's cell around six-thirty from my place rather than my office. Flora possessed amazing hearing when she wanted to listen to calls, and I didn't want her to overhear this one.

"Hi, Gérard, it's me. I missed that original news broadcast and your calls. Can't believe how Pinkowski blew this out of proportion."

"She has made a nasty kerfuffle, eh?"

"I got an angry message from O'Brien. He wants me in his office early to explain myself. Then a meeting with Quinn to clear things up and update him on our case."

"Connelly phoned me, too. I told him that we didn't say anything like that to Pinkowski. Only doing our job by looking at all the angles. And we never spoke of any prime suspect. Certainly no one in Thompson's group. He will speak to O'Brien about what really happened."

"Was he angry?"

"No. He wanted to be certain that we promised Pinkowski nothing."

"We didn't. That's why she took to the airwaves. Hoping to corner us into investigating those Messengers," I said.

"This is the real reason for which she spoke to us. But call me if you would need help."

"Thanks, Gérard. I'll tell them what happened. Just doing our job. Excluding some possible suspects. Eliminating reasonable doubt."

"Right. Let me know what happens, eh?"

"Definitely."

"*Bonne chance.*"

"Thanks. I hope I won't need luck. Talk to you later."

As I put my cell phone down, I felt relieved to have someone in my corner on this one. Yet part of me simmered with anger about needing any backup. O'Brien knew better than anyone that we needed an airtight case. We couldn't leave Pinkowski's claims hanging out there if we wanted to cream Kiley at trial. How could Quinn argue with that reasoning? As I got dressed for work, I wondered if this day was going to be my last one on the job. Susan was right. I should have started networking long ago.

Unfortunately, when I arrived at O'Brien's office, he was already there. He sat calmly on the edge of his desk, cradling a cup of coffee.

"Montez. This better be good." He closed his office door behind me. "Quinn's already received calls from the Cardinal, top representatives of the Center for Family Values and his own parish pastor. They're all demanding apologies. You've stirred up quite a hornet's nest."

"Saint Cyr and I found credible evidence of threats against our victim for her volunteer work at an abortion clinic. We had to nail everything down or else the defense will eat our lunch at trial. I didn't want to leave behind any loose ends."

"Tying up loose ends is one thing. But telling that clinic director we think members of Thompson's group are prime suspects is another."

"We never told her that," I said. "She made that up to try to draw our office into her fight with Thompson's group. We asked her and her staff about those threats against Miriam Carpenter and other protest activities at her clinic. And we showed her a photo of one of the protesters we found in some FBI files to see if she might help identify him. That's it."

He gurgled down some more coffee and let out a deep sigh. "Lucky for you Connelly got that same story last night from his Canadian detective. Not even a real American cop. Doesn't even vote in the county," said O'Brien. "But Connelly's a good man. He wouldn't screw with the truth. Neither do I."

"I'm telling the truth about Pinkowski," I said.

"It looks like it, so that's why I'm not kicking your ass out of here today. Just write it up for me and I'll get it to Quinn before our 11:00."

"So writing it up will square things with Quinn?"

"Hell, no. He'll be completely pissed at you." O'Brien chuckled as he leaned back in his creaking office chair.

"Why?"

"He'll be angry about any bad publicity. And he knows Thompson from their law school days at Harvard. But that doesn't mean you weren't doing what you're supposed to do," said O'Brien.

"So if I didn't do my job, he'd be happy."

"No. He'd be pissed at you later if we lose the case by not investigating deeply enough and leaving an opening for reasonable doubt."

"So if I do my job, he'll be pissed now. And if I don't do my job, he'll be pissed later."

Barely able to suppress a huge grin, O'Brien took a hearty swig out of his coffee. "You got it. Everybody gets their ass kicked for no reason in these high-profile cases."

"But doesn't my doing the job right count for anything?" I asked.

"Yeah. If you see your job as putting bad guys in jail for good. You gotta be satisfied with doing that if you're going to make it in homicide. Don't ever expect a big bouquet of flowers from Quinn or anybody else."

O'Brien had me there. I couldn't expect to please anybody, even Quinn, if I did my job right. Ruffling feathers came with the territory.

"Okay, I'll write it up," I said.

With a wave of his hand, O'Brien dismissed me. As I walked to my office, he called out, "Welcome to the big leagues, Monty."

It was the first time he had used my nickname since I got promoted, so it was a small victory. I returned to my desk and pounded out my report on my computer. Around ten, I handed it over to O'Brien. He read through it and seemed satisfied, passing it along to Quinn's office. Eleven o'clock couldn't come fast enough for me. I filled up my remaining time making phone calls to dealers in wet explosives on the subway project. I managed to clear two invoices from Carpenter, leaving nine invoices for explosives unaccounted for—or possibly faked.

I also called Harvey George's office about Carpenter's financials and Harvey advised me of what we already knew. Our office was either missing some business records or Carpenter had created dummy purchase orders and invoices to hide improper or illegal conduct.

I asked him if he had much experience with offshore banking.

"Some of my clients go offshore to try to reduce their tax liability, but the IRS is closing those loopholes. Others do it in hopes of getting higher returns on their money, Margaret," he said, with his needle stuck on calling me by that name.

140

"What about banking in the Grand Caymans?" I asked.

"Usually done to hide money from the IRS or perhaps a soon-to-be ex-spouse, since they have very strong banking secrecy laws, Margaret."

"So its secrecy laws make it a popular place for money laundering?"

"Yes, Margaret. Silence is what makes the banking world go round," he said.

I thanked him for his help and told him I might call upon him again in the future. Then Flora came into my office wearing a curly brown wig and handed me a fax from Mrs. Childs' business managers. She could tell I was feeling down.

"Honey, remember you gotta break a few eggs to make a cake."

"Thanks, Flora," I said, scanning the fax.

When I contacted Mrs. Childs' business managers, they noted their receipt of cancelled checks which Patrick Carpenter had endorsed but then signed over to a third party. These cancelled checks, totaling about $30,000, bore a deposit stamp for Archangel Investment Trust. Between these earlier wire transfers and the cancelled checks, Carpenter sent about $90,000 to the trust over the past two years. Was he was laundering money from illegal explosive deals, or paying off some other obligations? My mind reeled with this new information.

Before I could untangle it all, O'Brien and I were headed to Quinn's office. I filled him in on the latest financial news on our way, perhaps as a parting duty before my possible demotion to traffic court. My heart pounded in my chest.

"The main thing right now is to go with the flow. Don't say a word. I'll do all the talking unless Quinn asks you to say something."

As we entered a vestibule before Quinn's office, several secretaries typed away and one of Quinn's political handlers walked over toward us, addressing himself solely to O'Brien. "Mr. Quinn wishes to speak with you first. Then she can apologize."

He pulled O'Brien into Mr. Quinn's office. As the door closed, I felt foolish waiting there. My mind began to race with questions. Apologize? For what? Doing my damn job! I couldn't believe that yesterday's barrage wouldn't be the last time I'd get egg on my face this week. Anxiously scrolling through my cell phone messages, I noticed another public posting on Ginny's website.

"Luisa deserves a decent burial among her own people. *El Galo.*"

I frowned at this bread crumb tossed my way and wondered how I'd make any headway on these cryptic missives, especially if I got canned this morning. But then I'd have plenty of free time to track down Luisa.

Eventually, Quinn's adviser stuck his head out of Quinn's office door and waved for me to come in. "Ms. Montez. Please wait here." He pointed to a spot near Quinn's doorway.

Then he returned to Quinn's side and hunched over some documents as they commiserated with each other. I'd never been inside Quinn's office before, a cavernous space with high ceilings and heavy oak bookcases filled floor-to-ceiling with hundreds of law books. An oval conference table with six chairs was arranged to my immediate right. On my left, a comfy seating area featured a cocktail table sandwiched between two small loveseats.

Quinn sat about a mile away from me at a gigantic oak desk. Behind him was a long credenza crowded with photos of him smiling with his family or shaking hands with local politicians and celebrities. Two tall schoolhouse windows, above the credenza, displayed an unbelievable view of the city across the river. His desk faced two burgundy wing-backed chairs with brass upholstery studs. O'Brien sat in one wing-backed chair, and I couldn't see who sat in the other, except for his white sleeves, cuffed pant legs of a gray pin-striped suit and backs of a pair of wing-tipped shoes.

Quinn drew a deep breath and then stared at me for several long seconds. "The role of the district attorney's office is to inspire confidence in the public that investigations are being appropriately handled and that the needs of public safety and justice are being properly served. When there is public confusion about the workings of this department, we endanger the public trust, which is so crucial to our role here. We cannot have confusion about our investigations."

At first, I thought he was lecturing me, but then it became clear that he was reading from a prepared statement on his desk.

"Although Ms. Montez thought her actions appropriate, she

unintentionally caused confusion during a very delicate time in this investigation. And for that, my office apologizes to Mr. Thompson and the Center for Family Values."

"Sounds good," a familiar voice said. Edgar Thompson? I stood stunned, frozen in my tracks.

He continued. "Thank you for handling this so quickly, Frank. I read about this case in the papers. Saw photos of this victim and her young family. So disturbing that it should happen in a church. Please give my condolences to them. Certainly, it's anathema that any member of our organization be accused of taking any innocent human life, born or unborn."

"Of course. This press release will make that crystal clear."

Quinn turned to his political wrangler. "Be sure this goes to all the major media outlets within the next hour."

"Yes, Mr. Quinn," he said. "I'll fax a copy right over to your hotel and your national headquarters, Mr. Thompson. As well as to Ms. Harkins' firm. We have all of those numbers."

"Thank you. I'm greatly relieved that our organization is not truly under investigation by your office for any criminal act, especially homicide."

"And Ms. Montez wants to offer her personal apology to you, Mr. Thompson."

"Ms. Montez," said Quinn, not looking at me. "I'm sure Mr. Thompson wishes to hear from you now."

I tried to step forward, but couldn't move for a several interminable seconds. O'Brien peeked around the chair's leather armrest, nodding for me to come forward. Pure survival instincts took over and I lurched toward the left side of Quinn's desk. I soon found myself standing about two feet away from Edgar Thompson who sat, relaxed, in one of Quinn's leather chairs.

"So this is the young lady who's caused all of this trouble," he said. "I believe we've met before. I never forget a face."

"Yes, we met at arraignments for violations of buffer zones in district court."

"Oh, yes," he said. "Lillian normally handles those, but I like to be able to do my part when I can," he said, talking past me to Quinn.

"Perhaps you may be seeing her again soon in district court," Quinn said, hinting at my inevitable demotion. "Well, Ms. Montez, as you were about to say."

I felt a rush of blood to my face. I gulped back my anger and fought off a volcano of fury tightening my throat. Think fast on your feet, girl, you're a lawyer. I stared right at Thompson. "Mr. Thompson. I apologize for any misunderstanding which may have resulted from our efforts to professionally and objectively investigate Mrs. Carpenter's murder."

I would apologize only for the misinterpretation, but not for my conduct. I did the right thing tracking down those leads.

"Ms. Montez, I'm sure you'll be much more careful in the future."

"Thank you for being so understanding," Mr. Quinn said, breezing past me. "Let me walk you out, Edgar. I'm sure you have much more important things to attend to today."

"Yes, Astrid and I are holding a press conference at noon to announce our new charitable campaign for homeless families. I hope you might be willing to donate, Frank." Thompson rose from his chair and walked past me.

"Absolutely. Will you be joining us at the governor's breakfast this Sunday, Edgar?"

"Ah, yes. The governor's an old family friend. Perhaps, Frank, I can talk you into joining me for the Beanpot Competition. The Crimson has an outstanding goalie this year. And Lillian's loaning me her firm's suite overlooking center ice."

"If I can make that game, I'll give your office a call."

As soon as they closed Quinn's office door behind them, his political adviser lowered himself into Thompson's vacated chair. He mopped his brow with a starched handkerchief.

"What a disaster! I recommended to Mr. Quinn that he put a woman in a high visibility post. To satisfy the liberals. And to pay dividends in other areas, too. Like placating your own Puerto Rican community. I now regret that recommendation, Ms. Montez."

"I'm not Puerto Rican."

"What?" Quinn's handler fixed his gaze on me.

"I'm not Puerto Rican. I'm Portuguese."

"Well, you look Puerto Rican. And that's what counts. But now you've delivered us this nightmare."

O'Brien spoke. "Take it easy. She did fine. We dodged a bullet here."

"Try to keep us out of the line of fire for the rest of this investigation, O'Brien. Put her on a very short leash." He shifted restlessly in his chair. "And don't go blabbing about that Portuguese thing. You've done enough damage for one day."

Our brief audience concluded, he booted us out of Quinn's office. I boiled with anger, my face and scalp burning red-hot.

"Remember. The big leagues," said O'Brien. "Take a day or two off. Then lay low for a couple of weeks."

Lay low. How much lower could I get with a shotgun apology followed by a press release publicly rebuking me? I headed straight for my office, disgusted by the whole scene. I imagined Kiley reading Quinn's press release and laughing his ass off over his afternoon cappuccino. I looked out the narrow window in my office onto City Square and thought about resigning.

"Thinking of jumping, eh?"

I turned to see AngelEyes in my doorway.

"The idea has its charm." I looked back out my window, still steaming mad. I didn't want to look at him, afraid I might burst into furious tears at any moment. If you're a woman who wants to be taken seriously, never cry at work, no matter what.

"Did you have your meeting?"

"No. They had their meeting."

"How did it go?"

"Which part? My degrading personal apology to Edgar Thompson? Or that humiliating press release that's going out to the entire world in about an hour?"

"*Sacré*! This unfairness is hard to believe."

"Believe it. It'll be in all the papers. Montez Screws Up. Apologizes for Doing Her Job Right. Film at eleven."

My voice quaked with anger. In a matter of days I'd gone from the next Nancy Grace to Nancy Disgrace. And right on time for plenty of full-scale friend-and-family embarrassment at my sister's anniversary celebration this Sunday afternoon.

"Did you get fired?"

"Sort of. I get a brief vacation and then I show up every day as long as I don't do anything like investigating this case. And if I'm lucky, I'll be demoted back into district court once this blows over."

"I'm sorry things turned out this way." He squeezed my right shoulder.

"No need for you to apologize. I think there've been quite enough apologies today from people who haven't done anything wrong."

"Let me bring you to lunch."

"Nope. I want to feel sorry for myself for a little longer."

We stood without speaking for a few moments. "I know a good drinking place," he suggested with a mischievous grin.

My initial instinct was to refuse. But then I thought for a moment. "I know a very good drinking place," I said.

Hey, why the hell not? Lousy morning at work. A good-looking guy like AngelEyes. A few drinks in the middle of a workday. All the makings of some splendid trouble. At least if I got caught drinking and fooling around on the job, I'd have a real reason to apologize.

CHAPTER 21

We headed to an old law school dive, *Red Beret*, two blocks from the courthouse and hidden away in a basement of a rundown brick building. Its dirt-cheap drinks, tall on liquor and short on ice, made it a nighttime haven for cash-strapped law students looking to unwind after burying their heads all day in dense law books.

We pulled open its heavy black door and entered a narrow pub with its long polished bar. Smells of stale cigarette smoke and spilled beer lingered in the air. A dizzying array of hats hung from ceiling tiles and sprouted from tacks on its walls. Several straw cowboy hats. Clumps of knit ski masks. Two yellow hard hats. A crisp white nurse's cap. A black silk yarmulke. Tons of baseball caps bearing sports team or college logos. An amazing gray fedora with a large topaz plume. And what looked like a cardinal's scarlet skullcap.

Iron grates over its low tinted windows made it virtually impossible to see into this bar, making it a favorite cheater's lounge during daylight hours. Its dim lighting and series of high-backed booths allowed for a private rendezvous for two. Anyone who bumped into you at *Red Beret* while the sun was up wouldn't be in any position to blab about it to anybody else. Isolated, dark, and cheap made it the right spot to play a little hooky.

Not that I claimed to be a great expert in playing hooky, since I spent nearly every waking hour striving to do something. After a couple of vodka tonics on the rocks and looking into AngelEyes' baby blues for nearly an hour, the concept of playing hooky started to grow on me. We spent much of that hour talking about pretty safe subjects, like our jobs.

"My dad worked as a cop. And I idolized him in my childhood. He died young, in his fifties, he had a heart attack during a routine patrol in the old part of Québec City." He shrugged. "For me, it was a natural choice, eh? I became first a police sketch artist. But then I wanted to be more in the action."

"Is your mom still alive, Gérard?"

"Yes, she still lives in the house where we grew up."

Our hands bumped into each other's reaching into a peanut bowl. "Ladies first," he said, giving way.

"She must be very proud that you followed in his footsteps. And that you've become a detective in homicide."

"Yes... and no." His hand balanced in a so-so gesture. "She is very proud of my work. But she knows many difficulties for a policeman and his family. She knows the long days and the crazy hours and the high stress. She has lived it." He shrugged again. "And you, Marguerite? For sure, a family of barristers?"

"No, my parents own a bakery and I have four sisters. We're all pretty close in age. But no lawyers. I'm the first in my family to make it through law school. Or any kind of grad school."

"You're the family success story, eh?"

"Not really," I said, thinking of my mother's view of success. "My sisters have chosen their own interesting paths, so there's plenty of family success to spread around."

"Why not become a rich barrister in a big Boston society?"

"Never wanted the big-firm scene. All of those awful billable hours for fat-cat clients."

"Long hours, but very big rewards."

"So they tell me. But just like you, I prefer crazy hours, high stress, and lousy pay. Hard to find great jobs like ours every day."

AngelEyes laughed. "Touché. But really, I am interested. Why pick the prosecutor's office?"

"Goes back a long time ago." I munched on peanuts and sipped my vodka tonic. "When I was a kid, a friend of mine got murdered. My best friend."

I stopped for a moment. It had been a long time since I'd discussed Ginny with anyone else. Her story had bounced around for decades inside my mental echo chamber. Like most unpleasant realities, my parents never broached this subject with me, and my sisters still seemed uncomfortable asking me about it. *Ficar face* prevailed.

"Wow. What happened?"

"Ginny Viera. A really sweet person. Big brown eyes full of fun and mischief. A very talented dancer. We did everything together." I twirled the stirrer in my right hand for a moment. "Both of us could be real tomboys."

"I don't see you as the tomboy type."

"Oh, yeah? Let's arm-wrestle right here to prove it," I said, laughing.

"Hey, watch it. My strength is mighty." He raised his right arm, flexing his bicep.

"Yeah, right."

I had to admit he looked like he was in damn good shape.

"We had a favorite shortcut to school through a couple of deserted mill buildings near the Charles River. We'd sneak over there to play before and after school. Trapped some frogs. Climbed trees. Built a makeshift fort inside one building. Really only a couple of rotting boards propped up on some rocks with an old blue blanket draped over a pole in the middle."

"Your parents knew nothing of that shortcut?"

"No. It was our little secret. Our parents would've killed us if they knew about it. A couple of weeks later they found Ginny raped and strangled in a sewer drainpipe. She was only thirteen years old." I paused and felt the weight of my words. "It destroyed her family."

"Such a terrible thing." He touched my forearm. "Did they ever find the killer?"

"No. It remains an unsolved case."

I didn't dare tell him I was still chasing down leads on her website or that I was wracked with guilt because I didn't tell the truth when Ginny might have remained alive.

"The search for justice."

"Yeah. Something like that." And maybe a tad bit of a stubborn control freak who jettisoned any thoughts of relying on anybody for help, real or divine.

"And since you're a good student but a bad shot, you ended up in the DA's office, eh?"

I laughed and talked with AngelEyes about the trials and tribulations of law school. As I approached my new world record of little sleep, no breakfast and three vodka tonics in less than two hours, I found myself answering those inevitable questions about the ex. I avoided mentioning Kiley by name to AngelEyes. I wasn't *that* buzzed yet.

"You met him in law school?"

"Yup. I'd taken two years off to work as a paralegal in a law firm and save money for law school. I went four years at night. It took a lot of sacrifice, but I plugged along. My ex taught criminal procedure part-time at night as a young lawyer."

"I bet you got an A in that class."

"Yes, I did."

I paused and sipped my vodka tonic. "But he wasn't my professor. My ex taught another section. We met in a law school break room. He was a real charmer. A whirlwind romance and we eloped. So unlike me to be so impulsive. Not long after we got married, he landed some major criminal cases and success changed him. He fell in love with being a celebrity and all its shallow trappings."

"What made you attracted to him?"

"Very intelligent. I've got a soft spot for brainy guys. Much more important to me than looks." Although AngelEyes was a rare exception, smart and good-looking.

"He could not have been too smart: he let you go, eh?"

I had to bite my tongue not to reply with some self-deprecating remark, having long ago perfected the art of deflecting compliments, especially from a handsome man who could speak French. Watching his lips, I wondered if he'd been hitting on me at all or merely being nice to a slightly tipsy, bummed-out ADA. "That's nice of you to say," I answered.

"No, I mean it. To me, you are quite remarkable." He ticked off attributes on his fingers. "You are smart. You are attractive. You are lively. You are dedicated to your work."

"Thanks."

I appreciated that he didn't nose into why Kiley and I'd split up. Unlike some divorced folks who wallowed in their angst, I guess I'd never really enjoyed talking about my failed marriage. I didn't like to fail, especially in such a mundane way as being dumped for another woman, and then another, and another. At least if Kiley left me for another man, I'd have a much more interesting story to tell.

"What about *you*?" I asked, ticking off the same qualities on my fingers. "Smart. Attractive. Lively. Dedicated to your work."

AngelEyes started to laugh. "Hey, it is no fair to make the table turn." He took a swig of his beer.

"I mean it, too."

He smiled. His chance to be flattered and flustered for now. But I think he enjoyed our banter.

"No lady love able to capture your heart?"

"No."

"Not even close?"

"Well, once. Five years ago, I got engaged. It was a long-distance relationship, because I lived in Québec City and she lived in Montréal."

"Why did you break up?"

"Because I lived in Québec City and she lived in Montréal."

"What? Couldn't you both find a house in the same town in your price range?"

"No. She got a big promotion in her job with an ad agency in Montréal. I'd just passed my detective exam and wanted to move up in the force. Neither of us desired to move. Told us all we needed to know, eh?"

"Dating anyone seriously now?"

I couldn't believe I asked that one, but why not? I'm sure Dr. Ronni would've booted my ass for not being more aggressive.

"No. I am dating different people, yes, of course. But there is nothing serious."

I shook my head in disbelief. A guy this cute wasn't dating anyone and I might have an open field in the romance department if I wanted it. Deep down inside I wanted it, but did I really need to add to my travails right now?

"It's hard to find people to connect with," he said. "It seemed so easy in my parents' day, eh? People met, they fell in love, they got married, they had a family, they stayed together, *voilà*. Today, a simple thing, such as like connecting with someone nice, it seems so hard. As for love, marriage, family—they seem impossible."

Hard to believe any guy ever mentioning the "l" or the "m" word first. Yet before I could rant about troubled modern-day relationships, his cell phone went off. He looked at his caller ID. "It is Connelly."

He answered it and his smiling features melted into seriousness.

"Okay, I'm on my way."

He slid his cell phone shut. "I need to go."

"What happened?" I asked.

"Connelly got major results back from our lab. Want to come?"

"Absolutely."

O'Brien wanted me to lay low in the courthouse, take some time off. I could do whatever I wanted on my vacation days, even visit our county's police department.

AngelEyes ignored my request to help pay our tab, and then we bolted out. As we reached a top stair, he suddenly stopped and looked directly into my eyes. I felt a bit weak in my knees. Too many vodka tonics or something more? He rested his hands on my shoulders and leaned forward. Was he going to kiss me? It had been a long time.

He came very close to my mouth and then he sniffed, and sniffed once again. "Your breath smells like you've been drinking. Here, take one of these." Fumbling for something in his pocket, he took out a tiny pack of breath mints. "For sure, we each take a few or else we'll both be in more headaches, eh?"

He spilled out four green mints into my hand.

"Plenty enough for two," I said.

I felt quite stupid about crossing wires there for a moment. Hopefully he hadn't noticed, and I reminded myself to keep a safe distance. He picked a couple out of my hand and I popped two remaining ones into my mouth. We stood face to face, quietly sucking on our mints.

Yup, getting awfully hard to connect with people these days.

CHAPTER 22

Connelly didn't look very happy when Saint Cyr and I got back to his precinct. Bifocals perched at the tip of his nose, he was examining preliminary forensic reports. "Houston, we have a problem," he said. "The professor ain't matching up."

"Which parts?" asked Saint Cyr.

"Height. Hand. And shoe size," said Connelly. He began to read the report out loud. "The converging point based on blood splatter patterns suggest that Miriam's killer likely ranged in height from five-eleven to six-two. The professor couldn't be more than five-seven or five-eight."

"But maybe he stood on a pew or kneeler. And she probably knelt at that chapel railing. Did they take those things into account?" I asked.

"They did. But there's more." He flipped to another page. "From an analysis of a probable converging point, her assailant likely used his right hand to deliver fatal blows to her head. The professor's a lefty."

"Perhaps he made use of his right hand," said Saint Cyr.

"Did he use his bigger feet that day, too? Because according to this report, our killer wore a size-twelve waffle-print boot. Our professor prefers size-ten sneakers."

"Maybe he found the boots in the trash and put them on over his runners," said Saint Cyr.

"Yup, we thought about that, too. But we've gone through our evidence list of everything in his tent. Not a single pair of size-twelve anythings. And just to make our day, forensics found that besides church items he used as dinnerware, none of the other stolen items from Miriam or the church has any fingerprints on them."

"Not the professor's?"

"Not anyone's, Monty."

"He may have worn gloves. It was at least ten below Celsius that morning," said Saint Cyr.

"Maybe. It's hard to swallow that the professor was so careful that after he put on a big pair of boots, slipped on some gloves, changed into a righty, and then killed and robbed Miriam. Yet he never got around to taking any cash or IDs from her purse. It doesn't make sense. You saw him. He can barely remember his name, never mind plan this out. Nope. This was no robbery gone wrong. Somebody else was hiding in that church. And that person found a convenient dumping ground in his shopping cart."

"Mrs. Silva told us he parked it there regularly, so someone could've planned it that way," I said. "Did you get a chance to ask the professor if he saw anybody else in the church?"

"According to his public defender, the professor claims that he only saw a ghost, all in white."

"A ghost?" I asked.

"Yup. A ghost," said Connelly. "More like the ghost of Jack Daniels past."

"Wait. That's what Daniel Silva claims he saw. A hooded white ghost. Father Mac told us that a white hooded vestment, a supplicant, was missing from his sacristy chamber. The murderer could've been wearing that vestment when he killed Miriam," I said.

"Patrick Carpenter could've worn that vestment to prevent blood splatters on his work clothes," said Connelly.

"Does Carpenter match anything?" asked Saint Cyr.

"He'd be okay on height. But we didn't seize any of his boots from his house. We've contacted his lawyer to check out other particulars."

"I don't think Kiley's gonna give up any more info without a fight," I said. "O'Brien is supposed to go to court this week on Kiley's motion to reconsider trying to get back Carpenter's household and office items." I wouldn't mind a few rounds in the ring with Kiley, particularly if I got to deliver a knockout punch on this case. "Does O'Brien know this yet?" I asked.

"I called, but he wasn't in."

"I also got an update on Carpenter's financials for you guys. Our outside experts agree that records are missing or Carpenter faked some of his records. Mrs. Childs' business managers also claimed they received cancelled checks with Archangel Investment Trust on some of them," I said.

"Archangel again?" asked Connelly. "Do we have a line on these folks?"

"They're based in the Grand Caymans. Virtually unreachable under that country's bank secrecy laws," I said.

"He's probably laundering dirty money through it. Nolan must have been lying to us. Carpenter's neck-deep in illegal sales, not some innocent target of thieves," said Saint Cyr.

"I agree with Gérard. Can you squeeze anything out of them on our case?" I asked.

"We can always threaten to blow their investigation to get them to cough something up," Connelly said.

"Worth a try, eh?" said Saint Cyr.

"Do you mind delivering this good news to him?" asked Connelly. He handed me a copy of his report. "Remember, delivery only, Monty. No need to investigate each aspect of this report. Gérard and I will do that."

"No problem," I said.

I had my own angles to investigate anyway, although it would be humiliating to go back to the courthouse today. Everybody was sure to be blabbing about Quinn's embarrassing press release. But at least I would be giving O'Brien information he could use against Kiley's motion later in the week.

I left Connelly and Saint Cyr and headed back to City Square. Shuddering as a blast of cold air rolled across the open square, I tightened a blue scarf around my neck. I stopped for a moment to watch a cluster of six or seven protesters marching in front of our courthouse.

I'd often viewed their presence as a mildly annoying but strangely reassuring sign that free speech remained alive and well in our commonwealth. I hoped none of them moonlighted by making menacing calls or planting bombs. Before returning to my office, I decided to take the place's temperature on the Quinn's public rebuke of me and stopped by to see Cranky Albert.

"Well. If it isn't the divine Miss M."

"It's me for sure. Although I think the M stands for mud around here right now."

"Hey, not to worry. You running with the big dogs now, girl. Always gonna get a bit dirty. How you holding up?"

"I'm stumbling along okay. Trying not to fall on my face too many times."

"As long as you're falling forward and not backward," said Albert.

"Thanks. I'll try to remember that."

"You sound pretty weary. "

"Albert, I'm not getting much sleep these days." I reached for a Styrofoam cup for tea. "I'm trying to sort through some complicated stuff. Trying to get all these pieces to fit."

"Sometimes it's a good idea to get away from it for a few hours. Go for a nice walk to clear your head. Come back to it fresh."

"Maybe so. I feel like I must be missing something. It might be something right in front of my face." I paid him for my drink.

"Or could be something that's not there to see. Something that should be there, but is actually missing," he said.

"Good food for thought, Albert."

Maybe Cranky Albert's right. Perhaps I needed to step back and take a break from this mess. Unfortunately, stepping back wasn't ever my style.

I dropped off a copy of Connelly's forensics report with Flora. She told me that everybody was gossiping about Quinn's press release, a slice of news I could've done without. I let her know I'd be taking a couple of vacation days. Time off would free me up to do a little more nosing around on Simple Simon and Fetus de Milo. Maybe one of them wore a size twelve and a pair of warm winter gloves. Since I was persona non grata in Miriam's case, what did I have to lose?

CHAPTER 23

Most New Englanders head for tropical locales on their vacation days. But I decided on a staycation, touching base with my old cronies from district court below O'Brien's radar. Late afternoon, I headed to the courthouse basement and tracked down Baldy who served as bailiff on a number of these buffer-zone arraignments. With a promise of two dozen *linguiça* rolls from my family bakery, he took a look through his jailhouse transfer files.

Simple Simon's real name was Terry Randolph. Over at the court clerk's office, I pulled up Randolph's court files on an office computer. His file consisted of a cluttered list of nearly two dozen arrests in the past two years associated with buffer-zone violations around clinics, gay bars, and strip joints. Someone named Maria Rubio bailed him out every time. Perhaps she was Fetus de Milo?

A lawyer from Lillian Harkins' firm handled most of those group arraignments. I scanned the rest of this list and stopped on an entry for an individual arraignment last year for making harassing telephone calls. A judge dismissed this case when the victim didn't show. Ice Queen's firm again, even though it wasn't one of those Center rallies or protests. I'd need to dig up some old police files to get more details to see if those calls targeted Miriam or any other member of Pinkowski's clinic staff. Since Simple Simon's last known address was right off the subway's Red Line, I decided to pay him a visit.

Simple Simon's neighborhood had a misfortunate location squished between commuter rail tracks and a series of fenced rental car and towing company parking lots. A jumble of broken-down houses, mostly triple-deckers, jammed together on his street, punctuated by an occasional greasy spoon or cash-checking joint. I headed for Elm Street in an area devoid of any living vegetation. I followed sidewalk cracks and potholes and walked around two young girls drawing pictures with chalk on broken sidewalk pavers.

I soon found myself at the foot of 127 Elm, another ramshackle triple-decker with corrugated gray metal siding, probably chock-full of asbestos. A loose board covered a gap in stonework on a bottom step. Tattered junk mail flyers danced around in the wind on a front stoop. My cell phone jiggled and another posting on Ginny's website greeted me.

"Wash away our sins where we celebrate the Holy Ghost every year."

I furrowed my brow. *El Galo* had omitted his usual moniker from this posting. Yet for once I was getting a definite location, the Saugus Fairgrounds, a huge open-air park within untamed conservation lands at Breakheart Reservation. Every year, Portuguese people throughout the region converged for a weekend of food, wine, music, and parades in honor of the Holy Spirit.

It was a major *festa*, and in recent times other area residents joined in to learn about Portuguese culture. Several years in a row, Ginny's rancho dance troupe performed on its large wooden dance floor. My parents made us go to keep us in touch with our ethnic heritage. We spent most of this festival running around the park and playing with our cousins in thick forests. Had Luisa been abducted or even killed there decades before?

I tapped in a response. *Meet me at bandstand. Six o'clock. If you want to help.*

Putting away my phone, I dragged my finger down a row of at least ten names next to apartment doorbells. No Randolph on this list. Buzzing several apartments to see if anyone might let me in, I got no response. I walked down a narrow alley and found its rear entrance unlocked. Squinting as I entered into a dark hallway, I noticed a separate buzzer for a basement apartment. I pushed the buzzer. No answer. I nearly jumped out of my skin when I turned around and saw a dried-up prune of a man wearing a Bruins cap, a blue robe, and orange flip flops looking down at me from a first-floor landing.

"I'm the super. Dermott. Here about that apartment?" he asked in a gruff tone.

"Looking for Terry Randolph."

I flashed my ADA's badge.

"Arson squad, I hope? About time you damn folks showed up. That idiot practically burned this whole place down. Want to see the mess he left behind?"

"Sure," I said without correcting his misperceptions.

He shuffled down and pulled out a ring of keys, unlocking the basement apartment. As its door swung open, a powerful stench of stale soot and singed carpet rushed out. Two basement windows let skinny slits of natural light into this dank hovel. Dermott walked casually to the room's center and tugged a cord attached to a lonesome light hanging from its low ceiling.

I covered my mouth with a Kleenex and ventured inside. The apartment consisted of one grim room with no kitchen and a decrepit green-tiled bathroom about the size of a telephone booth. On one side, ceiling tiles and wall paneling were scorched black from fire. A metal trash can filled with charred particles sat on a thin rug, stained with soot. "What happened?"

"Damn fool. At first I thought he'd burned somethin' on his hot plate. Then smoke started pourin' into my place. I was smart enough to grab my kitchen fire extinguisher."

"When did this fire occur?"

"About a week ago. And when I knocked on his door, he didn't answer. So I let myself in with my master. And what do ya think I see? Randolph tryin' to put out a fire in the trash can with a towel. Crazy fool."

"Did he say what happened?"

"He's talkin' some crazy mumbo jumbo about offerin' it up to God."

"Offering what?"

"Who the hell knows? Whatever he burned in that trash can, I guess. I put it out and told him to pack his stuff up. To get the hell outta here."

"Did he leave right away?"

"I let him call a woman friend to pick him up and take his junk outta here."

"Do you know her name?" I asked.

"Mary, Marie."

"Maria?"

"Yeah, maybe. Wears a weirdo hat with a baby stuck to it. Another screwball for sure."

"Did he get a lot of visitors?"

"No, mostly that plastic baby girl. Although couple of weeks back, one of his pals had a freakin' car alarm blarin' at three o'clock in the morning. This big black sedan thing. Crown Victoria or somethin' like that. Can't bring some fancy car around here and not expect crooks to try to steal it. I ran into that guy when I came bolting out of my apartment with my Bobby Orr." He raised his hockey stick up in his right hand.

"Can you describe what he looked like?"

"Middle-aged guy. Full head of hair. Dressed nice."

"Do you think you might be able to pick him out of some photos?"

"I guess so." He scratched his scraggly beard.

"Any chance you got his license number?"

"Naw. Too dark out."

"Did you see what Randolph and that woman took with them?"

"Not much to take. A folding table. Couple of chairs. A cot. Computer stuff. And of course his damn video camera. I swear he's attached to that thing. Probably videos himself taking a crap. Bunch of boxes of camera gear and videotapes, too."

"Did you get any contact info from him in case you needed to get a hold of him about this fire damage?"

"You bet. At first, he thought he'd skate out of here and leave me to explain it to the landlord. I told 'em both that I'd call the cops if they didn't leave a forwarding. That sure got 'em scared. So she showed me her driver's license and I took down her address. Gave it to the building owner. He might even sue him for torchin' this place."

"Good thinking, Dermott. I'll call my office and get an investigation team here right away. Is that okay?"

"Great. If you need a witness against him in court, I'd love to put that dope behind bars. Could've killed us all."

"Thanks. I need to make a quick call and then I'll be right up."

As Dermott shuffled out, I called Saint Cyr and told him what I had found and got him to send a forensics team. Within a half-hour, he and three arson techs started scouring Randolph's former apartment looking for fresh evidence amongst the sooty remains. Dermott looked pretty happy to see so many cops working on his arson case now.

As I turned to leave, Dermott called after me. "If you know anybody that needs an apartment, you send 'em my way. I'll give 'em a good deal."

I smiled, but I had no plans to do any apartment-hunting. I needed to go home and change into something more comfortable before my date with *El Galo*.

CHAPTER 24

I turned on my headlights and motored north along Route One with its seedy no-tell motels, strip malls, bars, and pawn shops. Saugus, a perfectly respectable bedroom community, was nestled behind this highway blight. Its suburban neighborhoods thinned to rural fields and a single-lane road to Breakheart Reservation, a sprawling park with the Saugus River and fishing lakes in dense woods. I arrived an hour early to find the reserve's main paved entrance blocked with a heavy locked chain. I drove past it about a quarter-mile and pulled the Bomb into a gravel turnout adjacent to a riverbank. From years of playing in these woods, I remembered an old trail into the festival grounds.

I doubted an elderly *El Galo* would venture this way, and a younger ally might not even know about this overgrown path. I parked the Bomb behind a utility building. Remembering Connelly's warning about shallow graves, I turned on my cell phone's GPS locator and grabbed a heavyweight flashlight and a tire iron out of my trunk.

Dusky clouds shrouded an early evening sky as wisps of snow floated across my path. Dry twigs snapped under my boot soles and scrawny scrub trees gave way to thick evergreens. A scent of pine lingered as I breathed in damp cold air. With each step, I constantly looked around me. I wondered if Luisa had been abducted from these woods or if her remains were dumped in a watery river grave, yet to be discovered. Flicking on my flashlight, I kept its beam low to the ground, hoping to light my way without announcing my arrival.

At one point, I spied a familiar decaying stone foundation near a steep hill overlooking the fairgrounds. Decades ago, my sisters, Ginny, and I pretended to be wilderness pioneers protecting our cabin from our invading cousins, shooting imaginary muskets at their incoming arrow sticks. I remembered background noises of Portuguese music and dancing and smells of simmering soup and smoked meats as we mimicked the popping sounds of long guns.

Tonight, my flashlight picked out a couple of rusty beer cans discarded inside, its grassy floor scorched from a summer campfire.

Scrambling up a rocky outcrop, I crouched down and peeked over its sheer edge. Looking at the fairgrounds below, a lone halogen light on a clapboard cookhouse illuminated an empty parking lot. Rustic outdoor restrooms sat in the cookhouse's shadow. A large open-air pavilion, where bands played and visitors danced, remained in complete darkness. If I had known better, I would have told *El Galo* to meet me at the well-lit cookhouse. But it was already five-thirty and likely too late to change plans.

I turned off my flashlight and remained perched on top of the hill, waiting for *El Galo* to walk up the paved entrance to the bandstand. Rubbing my gloved hands together and waggling my feet, I tried to stay warm as I waited... for over an hour. I checked for new messages on Ginny's website and found nothing. Aside from a few scurrying squirrels, I didn't see any movement in the fairgrounds. By seven o'clock it became apparent that *El Galo* was a no-show.

Rather than trudge through pitch-black woods, I decided to head back on the main road. Clicking on my flashlight, I stood up, my body stiff from sitting in a damp cold. Gingerly, I picked my way down this steep slope and used my tire iron as a walking stick. My boots slid on the glistening black ice covering a cluster of rocks. I grabbed hold of tree trunks and branches to steady myself. As I neared the bottom, I felt my left knee lock, then completely give way. I toppled twenty feet in mucky leaves and landed alongside a back wall of a set of foul-smelling restrooms.

Taking inventory, I realized I hadn't broken anything, as my bulky coat helped cushion my fall. But my left knee alternated between throbbing and stiffening up. About fifteen feet up the hill, my flashlight beamed in the darkness. My tire iron was nowhere in sight. I rubbed my knee, hoping to ease my muscles and get normal circulation going again. I glanced around warily in case *El Galo* made an overdue appearance. Five long minutes later, I slowly eased myself up and haltingly lumbered though muddy patches toward my flashlight. Retrieving it, I looked around for my tire iron and found it sticking out of a pile of soggy leaves.

I plodded down the sodden hill and stopped to run my light across an empty bandstand and dance stage. In my mind's eye, I imagined music playing and Ginny and her dance troupe twirling in their colorful skirts and scarves and slamming their heels on these floorboards. Festival-goers would clap and cheer from benches ringing this dance floor or lawn chairs arranged near its bandstand. Had Luisa performed here, too? I guessed I wasn't going to find out tonight.

Hobbling toward the parking lot, I heard a loud creaking sound. Like a lighthouse, I quickly shone my light back and forth, anxiously looking for *El Galo*. As I trained my light across the deserted grounds, I spied only a loose shutter rattling against a cookhouse window. Trudging along, I remained vigilant as I made my way to the main entrance and back on to the country road.

When I arrived back at the Bomb, I checked my backseat before unlocking my door. Shoving my flashlight into my coat pocket, I sat at my open driver's side door to pull off my damp boots. Under my car's dome light, I wondered why *El Galo* hadn't shown up.

At this pace, I'd be retired before I'd ever discover any connection between Ginny and Luisa. Reaching into my back seat, I pulled out a bag with a change of shoes and put them on. For once, I'd come prepared. I fired up my car to let her engine warm up. Popping open my trunk, I tossed my tire iron and dirty boots inside.

As I reached for my flashlight, someone suddenly grabbed my coat hood and yanked it back hard, choking me. My attacker dragged me backward. I struggled to breathe and tried to yell. Only scratchy peeps squeaked out. I kicked wildly and clawed at the grassy bank, trying to slow his unrelenting march. Sounds of a rushing river grew louder as my assailant hauled me down a wet knoll. I reached up and managed to grab my coat zipper and tugged it down several inches before it got jammed. Enough slack to let me gasp for air and start yelling for help.

Stopping, he clamped his pale, sweaty hand over my mouth. I looked up at intense brown eyes peering out of a black knit ski mask. I bit his right hand, hard, and he cried out. In that instant, I whacked his shin with my metal flashlight and he fell into the river's shallows.

Bolting for my car, I didn't dare look back. I raced toward the Bomb. I jumped in her front seat and threw her into reverse. Her tires spun as she roared backward. I shoved her into drive and gunned her up the dirt path. My car shimmied and groaned as she skidded on to the paved roadway. My heart didn't start beating normally again until I was halfway home on Route One.

I didn't know if it was *El Galo* or somebody else who attacked me. But one thing was certain, somebody had tried to kill me, and there was no way I dared to report it to anyone.

CHAPTER 25

Arlington Heights seemed way too upscale for Simple Simon's crowd. Trendy boutiques, coffee shops with comfy couches, and gourmet food stores offering the finest foods at twice their actual value dotted a quaint center in the Heights. A little slice of yuppie heaven tucked quietly between conservative, wealthy Belmont and the liberal bastion of the People's Republic of Cambridge.

The owner of Dermott's building had been very pleased to pass along Rubio's contact information this morning to me. As Saint Cyr drove along hilly Route Two, I never let him know about last night's attack or that I supposedly was on vacation from my job. Instead, I made sure my turtleneck shirt covered my abrasions and looked back over my shoulder to admire a hillside view of Boston's skyline.

My phone beeped and another odd message flashed on its screen. "Missed you last night. Better luck next time."

I wasn't sure if I'd missed the real *El Galo* last night or if somebody was playing with me.

"Everything all right?" asked Saint Cyr.

I slipped my phone back into my purse. "No problem. Just a pesky reminder notice."

"Yeah, we're all slaves to our devices."

Saint Cyr pulled up to a giant Wedgewood-blue Victorian house with soft cream trim paint and gorgeous scrollwork on its wraparound porch. I lusted after Victorians with their slate roofs and shingled round turrets. A low stone wall surrounded this stately home, its bay windows overlooking a neighborhood park where locals walked their dogs on gravel paths.

"Fetus de Milo must be doing pretty well for herself, Gérard."

"For sure. A queenly estate compared to Simple Simon's flat."

"Somebody's got to bankroll their movement. Lawyers and explosives are expensive these days."

We walked up a neat brick path sprinkled with rock salt to melt slick ice, and stepped onto a wraparound porch. After we rang the doorbell, a young Asian woman with a heart-shaped face and almond eyes peeked through a lace curtain on a side window of an oak doorway. Saint Cyr held up his police badge. She raised her dark eyebrows and only opened the front door halfway. "Yes?" she asked, smoothing her nurse's uniform.

"We're looking for Maria Rubio."

"Yes."

"Maria Rubio?"

"Yes."

Saint Cyr held up a copy of Maria's driver's license photo. "Here?" he asked, pointing to her license photo.

"Not here. Right now."

"Do you know when she'll be back?" he asked.

"Not here. Right now," she said.

"Will she come back later today?" asked Saint Cyr.

"Not here. Right now."

"Terry Randolph here?" Saint Cyr asked, showing her Randolph's picture.

She shook her head.

"That is the end of that line of questioning," Saint Cyr said. "She must be taking care of someone, eh? Anybody else home?" he called out.

"Keep your voice down, young man," boomed a husky female voice from inside the house.

She barked a few words in French to her young Asian nurse who stepped aside, revealing a white-haired woman with steely gray eyes, whirring toward us in a motorized wheelchair. Her commanding voice belied her fragile appearance, her rail-thin arms clamped onto each armrest. "My husband's not a well man and he's trying to get some rest," she said.

"I'm sorry, ma'am," Saint Cyr said. "Gérard Saint Cyr. Homicide. "

"Marguerite Montez. District Attorney's office."

She examined our badges closely and then stared up at us.

"And you are?" I asked.

"Augusta Wakefield. And you've wasted your time. I can tell you that no one's been murdered here, so you've come to a wrong address."

"Actually, we are looking for Maria Rubio. Your nurse couldn't tell us where to find her, Mrs. Wakefield," Saint Cyr said.

"It's Dr. Wakefield. I have a PhD in linguistics. I speak seven languages and taught for over twenty-seven years at Regis, young man. As you can plainly see, I don't need a nurse. Ms. Ling tends to my husband. She speaks three languages fluently, French, Vietnamese and Thai. The communication problem is clearly yours, not hers."

"*Mon Dieu.* If I'd only known about her French," Saint Cyr said.

"You speak French?" she asked, softening her tone a bit.

"*Mais oui, madame.*"

"One moment. I'm trying to place your accent."

She tapped her index finger on her chin and shifted a black sweater resting on her shoulders. I noticed an angel pin on the left lapel of her off-white blouse.

"*Je suis Québécois,*" said Saint Cyr.

"Lovely place if one must go to Canada. But certainly it pales in comparison to Paris," she said. She nodded her head toward me, like a demanding professor grilling her students. "Are you a French-speaking DA, to boot?"

"No, I speak some Portuguese."

"A regular United Nations of law enforcement. I suppose Portuguese is quite useful during Carnival in Rio or if you take a wrong turn out of Spain. Can't imagine that it's all that useful for homicides."

She may have been locked in a wheelchair, but Wakefield came out swinging like a heavyweight champ with that round of nasty remarks. All that sarcasm must be hiding something.

"Did your husband teach philosophy at Boston College, Dr. Wakefield?"

"Yes, recently retired and named Professor Emeritus."

"Father Mac at St. Stephen's spoke quite highly of him," I said, hoping my bluff would appeal to her vanity.

"You know Father Mac?" She touched an angel pin on her blouse.

"Yes, he's been helping with our investigation," I said. "So—could you help us locate Maria Rubio?"

"Why do you want to see Mrs. Rubio?"

"We have a few questions for her regarding a case. Is she here?" I asked.

"Mrs. Rubio is not here today. It's one of her days off."

"Do you have a home address for her?"

"This is her home. She's a live-in nurse and a skilled caregiver to my husband, George. He'd be warehoused in some nursing home if not for her diligence."

"Does she return here every night, even on her day off?" Saint Cyr asked.

"Sometimes yes, sometimes no."

"Do you have an address for sometimes no?" I asked, feeling impatient.

"I don't pry into her personal life. You'll have to contact her nursing agency."

"Which is?" I pressed.

"It starts with a "B". Bagley. Bechler. Something like that. In Boston somewhere. I'm not directory services."

"Thank you for your time, Dr. Wakefield. If she arrives home unexpectedly, I hope you'll be sure to call us." I handed her my business card.

Dr. Wakefield reversed her wheelchair, spun around and whirred away from us along a front hallway, signaling to Ms. Ling to close her front door.

"By the way, one last thing, Dr. Wakefield. Do you know a man named Terry Randolph?" I asked.

"I'm not the yellow pages, either. You'll have to do your own homework. *Boa noit*, Ms. Montez," she said, without turning or stopping her wheelchair. She disappeared from sight and only her wheelchair motor's hum and the squeaks from its rubber wheels echoed in her hallway.

"*Obrigado y boa noit*, Dr. Wakefield."

Perhaps she partied in Rio or took that wrong turn out of Spain long ago. Ms. Ling closed the front door with a thud behind us.

"What the hell was that?" asked Saint Cyr. "She's clearly

protecting Rubio. She never told us something, Marguerite."

"No, she gave us just what we needed. Not enough to directly betray Rubio, but just enough to keep us from coming back to bother her again. Check the Bs for home healthcare agencies. They're probably listed like she said. And she told us to look for Terry Randolph in the yellow pages, not the white pages."

"So what? White, yellow. She plays with us."

"No, she's a linguistics professor. Like a lawyer, she chooses her words carefully. White pages for residential telephone listings. Yellow pages for business listings. So he must have a business listing of some kind. Maybe doing videos or taking pictures."

"I think she's wasting our time while Rubio escapes town. But I'll call to Connelly. Send a couple of cops here if Rubio says *oui* to the Heights tonight," said Saint Cyr.

"Did you notice that pin on Wakefield's blouse?"

"Yes, a tiny gold angel."

"Same pin, again. Maybe a secret sign of the Messengers," I said.

"The whole of people wear angel pins these days for a million different reasons. Doesn't mean she's a crazed bomber, eh?"

"You're right. But something to add to a growing pile of circumstantial evidence."

Saint Cyr shrugged. "More like a growing pile of new suspects with plenty of reasonable doubt to keep us busy."

I took a quick glance at my watch. "Hey, I'm heading back to my office. I want to do some more research for O'Brien on Kiley's motion to reconsider. You hit the phone books and I'll hit the law books."

Before I could say it, AngelEyes gently covered my mouth with the tips of his gloved hand. "I know. I know. I'll text to you if I find out anything decent."

The office was quiet, as most prosecutors were already in court when I arrived back from Wakefield's place. Like clockwork, Flora took her lunch at high noon, so I waited until she left and then snuck back into my office unnoticed. O'Brien knew me better than I thought, because I found another sticky note from him on my office phone. "Here's amended from Kiley. Make us look good."

I left our offices and hid out in the main law library, digging up additional cases that O'Brien could use Monday morning in his motion hearing with Kiley. After three hours, I'd come up with several recent cases in other states to support the position that our investigation of Patrick Carpenter was ongoing and his property should not be released. I added them to our memo and emailed a revised draft to O'Brien. No way was Carpenter going to get anything back on Monday morning.

"How's that vacation going?" O'Brien emailed back.

"Wish you were here." I replied.

My phone beeped with a text from Saint Cyr. Simple Simon turned up in the yellow pages under Randolph Video Services and Repair, using the same address as his burnt-out apartment. Saint Cyr also tracked down Mario Rubio's address in Somerville, 18C Davis Place, through Baxter Nursing Agency.

He wrote, "Let you know if I find anything. Now get back to your real job.:-)"

I decided to take a break from my non-existent vacation and meet Saint Cyr at Maria Rubio's place. I knew Connelly wouldn't like it, but then I didn't report to him on my days off.

After our earlier visit to Wakefield's upscale manor, Maria Rubio, like Simple Simon, lived decidedly in the real world. Highway overpasses, fast-food joints, and junky auto repair shops hemmed in her neighborhood's dilapidated apartment buildings.

I found a parking space two blocks away and walked toward her address to meet Saint Cyr. He must have already been inside, since I saw his car parked across the street from her building, a peeling brown triple-decker. I found its front door securely locked. I wasn't sure if I might be making a mistake announcing my arrival by ringing any doorbells. A rusty side gate creaked as I headed along an alley to the triple-decker's rear entrance.

The alley opened up into a rear parking area where a dented pick-up truck being repaired rested on four concrete blocks. I looked up at three rickety wooden porches hanging from the building's backside. No curtains dressed its windows and no names were taped to any of its apartment buzzers. The building looked deserted. The only sounds were intermittent snaps of laundry flapping in the wind from a clothesline strung across a neighboring porch.

As I opened an unlocked rear door, a thunderous boom shook the building to its foundation. A second or two later, a forceful impact threw me across the alley right out of my shoes. My head whacked hard against the pickup truck and I fell to the ground, dazed. Broken shingles and shards of glass rained down on me and my vision went double. Pulling myself under the truck frame, my head throbbed and my hands and knees bled from scrapes. Black smoke poured out of the tenement's back door and then there was a series of lesser explosions. Someone wailed, like a wounded animal.

I peeked out from under the truck and saw an enormous fireball devouring a man as he tumbled over the top porch railing. He crashed onto pavement a couple of feet away in flames. Simple Simon, screaming and ablaze, writhed on the ground in fiery agony, tangled up in the clothesline. I tried to crawl out from under this truck to reach him, but the hood of my coat got caught on something metal in the undercarriage. Randolph was almost within reach and I struggled to tear my coat off, but my zipper lay frozen in its tracks.

Trapped under this pickup, I watched his body burn and heard his screams of pain. He furiously tried to beat out the flames on his coat sleeve with a bandaged right hand, which soon caught fire. Suddenly I heard yelling from the street and echoes of running feet slamming on alley pavement. Two men dressed in oil-stained mechanics' jumpers from a nearby auto shop bolted out toward Randolph. They grabbed some bed covers from the clothesline and tried to beat down fierce flames engulfing Randolph's tortured body. Intense heat and a putrid stench of burning flesh pushed them back. A third man joined them with a small commercial fire extinguisher spraying white soapy foam at the orange flames searing Randolph's skin. It doused the blaze enough so that the other two men could put out the remaining fire with the bed linens. Covered in white mist, Randolph's blackened body lay motionless, still knotted up in a scorched clothesline. His large cross smoked as it hung from his neck. An angel pin slipped out of the blackened fingertips of his right hand, glinting in the fading afternoon sunlight.

Two more neighbors dashed up a set of back stairs, calling out for survivors. They dragged out an unconscious Saint Cyr. They rested his bloodied body on the ground, next to Terry Randolph's charred remains. I felt my vision blur to a snowy haze. Only the howling fire engine sirens drowned out my sobbing.

CHAPTER 26

9:41 p.m. I lay down, exhausted, on a stiff couch at Boston Memorial. My eyes were closed, but I wasn't sleeping. Every time I closed my eyes, I saw Simple Simon's smoldering corpse or AngelEyes' battered body being dragged out of that smoky triple-decker.

Ponytail Craig told me he'd sneak me in to see Saint Cyr in intensive care at the three-thirty shift change. Texting my family and friends, I let them know I was okay, but that Saint Cyr had suffered serious compression injuries and the next few hours would be critical. Everybody told me to go home, but I couldn't leave without seeing him.

I got away easy with only a few minor cuts and bruises on my hands and knees, mostly from crawling under that truck. Patience was my least favorite virtue so I paced around like a caged tiger in a deserted waiting room. I leafed through a display of year-old magazines and hospital educational pamphlets before emptying my life savings into a nearby vending machine. Restless, I started wandering around and found a restroom at the end of a dimly lit hallway. Splashing cold water on my face, I thought I heard the clicking sounds of rancho dancing shoes against bathroom floor tiles. Looking up, I saw a cleaning lady entered the restroom, pushing a rolling water bucket with her mop.

As I trudged back to the ICU, I stopped under a sign for a contemplation chapel. I put my hand on the door handle, but didn't pull it open.

"Hey, Monty," whispered Ponytail Craig. "Let's go. I can get you in for a couple of minutes."

He led me through a back hallway intended for medical staff. "You'll have to make this quick. We're only supposed to let immediate family in here," he whispered.

I trailed him to Saint Cyr's room where there was a police officer standing guard outside. I glimpsed him motionless in softly lit glass room. The cop eyed me suspiciously until I flashed my ADA badge; then he let me pass. Inside a cacophony of monitors hummed and beeped as an IV quietly emitted drops into a clear plastic tube attached to his wrist. AngelEyes looked very peaceful in his hospital bed. Small bandages crisscrossed his chest, neck and forehead. A cast immobilized his left arm.

"Considering how severe those blasts were, it doesn't look bad. Gérard looks like he's only sleeping," I whispered.

"Looks can be deceiving. He only sustained a few external injuries, a broken arm, and some stitches in various places. But the sheer force of those explosions gave him a number of serious internal injuries, including internal bleeding and a serious concussion. The heat and smoke damaged his lungs, too."

"Can I touch him?"

"You gotta be careful. We are still evaluating his internal injuries. But his hand is okay to hold."

I put my hand over his right hand, giving it a gentle squeeze.

"Is he going to make it?"

Craig went quiet. "I don't know, Monty. The next few hours will tell."

"Has anyone contacted his family?"

"Yeah, the cops are taking care of it."

"Is there anything I can do to help?"

"If you got a God, say a prayer."

"And if I don't?"

"You can always donate blood. We never have enough. I can show you where to go in the hospital."

"Thanks. I'm a universal donor; I hope that helps."

It was difficult to let go of his hand, but Craig had other patients to attend to, so he sent me on my way to blood donation.

One pint down, I drove away from Boston Memorial in my Blue Bomb. My bandaged hands hurt as I gripped the wheel and my scraped-up right knee ached when I hit either the gas or brakes. Between my Machado's and my cuts and bruises, I probably shouldn't be driving, but the subway was closed and I couldn't bear to wait around for a taxi. I knew there would be no sleep for me tonight, so I weighed my all-night options.

I couldn't face Lucky Lanes with its flashing lights and blaring music. It wasn't a great place for me to unwind right now. There was always diner dives, but I wasn't hungry at all. It wouldn't be a bad idea to hit a Laundromat since I had tons of dirty clothes to wash. Yet I didn't want to go home and spend time sorting out my clothes. Like any good obsessive-compulsive, I decided to drag myself to work. Work, my emotional comfort food, was on the way and always waited for me, day in and day out.

Zipping my card key through an employee entrance reader, I entered the darkened courthouse and headed up to homicide. What would feel spooky to most people felt safe and calming to me tonight. The mundane thought of doing basic legal research seemed oddly comforting. As I went up, my reflection on the elevator panel showed I looked like absolute hell, a zombie with good tailoring. But nobody was around to notice.

I flicked on my computer, but instead I ended up sitting dazed and numb at my desk. How had this case spun completely out of control? I tried to look at case files, but found myself yawning and simply moved papers from one side of my desk to another. I rearranged my pens and pencils in my desk drawer, emptied my recycling bin and filled everybody's staple guns. I even loaded several reams of paper in all three of our office copy machines.

Only the ring of my office phone cracked the silence and shook me out of my haze. I picked up my receiver gingerly hoping it wasn't bad news about AngelEyes. "Hello. Marguerite Montez. Homicide."

"I can't believe you're there, Ms. Montez. But thank God you are. I didn't know how else to reach you. This is Rachel Childs."

"Hello, Mrs. Childs. This is a surprise. Everything all right?"

"Not really. Can you meet with me right away? It's very important."

"Certainly. We can talk now. What seems to be the problem?"

"I'd feel better if you came over to my condo. I think my niece might feel more comfortable talking to you here in person."

"Your niece?"

"Yes, I think you should hear it directly from her."

"May I contact one of my colleagues to join me?"

"I don't think that'll work very well. She's terribly upset. Bridget will be less anxious if it's only you."

"Okay. I'll be right over."

I immediately tried to contact O'Brien, but got only his cell phone's voicemail and left him a message. I tried to reach Connelly, but the duty officer told me he'd gone out on another homicide call. I paged him on his beeper with my callback number. Despite all this technology, I couldn't reach anyone, so I headed over to Childs' condo on my own.

CHAPTER 27

When Mrs. Childs opened her condo door, I noticed right away that the once-defiant ten-year old who'd shot us a nasty look at Boston Memorial appeared shaken up and frightened. Wrapped up in a lumpy quilt, Bridget tugged on her messy ponytail. Her feet, covered with Mickey Mouse slippers, dangled over an edge of a large gold winged-back chair in her aunt's sitting room. She was sniffling, her eyes swollen red from crying. A pile of white Kleenexes littered a rug beneath her chair.

"Bridget," her aunt said. "Ms. Montez is here."

Right away, Bridget began to cry. Her aunt sat on an arm of her chair and patted Bridget on her shoulder. "It's all right, honey. She's here to help. Help us find out what happened to your mommy."

I sat in silence on a fluffy couch as Bridget continued to wipe tears away.

"Why don't I get started, Bridget? You can help me if I forget anything. Okay?" Mrs. Childs asked.

The little girl nodded in agreement.

"Bridget had a hard time sleeping tonight. She's not used to this condo. Her nana's been caring for them since, since everything happened."

"Nana didn't feel good today," Bridget said.

"Yes, she's got a touch of flu. I offered to take the children for a few nights."

"I had a nightmare," Bridget said. "Woke me up."

"What happened in your nightmare?" I asked.

"Joey got sick again. And he died and went away forever, 'cuz we didn't get a match."

The little girl shuddered and tears rolled down her face.

"I heard her crying and I went to her room to see if everything was all right, Ms. Montez. And Bridget told me about her nightmare. She told me her family would never find a match."

"Never. 'Cuz Joey's adopted. Joey's real daddy can make him better," Bridget said, between sniffles. "But he won't."

"His real daddy?" I asked, trying not to fall out of my chair.

"Yes. He's mean and won't get tested. Mommy said so."

"Bridget, let's tell Ms. Montez about what happened last time Joey stayed overnight in a hospital."

She brushed a few more tears away and took a deep breath. "Mommy and Daddy had a big fight. They thought I was asleep but I had to go to the bathroom." She gathered the quilt more tightly around her shoulders. "I wasn't snooping. I'm not a snoop like Joey says."

"That's okay, Bridget. I don't think you're a snoop. What did your parents argue about?"

"Mommy cried. Daddy got mad because he didn't match Joey at all. Then Daddy punched a wall. He started yelling at Mommy."

"What did he yell about, Bridget?"

"He screamed that Mommy's a liar. That Mommy trapped him. Always knew who Joey's real daddy was."

"Did your parents say his name, Bridget?"

"No."

"Did Daddy or Mommy say anything else about Joey's daddy?" I asked.

"Mommy just kept crying 'cuz Joey's daddy wouldn't get tested. Mommy said she'd go see him. Make him get tested to save Joey."

"Do you know when, or maybe where, Mommy met Joey's dad?"

"No. I'm not a snoop."

"Yes, you're right. You're not a snoop." I added. "Bridget, do you remember getting any bad phone calls about Mommy? People saying bad things on the telephone?" I asked.

"No."

"Think hard now, Bridget. Did you ever answer the phone and have anyone say anything bad to you or to Mommy? So bad that you stayed home from school?"

"No. Mommy won't let me answer the phone. Only Joey's big enough."

I dug into my briefcase with my aching hands and pulled out a photo of Simple Simon. "Have you ever seen this man before, Bridget?" I asked.

"No," she said.

"How about you, Mrs. Childs?"

"No, never."

"Is he Joey's daddy?" asked Bridget.

"No, I don't think so. Just someone else who might've known your mommy."

"I'm sleepy, Auntie Rachel."

"I don't have any more questions tonight," I said.

I bent over toward Bridget and touched her arm. "I'm so sorry about your Mommy and all these troubles. I appreciate you being so brave. Thank you so much for talking to me tonight."

Mrs. Childs placed her hands on Bridget's shoulders and guided her back into a guest bedroom. After several minutes, Mrs. Childs reappeared, her brow furrowed. She began to rummage through her purse, and then spied a pack of cigarettes on her coffee table. She grabbed a pack and lit one up, her hands trembling.

"We'll probably need a formal statement from both of you, Mrs. Childs."

"Oh, we won't have to go the police station, will we? I think it'll be too much for Bridget. Besides, I don't want any of this popping up in the newspaper or gossip columns in the society pages."

The gossip columns? Just when I thought Mrs. Childs might display a softer side, she reverted back to her true nature, worried about her social status. She'd be lucky if this soap opera didn't scream from the front pages of every newspaper and TV outlet or end up in some hokey made-for-TV movie.

"I can send an officer over tomorrow morning. Any ideas who Joey's father might be?"

"I've counted back fifteen years in my head. When she became pregnant, she left college and married Patrick. I guess I've always assumed that she'd only been with him."

"I remember you told me that she had a bad break-up that led her back to Patrick. Any ideas about that person?"

"Yes. I thought about that, too. Her roommates or teachers at school back then might know more. I'm sorry I can't be more helpful. I was married and living in Paris at that time. We weren't very close back then, so I don't remember any names."

"Have you ever heard of Archangel Investment Trust?"

"No," she said.

"It looks like your brother-in-law sent wire transfers to them and signed over some of your checks to them. Totals about $90,000."

"What are you talking about?"

"Your business managers sent us information that indicates that Patrick was funneling some of your loans into this entity, an offshore account in Grand Caymans."

"The Grand Caymans. Patrick's never been out of this state, never mind out of this country."

"He may have been trying to hide money or laundering it to cover up some illegal business activities."

"Patrick couldn't even balance a checkbook, if not for my sister. How could he have been involved in some foreign high finance?"

"We're trying to figure that out," I said. "Did you know that your sister volunteered as an escort at an abortion clinic?"

"You must be kidding, Ms. Montez."

"We followed up some leads that indicated that your sister may've been threatened by an extremist group due to her volunteer work as a clinic escort."

"A clinic escort. Impossible! My sister's a very devout Catholic."

I reached into my briefcase and handed her a copy of Miriam's clinic application. She read it, puffing away on her cigarette.

"Your sister even used your name, Mrs. Childs."

She looked as if she might cry. "This application is about me," she whispered, tearing up.

"You mean, besides your name?" I asked.

"Yes. My social security number. My home address in Maine. My diploma from the MFA school." She stood up and began to pace around, dragging even more furiously on her cigarette. "This can't be right. Miriam's so religious. Even as a youngster. She wanted to become a nun at one time." Mrs. Childs shook her head.

"According to clinic staff, Miriam was a regular volunteer. She previously told a clinic director that she'd received threatening calls at home. Claimed that one time Bridget picked up their home phone and didn't go to school the next day because of the threat," I said. "Kids would remember a scary phone call, missing a day of school."

"That's ridiculous. Bridget just told you there weren't any threatening calls. You're wrong about my sister. If anything she'd be marching against a clinic, not volunteering for one. There must be some mistake."

"There's no mistake, Mrs. Childs. A clinic gave us this information."

"It's a mistake." She crumpled the copy of Miriam's application up in her hand and tossed it on her floor.

No inaccuracies, but plenty of contradictions that we'd need to untangle. As I left her suite, I turned to see Mrs. Childs lower herself on to her couch and smooth out that scrunched up form on a cocktail table, to read it once more. I think it began to sink in that she barely knew her own twin, years of distance catching up to her now.

CHAPTER 28

When I started my Blue Bomb up, she coughed and wheezed in damp early morning air. My hands ached and my vision doubled briefly. I closed my eyes and lay back against the headrest, trying to pull myself together. As the car warmed up, it hit me.

Cranky Albert was right. Time to look at this case in a new way.

We had always viewed Miriam as an innocent victim of either her husband or now extremists. But her sister claimed it was Miriam who possessed a high IQ, not Patrick. Miriam got into Harvard on scholarship, not her husband. What if she played double-agent as a clinic escort, using her sister's vitals to mask her identity? She could have worked against Pinkowski's clinic from inside, gaining their trust and learning more about their security measures for the Messengers. She may have made up those threatening phone calls to strengthen her cover. She could have worked with her husband on illegal sales of explosives and helped bilk her sister of money to pay for their crimes.

I flashed back to that tiny gold angel pin on the chapel floor. It could have been hers, not her murderer's. Her twin sister was probably right. Miriam was no clinic escort, more like a true believer for the Messengers.

But then why did they kill her?

I remembered Daniel's drawing with the bubble saying "Judis. Judis!" She could have betrayed them is some way. Got too close to clinic staff working and had cold feet about blowing them up. Or she could have been mixed up with the Messengers, but that association might have nothing to do with her murder. Out of anger, Carpenter might have killed her after he found out about Joey. What could be a worse betrayal than to get a guy to marry you because you're pregnant and then find out later he's not the father? This case made my head hurt.

My cell phone rang. "Hey, what the hell are you doing chatting up Mrs. Childs?" asked Connelly. "I thought I told you to leave primary investigations up to us."

"She called me in the middle of the night. Only wanted a woman to speak with her niece. And I tried to call you and beep you, too."

"You're not a police officer. You should have brought another homicide detective along."

"The only other one working this case is in intensive care."

Connelly fell silent.

"How's Gérard doing?" I asked.

"I called about a half-hour ago and nothing's really changed," said Connelly. "How are you doing?"

I really wanted to tell him that I felt awful. Awful that AngelEyes barely clung to life because he followed me down this rat hole. Awful because every inch of my body ached from fights, car crashes, and explosions. Awful because all of my hard work on this case made me a complete laughingstock at the courthouse. Awful because I hadn't enjoyed a decent night's sleep for months. Awful because I was gonna die of an incurable degenerative disease. Awful because I kept having visions of my dead best friend whose killer still roamed free.

But I didn't say any of that. Instead I gave Connelly a rundown of Bridget's story and Childs' denials about her sister. I even told him about my new theory that Miriam may have been working undercover with the Messengers.

"Your theories might help explain those forensic reports. We matched a boot print from one of Randolph's boots," Connelly said.

"Oh, my God. Randolph is her killer?"

"It looks like it."

"Did anything turn up on his autopsy about his bandaged hand?" I thought he might have been my attacker in Saugus, either pretending to be *El Galo* or merely following me.

"His body was too badly burned for them to learn much of

anything. But we also got some preliminary forensics on that trash can fire," Connelly said. "They found a patch of burnt cotton material and large quantities of cotton fibers. They match up to material used in church vestments. Also some microscopic traces of a material called endosperm in his burnt trash can."

"Endosperm?" I asked.

"No idea about that one. They'll give us a translation on the endosperm stuff later. The coroner also found some tokens inside that big cross Simon wore."

"What did he put inside his cross?"

"That thing's damn big. It slid open in back. Found some scraps of Scripture and a key."

"Revelation, by any chance?"

"Yeah, our friendly Messengers' favorite verses. And some lines out of the Book of Numbers, too."

"What about that key? Please tell me it's like the key you found under Carpenter's Virgin statue?"

"Exactly, except it's an original with a company telephone number engraved on it. No unit number, but a serial number. We've tracked down the self-storage company's manager. Are you up for a ride?"

"I thought I wasn't supposed to be involved in primary investigations."

"Not without a homicide detective. As the chief detective, I'll take you along, but remember I call all of the shots."

I laughed. "Okay, boss. Did you find Fetus de Milo?" I asked.

"Not yet, Monty. But the world's got her photo now. Don't worry. We'll get her. Luckily, no more bodies after a fire department search of her building. Besides Randolph, it looks like everybody else was at work or school when her place blew up."

"Except for Gérard."

"He's gonna pull through. I know it," said Connelly, straining to cheer me up.

We left in a squad car for Dorchester Self-Storage, a small facility of about two dozen garage units just outside of downtown Boston. Connelly knocked on the manager's door, but no one answered. We waited a couple of minutes watching our breath rise in puffs of white cold smoke. A giant baby-blue Caddie squealed into the lot and out popped a sixty-something woman swamped by an oversized black mink coat with her blue-gray hair piled in a loose bun on top of her head.

Even with her bun, she stood probably no more than four-feet-ten. I felt like a giant next to her as I met her outstretched hand.

"Ida Lichtenstein at your service," she said. "Call me, Ida."

"We apologize for getting you out of bed so early, ma'am," Connelly said.

"Not to worry. I do my mall walk in about an hour so it's good to loosen my joints up beforehand anyways." She pointed to her perfect white sneakers before unlocking an office door.

"Hello, baby cakes, baby cakes!" someone screeched.

I jumped back, startled, and Connelly instinctively moved his hand to his pistol butt at his waist.

"Hi, sweetie. You behave yourself last night?" She nonchalantly switched on a fluorescent office light, revealing a caged parrot in her office.

"Hello, baby cakes! Hello, baby cakes!" the bird repeated, whistling and cawing at a piercing decibel level.

"Lucky I didn't blow sweetie's head off," Connelly said to me under his breath.

"Settle down now, sweetie. We have some special guests."

Ida reached into a desk drawer, pulling out a plastic sandwich bag of birdseed to feed him. "He's such a good little boy. Better than a watch dog. With all that chatter makes people think there's somebody in here all day and night."

She pulled off her mink coat to reveal an orange sweat suit decorated with shiny tropical appliqués that cried out K-Mart.

"Hello, baby cakes! Hello, baby cakes!"

I wondered if he said anything else, but didn't want to ask. Things seemed weird enough at this point.

"Now let's have a look-see at that key, detective."

"Key, baby cakes. Key!"

Connelly handed her Randolph's key. She pulled out a giant handwritten logbook and thumped it on her desk. She ran his key beside a list of serial numbers. "I keep meaning to put all this on a computer, but I just never get around to it. Here we go. It's unit fourteen around back."

"Back, baby cakes. Back, baby cakes!"

The idea of Connelly's shooting the bird began to grow on me. "Does it say who rented that unit?" I asked.

"Archangel Investment Trust," she said.

"We'll take it from here, ma'am," said Connelly.

We walked around to unit fourteen. Connelly unlocked it and pushed its door open. I groped for a wall switch. As I flicked it on, Connelly let out a whistle.

"Hello," he said.

I could barely believe my eyes. The unit contained dozens of tall wooden shelves filled with thousands of videotapes. Wooden crates overflowing with wires, unopened video cassettes, and lots of other computer and camera gear lined its walls. Simple Simon's landlord knew his tenant well. Randolph must have filmed nearly his entire life, by the look of things. I ran my finger along spines of tapes, each labeled by hand with a date and protest location, going back at least four years.

"The Messengers' home videos," I said.

For the rest of the day and into the weekend, I worked with two techs, sifting through Randolph's videos to locate ones taken at Pinkowski's clinic. Since I knew most of our major players by sight, I helped another specialist start the tedious task of watching them for any clues. With Connelly's team, we viewed hours of repetitive Messengers' videotapes, mainly of people holding protest signs, kneeling in prayer, and yelling warnings about eternal damnation at people entering clinics, strip joints, and gay bars. No big news there. We knew Randolph was our man, but his links to the Carpenters weren't completely clear yet.

However, some initial computer forensics discovered that Randolph had entered my name into a search engine and a WHOIS database of website owners, along with Connelly and Saint Cyr's names. If he learned that I owned Ginny's site, he might have made some of those postings to distract me from Miriam's case, or to lure me to those fairgrounds. I'd never know for certain. Since Randolph wasn't at our neighborhood soccer club, *El Galo* must still be out there. Under the radar, I planned to continue my investigation into Ginny and Luisa's murders, with or without *El Galo*'s help.

As Connelly's team tried to nail down those connections, I

kept busy researching Carpenter's financial misdeeds and federal and state violations of his sale of explosives as a basis for retaining his records. I started drafting up event summaries of Randolph's videotapes, too. This flurry of activity helped to keep my mind off AngelEyes' condition, which remained largely unchanged.

With Kiley's motion hearing delayed until Monday, I had a little more time to further heal from my injuries and to help Connelly's techs in reviewing Randolph's videotapes. I even managed to get a good night's rest. My meds must finally be leveling off, I thought. As we amassed evidence about Carpenter's possible criminal acts, O'Brien chances of kicking Kiley's butt on that motion seemed to be looking up.

I couldn't wait to have a front-row seat.

CHAPTER 29

Before Monday, there's always Sunday. Although the Almighty rested that day, I had to face my family—and pretty much our entire neighborhood—at my sister's fifteenth-anniversary mass and reception that afternoon. The Thompson mess hung over my head, but I pasted on a happy *ficar face* and bought a lovely crystal vase for her celebration.

My second-oldest sister, Fatima, was a sister and a Sister—as well as a saint. Being a modern woman, Fatima never wore an old-fashioned nun's habit, but had close-cropped dark curly hair and wore modest clothing with a tiny silver cross pinned to her blouse collar or sweater pocket. As a nun, she'd considered herself married to Christ for fifteen years and seemed to find great joy in her calling. Maybe being wed to someone who listened to your prayers and sorrows, but was never around to talk back, leave a toilet seat up, or cheat on you, was the key to a long satisfying union.

It had been a tough roller-coaster week for me, but I loved my sister and knew I owed it to her to be there to honor her life, not bemoan mine. I hopped on a subway train at Kendall to avoid the nightmare of finding on-street parking in her crowded urban neighborhood. Happily, I arrived at Our Lady of Lourdes right before mass started, early enough to avoid the evil eye from my mother for being late to mass, but not so early for the inevitable demoralizing chit-chat about the Thompson debacle. I'd have plenty of time for that crap at the reception. An enormous granite statue of the Madonna in the church vestibule momentarily sent me back to Miriam's crime scene, but I swept away those thoughts.

Skipping the holy water, I slid into a pew where my mother and two of my sisters sat along with their husbands. My mother had gotten her hair done and it was nice to see her out of her bakery apron, wearing an attractive soft peach dress. They all smiled and nodded to me, except for my younger sister, Delia, who smirked as she flashed open her jacket to reveal a small liquor flask. Good thinking, Delia. I gave her a quick wink for remembering a little something for the reception punch. Our baby sister, Bianca, was missing in action as usual.

When I was a kid, I remembered always being bored to tears in church. Priests always lecturing us about being good and avoiding a laundry list of sins that lurked around every street corner, every relaxing moment, every fun time. In elementary school, the nuns often kept me after class or sent notes home to my parents for disrupting religion class with too many pointed questions. Why can't women be priests? How come innocent dead babies go to limbo instead of heaven? If God is love, then shouldn't he stop suffering? And later on, Why did God let my best friend get killed?

Luckily, my parents couldn't afford the tuition for parochial high schools, so we bolted to local public schools, but I never escaped my questions. When I got older, the questions got harder and I couldn't square my beliefs with those of the Church and we parted ways. But I'd be lying if I claimed that those old tapes of Catholic do's and don'ts didn't still play inside of my head lots of times.

But today, I enjoyed listening to people talk about all the wonderful things my sister, Sister Fatima Marie, had done at the school. A Daughter of Charity of St. Vincent de Paul, she taught English to the poorest immigrants in our city's most violent neighborhoods on a shoestring budget. Despite the misery, dysfunction, and hardships she witnessed daily, Sister Fatima Marie was a remarkably upbeat person and dynamic teacher. She spoke five languages and glided in and out of them like an Olympic figure skater, one second speaking Spanish, then double-Lutz jumping into French Creole or triple-Lutz jumping into Vietnamese or Mandarin Chinese.

My nieces and nephew were also involved in this mass, reading verses as lectors and bringing up gifts to concelebrants Father Clarita and Father Nguyen. Local kids sang upbeat hymns with an adult church choir, accompanied by two guitars and a set of conga drums. A couple of her fellow nuns even did a liturgical dance up and down the church aisles. All in all, it was a pretty uplifting service that celebrated and reaffirmed the good in people, which is probably what I needed after week of heartless murder suspects, self-centered millionaires, and power-hungry politicians.

After mass, my mother proudly stood next to my sister in a receiving line in the parish hall as our family and friends, local church community, and old neighborhood came together. The kind of diverse reunion of your life that might only occur at your wake after you died. Presents on the gift table were piled high. Disparate tangs of Asian, Haitian, Portuguese and Hispanic delights from parents and neighbors filled this church hall. My ma made sure a dessert table overflowed with fabulous desserts, breads, and pastries from our family bakery. A cacophony of different languages and accents drowned out light music being piped into this room.

I gave my sister a big hug and a kiss in the receiving line. "Congratulations, Fatima. What a wonderful service. And all so well deserved."

"I'm really overwhelmed with happiness and gratitude," she said, beaming. "How are you? Is your shoulder doing better?"

"Ready to pitch a double-header for the Sox any day now," I joked, not wanting to rain on her parade. "We'll talk later," I said. "Your public awaits."

She laughed and continued to greet a throng of guests pouring into the community center. I gave my mother a hug, too. "Beautiful dress, Ma."

"Still employed?" she whispered anxiously in my ear.

"Drawing a paycheck as we speak," I said. Although for how much longer remained to be seen.

As I waded through the happy crowd, I saw a tiny angel pin attached to a black man's jacket lapel. "What a lovely pin, sir," I said.

"For Mother. Sleep in heaven," he said in broken English, with a lilting Caribbean accent.

I smiled. Everybody seemed to have their own reason for wearing that pin.

"What? No police escort?" Delia shoved a cup of fruit punch

into my hand. "Old family recipe. Just a touch of vodka."

"*Saude*," I said.

"To your health, too," she said. We tapped the rims of our plastic cups together. "You surviving in that shark pool?"

"Barely. I may be back baking *Dona Amelia* cupcakes sooner than you think."

"Bullshit. You can work with Marcus and me on our business. We could use your help on our legal and marketing stuff. We need someone who knows how to spell and draft decent content."

"Glad to hear computer consulting is still working for you guys. I'll keep it in mind," I said, sipping spiked punch. "Rocco is adorable. Can't believe he's already six."

"Yeah, he's six going on forty-six. He's much smarter than we were as kids."

"Anything new on Bianca?"

"Last contact we had she was trying to borrow some more money from us. Caridade, too. Claimed she was thinking about a fresh start, becoming a nurse for expats and retirees in Nicaragua," said Delia.

"I bet it's a lot easier to steal scripts for OxyContin down there," I murmured.

"Bingo. I think that's her plan."

Our sister Caridade found us in the crowd and hugged us both. A successful real estate broker with her husband, Leon, she got those skinny genes from my mother's family, while Delia and I inherited the "look at a cookie and gain weight instantly" curves of the Montez clan. She retained her bossy nature as our eldest sister and would never be mistaken for a diplomat in our family tussles.

"I read about that murder. Did you get fired for screwing up that case, Marguerite?"

I huffed. "No, on both counts. I didn't screw it up. And I didn't get fired."

"That boss of yours really trashed you in that press release. We all saw it in the newspapers."

"Don't believe everything you read, Caridade."

"You should Google your name, Marguerite. That info is everywhere."

"Not a good idea, Marguerite," said Delia. "Moving right along, how's that foreclosure market?"

"Really great. Rock-bottom prices. Lowest interest rates ever. Great time to buy an investment property," she said, always happy to talk up real-estate values.

"I don't see myself as the vulture type. Swooping in and feeding off of other people's misery," said Delia.

"You snooze, you lose, ladies."

"How are the girls doing?" I asked, moving to neutral territory. "They've gotten pretty tall."

"Fantastic. They're both doing well in school and Caroline's showing some musical talent. Thankfully, they haven't discovered boys yet, so no headaches on that front so far. They're running around here with Rocco."

"Girls, girls."

I could hear my mother calling out over the din. She waved for us to take a picture with our guest of honor.

As we gathered for a family photo, my cell phone began to vibrate. I glanced at my screen. O'Brien had sent me a text listing further changes he wanted me to make to our memo before tomorrow's hearing on Kiley's motion. As I was about to reply to him, a school photographer interrupted, directing us to turn our shoulders and lift our chins. He tried to position us perfectly for a commemorative photo. Family friends jockeyed for positions to take their own photos of the Montez women. I turned my cell phone off. I'd get to his damn memo later.

Right now it was all about my family and smiling broadly as we sang out, "cheese!"

CHAPTER 30

Early on Monday morning I ran another quick computer check on the cases in our memo. Nothing new, so I headed to Judge Walters's courtroom. When I got there, O'Brien was chatting up a new bailiff, Amber, whose golden locks had come straight out of a bottle. I tried to get O'Brien's attention, but he seemed pretty taken with this court officer. As I sat at the prosecution table, I heard someone whistling behind me, "Take Me Out to the Ballgame." That damn cologne. I turned around, and there was Kiley beaming at me, not saying a word. I faced forward again and perused our memo once more. He kept whistling that tune for several more bars and then plopped right down beside me.

"Whistling in the dark again with this motion to reconsider," I said.

"I hear you took some batting practice with a Louisville slugger recently," Kiley said.

"Really? You must be confused. Spring training's still two more months away."

"If they press charges for battery, I'd be happy to defend you. Didn't know you liked it rough," he purred. "Too bad we never had the chance to explore that side of you."

Before I could give him a good slap, O'Brien tapped Kiley on his shoulder. "Do you mind? Judge is about to show and you're in my seat."

"Keeping it warm for you," said Kiley. He stood and strode over to the defense counsel's table.

O'Brien pulled out a handkerchief and pretended to sweep his chair clean.

"I've got a lot to tell you," I said.

"Save it. Connelly woke me Saturday morning to fill me in. I also found out you been working video forensics this past weekend. I thought I told you to keep a low profile," he said.

"You told me to keep a low profile at the courthouse. None of this work was at the courthouse, O'Brien."

"Don't get smart with me. You know what I meant."

A bailiff's voice interrupted us. "Oye, Oye. The court is now in session. All those having business before the court now rise and make themselves known. May God save this court and the Commonwealth of Massachusetts."

As the judge entered, we all rose to our feet. Judge Walters was an old Dukakis appointee, so I knew he'd be tough on any search-and-seizure issues. He pulled the collar of his black robes around his neck and rubbed his hands together. "Is the damn heat on in here?" he asked.

"Yes, Your Honor," said a bailiff.

"Turn it up, for God's sake. It's warmer out in City Square," he shot back.

A bailiff scurried over to a wall thermostat and turned it higher.

"Counsel for the moving party?" asked the court clerk.

The judge shuffled through his court papers.

"Theodore Kiley, for the defendant and moving party, Your Honor," Kiley said, rising to his feet.

"Counsel for respondent?"

"Your show, kiddo," whispered O'Brien at the last moment. I couldn't believe it and scrambled to my feet. "Marguerite Montez, for the prosecution and respondent, Your Honor."

All those years in district court taught me how to handle last-minute curve balls, but I never expected O'Brien to give up a chance for a direct face-off with Kiley.

"Mr. Kiley, why do you think I should reconsider my earlier motion upholding the seizure and custody at Mr. Patrick Carpenter's home and office items?"

"Your Honor, under Rule 61, we are requesting you to reconsider our earlier motion for the return of property to Patrick Carpenter, which included household items and commercial records integral to the continuation of his family life and business," said Kiley.

"Mr. Kiley, weren't these items seized as part of a murder investigation?"

"Yes, Your Honor. But the prosecution recently arrested a homeless man who appears to have committed the crime."

"Is that correct, Ms. Montez?" asked Judge Walters.

Out of the corner of my eye, I saw Tiffany rush into our courtroom and hand Kiley a note. Leaks R Us. It was probably breaking local news that Randolph was looking like our killer.

"Your Honor, we arrested Mr. Huntington for theft of items from St. Stephen's church. But he's not our prime suspect in the murder case."

"Nor is my client a prime suspect, Your Honor. I've just received word that a man killed in an explosion yesterday in Somerville is considered to be the deceased's likely killer in this case. His name is Terry Randolph. And in *Commonwealth v. Negron* and *Commonwealth v. Sacco*, cited in my brief, the prosecution must return all items, not contraband, to the defendant once there ceases to be probable cause to retain this property. There is now no reasonable basis to continue to hold these items, which are critical for my client to carry out his livelihood, to support his family and to return his household to normalcy."

"Ms. Montez, is it true that another man is now viewed as an actual murder suspect in his matter?"

"Your Honor, Mr. Randolph is considered a potential suspect, but we are still investigating whether he may have acted in concert with or under the orders of Mr. Carpenter in this murder. Our investigation has also revealed that Mr. Carpenter is implicated in a potential money laundering scheme and illegal sales of explosives to domestic terrorists and may have provided those explosives that resulted in Mr. Randolph's death yesterday. That explosion also seriously injured a homicide detective, Gérard Saint Cyr, who is fighting for his life in the intensive care unit at Boston Memorial."

I prayed that I was right and AngelEyes was still battling to stay alive.

"Your Honor, my client has not been indicted for any criminal action, be it murder or illegal dealings in explosives or money laundering. I renew my request based on the *Negron* and *Sacco* precedents," said Kiley.

"My brother at the bar has misinterpreted those precedents, Your Honor. Both of those cases dealt with the return of property illegally seized by law enforcement without a valid warrant or a recognized exception to the warrant requirement. In this instance, our officers had a valid warrant in compliance with Article Fourteen of the Declaration of Rights to search and seize items from the Carpenter home and business."

"Yes, I see a warrant here," said Judge Walters. Thank God we'd gotten a warrant before we searched Carpenter's place.

"In addition, this case involves an ongoing investigation, Your Honor. Return of the property at this time could result in the destruction or loss of key evidence possibly linked to at least two homicides, along with other serious criminal matters endangering public safety," I said.

"She's got you there, Mr. Kiley," said Judge Walters. "The officers wisely secured a warrant. *Sacco* and *Negron* dealt with cases of illegal searches and seizures without warrants being issued. That's not the case here. Until their investigation is complete these items will remain in the custody of the Charles County Police Department."

"But, Your Honor, how can my client continue to run his business without key records? He has two young children to support, including a son who's suffering from cancer."

"You *would* bring up the kids, Mr. Kiley," said the judge. "Next thing you'll be claiming that they're all going to be homeless orphans."

He turned to me. "Any chance, Ms. Montez, that you can work on giving defense counsel a copy of his business records so his client can keep supporting his family? And give back those items from his home that don't look to be connected to this case?"

"Your Honor, we take no issue with giving defense counsel copies of his business records. We'll also make good faith efforts to return any household property that isn't at issue in our criminal investigation."

"Sounds good to me," said Judge Walters. "Doesn't get any better than good faith, Mr. Kiley,"

"I wish to note my continuing objection to this order, Your Honor."

"That's your client's right, Mr. Kiley. Good luck in the appeals court."

Judge Walters rose and exited without hesitation into his chambers. I sank down into my seat. Kiley walked out in a huff with Tiffany in tow, still lugging that silly litigation case.

"I can't believe you did that," I said to O'Brien. "Gave up a chance to cut Kiley down."

"After this week's events and you working all those graveyard shifts on this case, I figured you earned it," O'Brien said. "Betcha it felt good to kick your ex in his ass."

"It did," I said, even though I felt mostly empty and worn out.

I couldn't feel any real burst of joy over this minor success, not until AngelEyes moved out of danger and this case was nailed down tight.

CHAPTER 31

After this morning's success, I got Connelly's approval to dig a bit deeper into Miriam's past. I walked through a labyrinth of alleys to a cluster of cramped houses. Over the years, Harvard had bought up private residences and turned them into quaint administrative offices tucked away in nooks and crannies of Harvard Square. An assistant director of residence life, who didn't look much older than a student, met me and reviewed an emergency court order giving me access to Miriam's school records. She handed me a file bearing the name Miriam Rogers and showed me into a windowless conference room.

When I opened the slim file, the fresh face of a youthful Miriam smiled back at me, the optimistic face of a young person ready to take on the world. She was about to embark on an educational journey that could've helped her have more life choices and break out of her working-class background, something that college and law school had done for me. How had it all gone so terribly wrong within a year? A quick succession of errors in judgment had erased all her dreams of becoming a doctor. A bad relationship, followed by an unplanned pregnancy, then dropping out of school to marry someone who hadn't fathered her child. I wondered if she knew that fact when she married Patrick... or was it a recent earth-shattering revelation from Joey's bone marrow tests?

I jotted down the names of her two former roommates, Jennifer Ellison and Sarah Woodley. Miriam had registered as biology major and joined Harvard's Catholic Newman Club and its choral society. Perhaps her old roommates, professors, or friends from her clubs might have useful information to help unlock our mystery man's identity.

Like most universities, Harvard kept a computerized database of its alumni for fund-raising purposes. I found that Jennifer Ellison lived in Washington, D.C. But Sarah Woodley Garrison hadn't ventured far, moving only to Weston, a nearby bedroom community.

When I called her, she seemed thrilled to be in the middle of a murder investigation, especially since she'd just started an evening class on writing your first mystery novel. She excitedly promised to try to dig up some old photo albums from her college days and gave me directions to her home.

The Blue Bomb needed a nice long ride in the country to charge up her battery as she chugged down a winding country road toward Weston. I missed a hidden entrance to her home and had to turn around to find an unpaved driveway to Sarah Garrison's home. As I putted down a gravel path, the springs on my car creaked over each frost heave and pothole. Eventually I saw a massive putty-colored colonial up ahead with white columns with horse stables in a nearby field. A large silver Land Rover stood parked out front.

Mrs. Garrison looked as if she stepped out of a J. Crew catalog. She possessed that casual, clean look that I never managed, even on my best day. Tall and slender, she pulled her sweater tighter around her shoulders, shuddering with the cold as she let me in. Her chin-length blond hair pulled back in a brown headband bobbed up and down as she showed me to an enormous family room with its towering cathedral ceiling.

"You caught Quentin and me in our morning French lesson. Say *bonjour, mademoiselle*."

"*Bonjour, ma'mzelle*," said a little curly-haired boy, about three or four years old.

"*Mademoiselle*," corrected his mother.

"*Bonjour*, Quentin," I said, in my flawless Boston accent.

"Quentin, here's your sheet music. Why don't you practice your song before Mr. Florence comes for your violin class?"

"*Oui, maman*."

She planted a kiss on Quentin's mop head and he obediently left the room.

"He's amazing. French. The violin. How old is he?"

"He's three and a half. And, frankly, he's behind schedule right now if he wants to be admitted into Lindell Preschool."

"Lindell Preschool?"

"Yes, if he's going to get into Harvard or Yale he's going to have to get into Lindell. I went there as a girl, and so did my husband Frederick. But nobody's a shoe-in. Their interview and evaluation processes have become so competitive. Those Asian whiz kids have raised the bar for everyone."

"I'm sure Quentin will do fine, wherever he ends up."

"It's Lindell, or his future is precarious," she said. "Maybe I should bring in that chess coach before it's too late?"

Poor Quentin. I think I was still learning how to get in and out of my flannel jammies at his age. I hadn't yet worried about destroying my entire adult future.

"I appreciate your taking time to speak with me, Mrs. Garrison."

"Yes, of course. I've read about it, but had no idea that it was Miriam *Rogers*. What a horrible thing. But then I guess you see lots of terrible things in your line of work."

"Unfortunately, it goes with the territory."

"Didn't they arrest some drifter already?"

"There's been an arrest. But our investigation's ongoing. We're looking into a past relationship Mrs. Carpenter may have had with someone while at Harvard."

"Somebody from way back then? Seems incredible to me that one of our classmates could be a m-u-r-d-e-r-e-r." She spelled it out, just in case Quentin might overhear us.

"It's too early to tell anything. We're not even sure if it was a fellow student. If he can be identified, we want to talk to him at this point."

"She only went there freshman year. On scholarship. A good student. Very pretty, but not stuck up. Sweet and a little shy. Always very nice."

"Do you remember any of her close male friends or boyfriends when she roomed with you? Or any one-night stands?"

"She really wasn't much into Harvard's party scene. Sort of a religious type. Not the kind of girl to bring some strange guy back to our dorm room."

"Anybody she might have had a crush on?"

"I did find one of my college photo albums. Miriam was very involved with Harvard's choral society. And I remember she liked some guy from our Christmas concert, but I'm not sure they ever dated. Oh, what was his name?"

Mrs. Garrison looked up trying to summon his name from her memory. She then picked up a floral photo album and leafed through its pages. "I think he's in this photo, taken at one of those freshmen mixers they used to run back then. Had to watch out for those flirty Simmons girls, always trying to horn in on our guys," she said.

After turning through several more pages, she stopped. "Here it is."

She handed me a blurry photo of a half dozen grinning students crowded into a party photo, raising their plastic cups in the air in front of a camera.

"There's me with Miriam. And here's my freshman boyfriend, Donald. Oh, Donald," she cooed. "My first serious boyfriend. Great tennis player. An economics major. Indicted for insider trading a couple of years back. He's at Danbury," she confided.

"I'm sure he'll have lots of time to work on his game."

She laughed. "I'm not sure about this guy next to Donald. Or this guy either. But this one is Miriam's friend from that concert."

I looked at half the face of a young man with sandy brown hair and sort of handsome, at least what I could see of him in this out of focus shot. Perhaps FlashPhoto Phil could enhance it for me. "A Harvard student?"

"I'm not sure. Those mixers tended to draw on students from all the good schools in town. And our choir was known for collaborating with students from other colleges, like BC and BU, especially for our big Christmas concert."

"Do you remember his name, first, or last, by any chance?"

"Not sure. But it was a funny name, like Herbert—or something. Or maybe Chauncey. You know one of those names you could never imagine giving to a young person."

Sort of like Quentin, I thought. Or possibly Xavier, like Father Mac. "May I keep this photo until we wrap up our investigation, Mrs. Garrison?"

"Oh, certainly. I have some other albums up in my attic that

I'll take a look at this afternoon. Do you think this guy might be her k-i-l-l-e-r?"

"Don't know. We're mainly trying to clear up any outstanding issues right now." I wanted to downplay this possible connection. Didn't want her to go tattling to her mystery group about this case at such a sensitive time in our investigation. "Do you think Ms. Ellison might know him?" I asked.

"I don't know. That Jennifer. Really a wild one. Surprised she graduated from Harvard. And cum laude, too. Probably slept with her professors. I think Miriam was in awe of Jennifer's worldliness. I do remember Jennifer trying to talk Miriam out of leaving Harvard."

"And you graduated from Harvard, right?"

"Magna cum laude. Class of 1993. A medieval history major," she said with pride.

Now that's truly a useless degree, I thought, likely to yield some hearty laughs over at the student placement office of Boston City College, my own alma mater. But then she lived in a big-ass house in Weston with stables and a Land Rover, so perhaps she'd done pretty well by that choice.

Driving back to the office, I dialed up Jennifer Ellison's home phone in DC and left a message on her answering machine. Then I realized I should have asked Mrs. Garrison to take a look at her yearbook, in case our choirboy showed up in any obligatory photo line-ups of college clubs or stock photos of campus life. I called her on my cell and asked her if she would also review her yearbook just in case this mystery choirboy appeared in it. She could barely contain her excitement.

"My mystery class is going to be sooo impressed," she said with glee.

Yup. I could see it now. C is for Choirboy.

CHAPTER 32

I could have strangled Maria Rubio.

Lucky for her, O'Brien and four inches of two-way mirrored glass prevented me from throttling her. While AngelEyes lay unconscious in intensive care, she was refusing to answer any questions from Connelly about Simple Simon until her lawyer showed up. Just several days ago, her friend had died a horrible death—and she wouldn't say one word that might help us find out what had happened. She sat in the interview room wearing her plastic fetus baseball cap with a tiny gold angel pin clipped to it.

Connelly left her under guard in this interrogation room while we gathered in his office.

"For a gal facing serious charges, she's one cool cucumber," said Connelly. "She dialed up Lillian Harkins' firm, so we're stuck waiting on them."

"We'll get nothing out of her once Harkins starts breathing down our necks," said O'Brien.

"Don't worry. She's not going anywhere. We've already got her for illegal possession of explosives. Those files in her and Randolph's self-storage unit show that Archangel underwrote the Messengers, so she may be looking at money laundering and domestic terrorism charges, too. We're still looking through two past years of video for anything else of value."

"What's the word from the fire marshal on that explosion?" asked O'Brien. "Did Randolph accidentally blow himself up or did he do it on purpose?"

"They found chemical traces of explosives. They don't know if it happened by mistake or he got a little help through remote detonation."

"Wet or dry?" I asked, remembering my earlier Explosives 101 talk with Dynamite Doug.

"They found traces of both at the scene."

"Did they identify any chemical signatures to help track down possible manufacturers?" I asked.

"Not yet. We're checking to see if we can link these explosives back to Patrick Carpenter. I also got a call from Nolan. He's fuming about Simple Simon. Claims we're screwing up ATF's investigation. That bastard lied to us, wasting our precious time and endangering our lives," said Connelly.

His office phone rang. "Hey, I said no interruptions."

"Stephen Nolan from the ATF is in our lobby."

"Speak of the devil," said O'Brien.

"Okay, send him up." Connelly clicked off his speakerphone. "He better have a damned flak jacket on if he wants to get out of here alive."

We watched through Connelly's office window as Stephen Nolan walked through the homicide unit in a tailored blue suit and starched white shirt, every strand of his hair in its proper place. He carried a large gym bag in his right hand. I felt my angry stare boring right through this office glass and drilling right into his chest.

Connelly swung his office door open before he even knocked. Nolan stood in the doorframe, unrepentant. "It seems that you people are trying to destroy two years' worth of undercover work into international terrorism. We were collecting important information. Then you people start pushing too hard and too fast on Carpenter and his customers, trying to solve your little murder case. That explosion yesterday sent all those rats scurrying. It may take years to tunnel into that network again."

"One of my men might die in a local hospital from that explosion, thanks to you holding out on us. You said your goons were looking into stolen explosives from that subway project, not international terrorists. Nothing to do with Patrick Carpenter or his wife's murder, you told us back then." Connelly pointed his finger in Nolan's face. "You're lucky I don't haul you in for obstruction."

"That was merely our cover story. Carpenter's a low man on a global totem pole, but we planned to use him to start to trace links to bigger domestic and international fish."

"From our vantage point, it looks like we're going to help you catch some terrorists. Do the Messengers ring a bell?" asked O'Brien.

"Little fish to us. Thanks to you, Ms. Montez, you stumbled upon some minor domestic disturbances at an area clinic and screwed up our chance to crack rings of hard-core terrorists."

He paused and slicked back his hair. "Any more nighttime baseball?" he asked, motioning to a few bandages remaining on my hands and knees.

Before I could respond, Connelly let go a right upper cut that sent Nolan flying. Connelly grabbed him by his lapels as Nolan stumbled back against an office wall. He shook him violently and then put him in a headlock. I froze in shock. O'Brien seemed to be enjoying every minute.

"I should kill you, you son-of-a-bitch. Two of my people nearly died because you sandbagged us!"

"You're choking me!" Nolan gasped. "You're crazy!"

"That's what I love about him." O'Brien was sitting calmly, unperturbed by this turn of events.

"You better hope my man doesn't die in that hospital. Or you'll be lucky if you get to check liquor licenses in Alaska."

"Let me explain," he gurgled.

But Connelly wouldn't ease up.

"Connelly, stop!" I cried out.

A moment later, he let go of Nolan, who collapsed onto the floor, his blue suit torn on its right side and his neat hair tousled into a complete mess.

"Never a good idea to poke a bear in his nose," O'Brien said, laughing.

Nolan coughed for a few seconds, pulled out a white handkerchief and wiped some blood from his split lip. Slowly, he got up, straightened his tie and adjusted his suit.

"You won't be laughing when I swear out a complaint against him," Nolan said.

"Yeah, and who'll be your witnesses, wise guy? Say your piece, and then get the hell out of here," said O'Brien.

"Steer clear of Carpenter in your murder investigation. He's not your man."

"We already know that Terry Randolph killed Miriam Carpenter. Now we're just trying to figure out the why. And that keeps Patrick Carpenter in the picture," I said.

"Carpenter wasn't involved. He was with one of our undercover guys that morning in a subway tunnel. Working out some details for an illegal sale at the time of his wife's murder. He ran because he thought you were on to his side business."

"He could've sent his pal, Randolph, to kill her. Either to keep her quiet about his illegal deals or to bail out his failing business," O'Brien said.

"There was no need to keep her quiet."

I finished his sentence. "Because she was one of the Messengers, right? We already figured that out. But you could've saved us a lot of time and kept Detective Saint Cyr out of ICU if you told us that earlier," I said.

"Yes, you're right. The Carpenters and Randolph have been subjects of our wiretaps and surveillance efforts for over a year because of their involvement with Archangel and the Messengers."

"You didn't happen to see who killed her?" asked O'Brien.

"No. We weren't tailing her. We followed her husband that morning."

"So why are you here?" I asked.

"I want to make a trade."

"A trade?" asked Connelly.

Nolan tossed a gym bag at Connelly's feet. "Here are our wiretap transcripts and surveillance reports for the past year. They should tell you what you need to know about Miriam Carpenter's connection to the Messengers. They'll shed light on a possible motive for her murder."

"What do you want in return?" asked Connelly.

"We want to see what you found in that self-storage unit. It could help us bring federal charges against Carpenter and the Messengers. And give us further intelligence on Archangel that we may need regarding some of their other offshore projects."

"No deal until we see what's in these wiretaps and reports. If it's worth anything, then you've got a deal," said Connelly.

"I can live with that."

"Anything else you want to tell us before we kick you out of here?" asked O'Brien.

"No. I'll show myself out."

Nolan turned on his heel and strode out of the unit as if nothing happened.

"Remind me not to ever get you mad," I said to Connelly.

"Sorry about that. I didn't mean to scare you. But he asked for it." Connelly winced as he massaged his knuckles. "Damn hard head, that Nolan."

"Not as hard-headed as me," I said. "Would love to see what's in that bag." I was already reaching down to pick it up.

"Nice try, counselor. But I still call the shots around here. My team's got first dibs on that bag. We'll let you know if we need any help."

My cell phone rang. It was Mrs. Garrison.

Looking through her college albums, she'd had a memory flash. Miriam's special friend's nickname was Mac.

CHAPTER 33

Confession is supposed to be good for your soul, but there were few takers at St. Stephen's on this snowy afternoon.

I brushed soft white flakes off my shoulders and the front of my puffy parka. I pulled off my coat and sat down in a pew near two confessionals beneath the watchful gaze of a Virgin Mary statue. A lingering aroma of burning votive candles remained in the air. I watched an elderly woman disappear into one confessional that flanked a priest's center booth. I heard a kneeler squeak as she knelt down inside. A white light in the shape of a cross flashed on above her booth, telling members of the waiting faithful that it was occupied. But there was no one else to signal.

Except for me, the other pews remained empty. Besides, I hadn't come there to confess, but to try to get Father Mac to do some reckoning.

I checked my watch. Where was Connelly? He'd planned to meet me here twenty minutes ago. Probably stuck in some nightmare traffic snarl from that unexpected snowstorm.

After the woman left the church, I decided to step into a confessional for a private conversation with Father Mac. I pulled back the thick purple velvet curtain and eased myself onto a kneeler, trying not to put too much weight on my scraped knees. Father Mac slid his window screen open. A dim confessional light above him muted his features, but I could hear his rhythmic breathing. I remained silent in the darkness for a several moments.

"How might I help you reconcile yourself today?" he asked, in a hushed tone.

"That's my question for you, Father Mac."

"Ms. Montez?"

"Yes."

"Are you here to confess?"

"No. I need to discuss a few developments on Miriam's case with you," I said.

"This sacrament doesn't seem like the right time or place for that. Maybe we can talk later today. I'm handling reconciliations until three o'clock. Then I'm off to the hospital until at least seven or eight tonight. Perhaps we can meet after right o'clock this evening—or tomorrow morning?"

"This matter can't wait, Father Mac. And it'd be better if we talk privately first without any chance for interruptions."

"If you insist." He switched on a main light inside his booth.

"We've found remnants of your missing church vestment. A long white surplice with a hood."

"Where?" he asked.

"In an apartment of a man named Terry Randolph. Do you know Terry, Father?"

"I don't believe he's a parishioner here," he said.

Nice deflection on that one, padre. "He isn't, but do you know him anyway?"

"His name isn't familiar."

"Seems he burned that surplice garment in a trash can and left a few matching fibers behind," I said.

"Why did he steal a church vestment to burn it? Some kind of satanic ritual?"

"I'm not sure he stole it. Perhaps someone at your church lent it to him."

"We don't lend out church garments," he said.

"Maybe just a one-time thing," I replied.

"I don't know what you mean."

"Father Mac, he needed it to mask his identity. For this one time. Dressed all in white with a hood draped over his head while he crept up on Miriam and bashed her head in. Both Daniel Silva and the professor mistook him for a ghost. Good way to keep her blood from staining his clothes, too."

"How awful. Are you sure he's a killer, and not simply a thief?"

"We found some traces of endosperm in his trash can, too."

"Endosperm?" he asked.

"Yes. Turns out it's a core element of wheat flour. It's used in making Eucharistic wafers. Explains why we didn't find any communion hosts left out on the altar. Mrs. Silva told us some of them were left behind after mass. But they never ended up in the professor's cart."

"He burned that, too? What a terrible desecration of our holiest sacrament."

"Randolph didn't think so. He didn't want to throw them away in the professor's dirty cart. Apparently, he saw it as a sin offering to God. A burnt sacrifice that he read about in the Bible, a passage in the Book of Numbers."

"Are you sure he killed Miriam?" Father Mac asked.

"Yes. Tread patterns and the size of his boot print matches a bloody footprint we found here."

"But why would this Randolph man want to kill Miriam?"

"I guess that's where I need your help, Father Mac."

"My help? I don't even know this man."

"Sure you do. Randolph wore a big cross around his neck. The strangest thing about that cross: he stored mementos inside it, like scraps of Scripture," I said. "And one of those angel pins, like the one you wear all the time."

"Scripture?"

"Yes. Along with the verses from Numbers, it contained Revelation 12:7-9. The mission statement for St. Michael's Messengers. They put it in all of their bomb threats," I said.

"I've read about that group in the papers. Didn't they recently catch their ringleader hiding out in some remote campsite?"

"Yes, but their underground network's still pretty active. Randolph's been videotaping for the Messengers for years at their various protests. Your friend's been storing them in a rental unit in Dorchester for years."

"He's no friend of mine," said Father Mac.

"But dear Miriam was. She and Patrick had a copy of that same self-storage key hidden under their backyard Virgin Mary statue. They're members of the Messengers, too. But you already know that. Those angel pins are a clever way to help identify who's on your team. That same sort of angel pin fell off Miriam's blouse when she tumbled dead on to the chapel floor that morning."

"I don't know anything about the Messengers. Or any angel pins they wear," he said.

"We found a box of those pins in a self-storage unit paid for by Archangel Investment Trust. A shipping label for those pins had your name on it. You passed it along to the Carpenters or Randolph who put it in their storage unit. What's your role in the Messengers, Father Mac? Secretly recruiting for them, or merely offering friendly absolutions after every bombing?" I asked.

"I don't have any idea what you're talking about. I don't belong to the Messengers. And I'm certain that the Carpenters knew nothing about that group."

"You do know that Patrick Carpenter isn't Joey's biological father."

He didn't reply for a few seconds. "As I told you when we first met, I'm bound by a confidential seal of confession with my parishioners. You should know that as a lawyer."

"I know that, Father Mac. Yet Miriam became pregnant way before you became a priest. You told us that yourself."

He said nothing.

"Back then, you stayed in regular contact with Miriam, even though you ended up at different schools. You both belonged to the same college chapter of the Newman Club. Even sang in the club's intercollegiate choir together."

"So what? There's no crime in belonging to a club or singing God's praises," he said.

"No, but obstructing justice is a crime, Father Mac. And you should have told us earlier that you knew that Patrick Carpenter isn't Joey's father. That's pretty vital info for our case, don't you think?"

"I don't approve of Patrick. His poor treatment of Miriam and her children. But I want justice to be done for Miriam as much as you do," he said.

"Yet you didn't mind leaving our investigation's spotlight on Patrick. You never liked him and you didn't seem to mind if he became the fall guy."

"This is crazy. I didn't kill Miriam." His breathing quickened to short gasps as he fumbled for his inhaler.

"No, you managed to get Terry Randolph to do your dirty work," I said.

"No, I'd never want her harmed. I loved her." He wheezed and gulped for air.

"But you didn't love her enough to get a paternity test. An old roommate told us that Miriam had a brief fling with someone nicknamed Mac. Even a whiff of another Church sex scandal ends your rise in the church hierarchy. Any hopes of becoming archbishop, and perhaps cardinal, snuffed out. So you told Randolph she planned to tell the authorities all about the Messengers and he killed her to protect that group."

"You don't know what you're talking about. I'm not so ambitious or so cruel that I'd kill my dearest friend and sacrifice an innocent man to a life in prison."

He raised his inhaler to his lips and sucked in a long puff. Father Mac held his hand to his chest as he appeared to try to ease his breathing.

"Then why not tell us about Miriam's panicked call to you when Patrick flew into a jealous rage about not being Joey's father? The Feds got it all on tape."

"Tape?"

"Yes, they've been wiretapping Randolph and the Carpenters for over a year. And she's on tape calling you a week or so before she winds up dead. She told you about bone marrow tests showing that Patrick was never Joey's father," I said.

"Again, that call is protected by the priest-penitent privilege."

"Father Mac, she didn't call you to confess. She called to get her old friend's help about a shared secret from your college days when you weren't a priest yet."

"We may have shared a secret, Ms. Montez, but never a bed," he said.

"Only a paternity test will tell for sure. And she planned to squeal about your connections to the Messengers if you didn't do it. Right?"

"Miriam never threatened me. I'm not Joey's father. And I wouldn't hurt Miriam or tell others to harm her."

"We'll let the DNA do the talking, Father. It'll all be outlined in our prosecutor's motion papers tomorrow. For the entire world to see, unless you want to tell me something to direct our attention elsewhere," I said.

He sat motionless in his confessional. He lowered his hand

from his chest as his breathing slowed. A tear rolled down his cheek. Father Mac began to speak haltingly. "Yes. Miriam told me she was pregnant when I attended BC."

Pausing, he wiped a tear away. "Naturally, she became very upset. Pretty scared. Almost hysterical. Even talked about killing herself. Or getting an abortion."

He drew a deep breath summoning up his strength to continue. "We'd grown up together, like brother and sister. I knew she'd never forgive herself if she took her child's life. I wouldn't let her damn her soul by taking her own life either. She was very committed to her faith. I begged her not to compound her youthful mistake with a mortal sin of murder. We talked a great deal over several weeks about her situation. Thankfully, she calmed down and decided to move on with her life and to have her child."

"Did she tell you the name of the father?"

"No. Miriam was unsure. Patrick and she had an on-again, off-again relationship while she went to Harvard. Miriam hinted around that she had a serious crush on a much older graduate student. She never gave me his name."

"Do you have any other information about him?" I asked.

"Not much. Just that one night she drank too much and things went too far. He used her for a one-night stand. He'd been engaged already to some wealthy coed at Wellesley. And when Miriam married Patrick, I assumed she had determined that Patrick was Joey's biological father."

"But that turned out to be wrong, Father Mac. Those bone marrow tests proved Patrick wasn't Joey's father."

"Yes, I was wrong. Wrong about a lot of things. But I didn't kill Miriam."

We remained in silence in the confessional box.

"Monty?" Connelly's stage whisper echoed in the church.

"You know you'll have to make a formal statement to him, Father Mac?"

"Yes, I know."

"And give us a blood sample?"

"Yes. I hope we can do it discreetly," he said.

"We can keep your test initially under wraps during our investigation, but not if it proves paternity. And I can't speak for the Feds."

"The federal government?"

"Yes. They have their own investigation. We've shared our information on the contents of that self-storage unit with them. You can expect a call from them, too."

CHAPTER 34

I missed the old Boston Garden. It had its charms, its history, not to mention its clogged-up bathrooms, obstructed-view seats, and terrible ventilation system that blew cold air in winter and hot air in summer. The Garden gave way to the new, more sterile environment of this sleek modern sports and entertainment complex. I took an elevator up to the rarified air of private luxury boxes on its seventh floor.

A boisterous college crowd roared as the Harvard Crimson was taking a serious thrashing from Boston University's Terriers in this year's Beanpot Hockey Tournament. I knocked on a door of a luxury box marked with a plaque for Harkins' law firm. Luckily for me, the Ice Queen didn't like hockey. Perhaps reminded her too much of her home planet. A young man carrying a serving dish of hors d'oeuvres answered it. He asked me to wait while he spoke with the host. Then Edgar Thompson came to the entrance.

"Ms. Montez, I didn't imagine that you're a hockey fan. Unfortunately, this is a private party for Harvard alumni, and you don't have an invitation."

"No, I don't. But I do have some old Harvard memories to share with you about Miriam." I said.

"Who?"

I held up a copy of Mrs. Garrison's photo from that college mixer. FlashPhoto Phil had zoomed in and sharpened up this partial image of Thompson's young face next to Miriam. He slipped on a pair of glasses and plucked it from my hands to take a closer look.

"I don't remember this," he said.

"How about this one?"

I pulled out a second photo of Thompson with Miriam singing at a Harvard choral society's concert copied from a yearbook photo that Mrs. Garrison had dug up.

"Looks like something from our school choir. Quite a few years ago."

He handed the photos back to me. "Still don't know what this has to do with me."

"Then perhaps a trip downtown might refresh your memory. In Quinn's office, you pretended you didn't know Miriam. Claimed that you learned about her case in the papers. Even saw newspaper photos of her, but never owned up to knowing her. Then here you are in two photos with our victim. I thought you told us you never forget a face."

"Is that her?"

He took a closer look.

"Yes. Before her head got bashed in at St. Stephen's."

"A terrible tragedy indeed. But again what does any of this have to do with me?" he asked.

"You wouldn't want me to spell it out right here. Not in front of all your guests. I'd rather handle this quietly, just between the two of us, Mr. Thompson."

"What do you mean?"

"I'm the only one who knows about your romance with Miriam in college. And if you'd like to keep things that way, then perhaps you and I should find a nice quiet spot to talk things over."

"Everything all right, Edgar?" called out one of his guests from inside.

"Yes, Charles. It's fine, fine. A few issues to straighten out," he said. He closed this suite's door behind him. "I'll humor you, Ms. Montez, for a couple of minutes. But solely to clear up your confusion. Then I must return to my guests," he huffed.

Thompson grabbed my elbow and led us to an exit and into an empty stairwell. Muffled echoes of skates scraping against ice, clacking hockey sticks, and booms of bodies crunching against backboards masked our voices. As an organ played cheerful fight songs, an animated crowd clapped and roared its approval. He rushed me up a flight of stairs, several steps below an emergency exit to the roof. I hoped he wasn't taking us too far away.

"I know you may wish to embarrass me and my organization with tales from my college days, but I have no clue how these pictures could be related to this woman's death."

"You were a law student at that time, and Miriam, a naive freshman. You both landed roles as soloists for an annual Christmas concert. All that time rehearsing together," I said.

"I remained active in Harvard's choral society throughout all my college and graduate school years. I sang with lots of people, years and years ago. I can't be expected to remember every shred of my educational endeavors." He ran his fingers through his hair several times.

"But she made four calls to you this past month."

"What are you talking about?"

"The Carpenters were under investigation by federal authorities for illegal sales of explosives. We've got her voice on tape contacting your office on four separate occasions to talk with you about meeting at St. Stephen's Church," I said.

I noticed a slight twitch in his upper lip.

"Some of our most ardent supporters are churchgoers. I often meet supporters at churches. That's hardly unusual."

"Do they all turn up dead?"

"Really. That remark's beneath even you, Ms. Montez. My calendar's packed with meetings. I'm sure she was merely another donor or someone calling on behalf of a group hoping to meet with me. If you check my calendar, I'm sure you've mixed up your dates. I haven't met anyone at St. Stephen's during this campaign."

"No, but you were supposed to. Miriam's family told us that she planned to meet the father of her seriously ill son. She needed to talk to him about being tested for a bone marrow match to save their son's life. And then these calls from her to your office."

"Ridiculous! I have only two children. Two lovely daughters with my wife, Astrid. You clearly have got the wrong person," he replied

"A simple blood test will help clear up our confusion."

His back stiffened up. "That's outrageous! Clearly another shameless attempt to slander our organization. You have absolutely no basis for such a preposterous demand."

"Sure I do. Both of Miriam's old roommates remember Mac quite clearly." I held up a photo of him at that mixer again.

Fortunately, Jennifer Ellison had called me back and confirmed Mrs. Garrison's memory of those unfortunate college events, and added to them.

"You went by the nickname Mac in those days. Shortening up your middle name. Your mother's maiden name, Macmillan. A lot less formal than using a stuffy name like Edgar with those nubile college girls."

"I won't listen to this for another moment," he said.

"One roommate clearly remembers when Miriam broke down into hysterics when she found out she was pregnant, right after you dumped her. She even asked her worldlier roommate for help in getting an abortion. Guess you didn't want Miriam to upset your well-connected fiancée with that tawdry bit of news. But lucky for you, Miriam married Patrick without ever finding out who the real father was. Until recently, that is," I said.

"This is insane."

He turned to go back down the stairs.

"Not as insane as sending poor Terry Randolph in your place to kill Miriam."

He stopped and looked up toward me.

"What? I don't know anyone named Terry Randolph."

"That's funny. He's got lots of videotapes of himself standing right next to you. You know, that chubby guy who wore a big wooden cross. His friend, Maria Rubio, took that video of him with his hero. You."

"I see, Ms. Montez. I'm guilty of having people standing next to me in photographs and videos. I'm a public person, so it is quite common for my supporters to want to appear in photos and videos with me."

"You did a lot more than stand next to him. He kept a nice library of extremist home movies for St. Michael's Messengers. They like to blow things up, when they're not blowing up each other. You were good enough to send Lillian Harkins' firm to represent him and Ms. Rubio on a number of occasions. You didn't want them accidentally blurting something out about those secret connections between the Messengers and your Center. Your regular donors wouldn't like it if they found out their funds were being funneled to violent extremists," I said.

"The Messengers? I have no connection with that group or

Randolph. Besides, Ms. Harkins' firm represents a broad range of clients. I have no control over which clients they offer their services to on a *pro bono* basis."

"But your organization paid their legal fees. There were no freebies from Harkins' firm. It's all spelled out in your demand for attorneys' fees in your civil rights cases against the County," I said. I owed Scarecrow Don for that tidbit.

"Even if that's true, our organization as a matter of principle supports many people who fight for our causes."

"Yeah, but not too many of them get you to pay their legal fees and also to visit them in-person in their squalid little apartment. Just a tiny hovel where a nobody lived. He almost scorched his place trying to destroy evidence from Miriam's killing."

"Clearly you found your man. How does any of this babble relate to me?" he asked.

"It wasn't very nice of you to lie to Randolph. You warned him that Miriam planned to tell the police about the Messengers and his bomb-making factory at Maria's apartment. Told him Miriam had a change of heart. She'd gotten too close to staff at Pinkowski's clinic and wanted to back out of bombing that place, spill it all to federal authorities. You knew Miriam wasn't going to do that, but you lied to Randolph anyway. Pretty easy for you to convince him he'd be doing the right thing. Promised him in the end that he'd be a hero for saving the Messengers from the Feds. And to think, you really used him to get rid of your own scandal from your past," I said.

"I don't know what you're talking about."

"He even called you when the deed was done. You asked how Judas was doing. And he told you Judas was gone and wouldn't be bothering you anymore." I thought back to Daniel's drawing. "It's all in the wiretaps."

"You're merely throwing delusional theories at me. You'll be out on the street and brought up on charges before the bar association tomorrow morning." He turned to go downstairs to his luxury box.

"Don't forget this. I'm sure your guests will enjoy it." I raised a videotape cassette in my hand.

"What, more video of people standing next to me?" he laughed. "Hardly anything special I'm certain of that."

"Definitely a special night for Randolph. The night that the almighty Edgar Macmillan Thompson came to visit. You know Randolph just loved camera gear and videos. So much so that he rigged his own apartment with a camera to take videos of all his visitors, including you. He didn't get a chance to remove that last bit of video before his landlord sent him packing after that trash can fire."

Thompson stood silent for a moment.

"Randolph didn't get many guests, but his super does remember seeing a very special visitor one night. He ran into you when your car alarm blared on your Crown Victoria," I said. Dermott had picked Thompson's picture out of a photo array Connelly showed him this morning.

"Why are you telling me all of this? Shouldn't you be off trying to impress your friends at the DA's office?" he demanded.

"I'm the only one who's put all the pieces together and who knows about these photos and this tape. Perhaps we can talk business and avoid any unpleasantness."

"So this is all about money. It doesn't seem like your style, Ms. Montez."

"I don't get paid that much in the prosecutor's office. And if Quinn loses this election, I'm out of a job. Nothing wrong with wanting some financial security for myself."

"I won't be blackmailed by you or anyone else."

"Is that why you had Miriam killed? Was she blackmailing you, too?"

"Miriam possessed a more noble motive than you. She didn't want money. She only wanted to save her son. But she couldn't accept why I didn't want to be tested. My personal weakness would create an enormous scandal, irrevocably damaging our movement," he said.

"Or maybe that no-good husband might find out and start demanding money from you, right?"

"Either way, I couldn't let my own personal problems endanger our work."

"You mean interfere with domestic terrorists, like the Messengers?" I asked.

"You call them terrorists. I call them heroes. Willing to make sacrifices to save our society from moral ruin."

"So why not sacrifice yourself for your son?"

"The greatest good for the greatest number. The deaths of innocents, like Joey, are holy sacrifices to God. One life, or even a dozen, pales in comparison with saving millions of unborn children and rescuing their parents' souls from damnation," he thundered.

"You'd let your own son die? I think you were worried more about your reputation and your senate candidacy than anybody else's damnation."

He lunged at me, but missed. I turned and ran upstairs. When I pushed open an emergency exit, a fire alarm began to honk in the still of the frigid night. The roof deck was dark with twinkling safety lights at each corner. A gush of bright highway lights from the massive Zakim Bridge hundreds of feet below illuminated the northern edges of this rooftop.

I bolted across the roof, spying the dim lights of another rooftop emergency exit. Before I reached it, Thompson grabbed my right arm and nearly pulled it out of its socket. We struggled over Randolph's tape. He pushed me hard and I tumbled across the roof deck. His tape flew out of my hands and skidded into a darkened corner. Oh, damn. I felt myself getting dizzy and my vision went double. Bad timing for a Machado moment. I squeezed my eyes shut and hoped they'd clear, but Thompson was towering over me when I opened them. He grabbed the hood of my red parka and jerked me to my feet.

"I hope you've enjoyed your little game," he said. "There are bigger issues at stake here than either of us. I won't let you or anyone stand in the way of our work. At times, sacrifices are needed if we're to succeed. And if pushing you off this roof will save our movement, then it's a necessary evil. It'll be written off as an unfortunate action of a despondent, failed prosecutor."

"Like Randolph's unfortunate death?" I gasped.

"No, his death was an accident. An unexpected explosion. But your death will get a helping hand from me."

I yelled for help, wildly kicking and punching in his direction, but missing my mark. We struggled as he tried to push me over a steel railing on an edge of the roof deck. I hugged an outside railing with all my might as sounds of traffic whizzed beneath us on the busy Zakim Bridge. Flailing around furiously, I tried to land a kick on Thomson. But he grabbed my coat's hem to flip me over the railing and down into the buzzing bridge traffic below.

"Police! Freeze!" yelled Connelly.

A flood of officers swarmed out from both rooftop doors. Thompson turned and slowly let me down.

"I'm glad you came by, officers. This crazy woman attacked me and I had to defend myself." He pointed at me.

"Nice try, scumbag," said O'Brien. "She wore a wire. We got it all."

"You okay, kiddo?" asked Connelly.

"Where the hell were you guys?" I panted, trying to regain my breath.

"You got out of range for a few minutes. We could hear you, but couldn't pinpoint your actual location. Setting off that emergency exit alarm let us know where you were," Connelly said.

He pulled out a pair of handcuffs and gave them to me.

"Your collar, Monty. You earned it."

I took hold of Connelly's handcuffs. As I approached Thompson, he took two steps back.

"Sometimes one must make sacrifices to achieve the greater good, Ms. Montez," he said.

Then in the next split second, he flung himself over the roof railing. Screeching car brakes echoed on the highway bridge below us.

CHAPTER 35

The EMTs rushed Thompson's broken body, strapped to a metal gurney, into Boston Memorial's emergency room. I hobbled out of the back of an ambulance under my own power. O'Brien demanded that I go to Boston Memorial to check out my bruised body parts and to make sure I hadn't damaged anything else of importance. As O'Brien helped me toward the sliding emergency room doors, Ponytail Craig stood just outside stubbing out a cigarette.

"Nice to see you again, Monty." He grabbed a wheelchair and offered me a seat. "You're sure good for business," he joked.

As he wheeled me inside, I asked, "How's my—" I stopped. "How's our friend, Saint Cyr, doing?"

"He's doing better. Turned a corner this afternoon. Stable right now. He's been asking for you. Come on up when you're done."

Ponytail Craig gave me the best medicine I could have hoped for—AngelEyes pulling through this nightmare and asking to see me. My shoulder ached and my neck throbbed from my battle with Thompson. After several hours in a waiting room, I stopped listening to O'Brien's running commentary on every new patient that stumbled in. I felt relieved when a duty nurse finally called my name. "Margarita Montez?" she said.

Although a good shot of tequila seemed like a great idea, I couldn't muster enough strength to correct her. "Just call me Monty," I said.

Ultimately, the emergency room doctors told me the same old, same old. Several bad bumps and bruises, but I'd live to prosecute another day. I headed up to intensive care and paused near a darkened contemplation room. Reaching for its door handle, my fingertips touched the cool metal. I thought about saying a prayer for AngelEyes or lighting a candle for Ginny, and Luisa, too. But I couldn't get myself to open it and go in. Instead I headed to ICU and Ponytail Craig escorted me to Saint Cyr's room.

Seen through a glass partition, he appeared to be sleeping, hooked up to fewer machines than last time and breathing on his own. "Has any of his family been here?"

"His mother isn't well, so she can't fly in. She's waiting for another son to return from Hong Kong. He's supposed to drive her here and they'll arrive late tomorrow. But we've been in regular phone contact with them."

I didn't want to wake him, so I watched him through the glass at first. "Can I?" I asked, turning to Ponytail Craig.

"Go on in," he said. "Gérard may float in and out. But he could use some company."

I smiled and then tread softly into Gérard's room. I sat in a hard plastic chair in silence, only interrupted by an occasional beep of one of his monitors. Connelly joined me and we barely spoke for about a half-hour.

"Wanna grab a bite to eat in their cafeteria?" asked Connelly.

"Nah, go without me. I don't have much of an appetite."

As he exited Saint Cyr's room, he turned to me. "You did all right," said Connelly. "For a lawyer. But remember…"

"I know, I know. You still call all the shots."

He nodded and left for the hospital cafeteria.

I got up and stood over AngelEyes. Reaching out to him, I caressed his cheek and stroked his silky blond hair. I kissed his forehead lightly a couple of times. It might be my only chance to do that. Several minutes later, his eyes fluttered open, then closed and then opened once more. He looked up and smiled weakly. I grasped his hand.

"I must be dead, because I'm looking at an angel," he said softly.

"Even on your deathbed, you're still flirting."

"Is there any other way to go?" he asked in a raspy whisper.

"How are you feeling?" "Like I got hit by a Zamboni. Do I look as bad as I feel?"

"You look fine." Damn fine, I thought. "But you did a nice job beating up your innards."

"Yeah, so they tell me, eh?" he said. "Did we get those bad guys?"

"Yup, we did." I squeezed his hand.

"You will tell to me all about it."

"Sure, when you're feeling better."

"Very much, I'd like that."

I didn't want to tell him that Thompson almost killed me trying to wrest a videotape of my law school graduation out of my hands. Or that Thompson was struggling for his own life this evening in this same intensive care unit.

In the end, Thompson wasn't a match for Joey. He died two days later from his injuries. His wife possessed enough inner strength to put aside her tragedy and donated his organs to give life to others. Only time would tell if any of Joey's new half-sisters might provide a bone marrow match.

"Craig says you've got family driving in to see you tomorrow. Your mom and your brother."

"I'm not sure alone I can face them," he said, smiling. He looked into my eyes. "Might need a good barrister."

"My fees are pretty high for a homicide detective's salary." I bent forward and softly kissed AngelEyes on his lips for the first time. "But then I might find a way to do some *pro bono* work for you."

ABOUT THE AUTHOR

As a kid, Bridges tortured her eight siblings by writing and directing annual family plays. Starting with a pad of paper, then moving to an orange Smith Corona typewriter, and now to her trusty laptop, she has always enjoyed the puzzle of finding the right word, phrase or plot twist. Her published works are both non-fiction and fiction. She has published three non-fiction books and numerous articles, manuals, and editorials in the legal, travel and business fields, and a novel and short stories in the science fiction, fantasy and mystery genres.

In 2015, she published *Bridles of Poseidon*, an underwater fantasy, about a shape-shifting mermaid, Aquan, racing to stop another Great Flood. That novel was chosen as a finalist in the 2012 Royal Palm Literary Awards (unpublished fantasy) from the Florida Writers Association. Her short stories *Clair de Lune*, based on the Celtic myth about Selkies, is published in *Mother Goose is Dead, Modern Stories of Myths, Fables and Fairy Tales* (Damnation Books 2011) and *Chasing the Moon*, about a werewolf with Parkinson's Disease who revels in his monthly transformation, is published in *Tails of the Pack: A Werewolf Anthology* (Sky Warrior Books 2013). Her non-fiction essay, *Brick*, honoring her late father, Joseph, and his love of words is published in *Living Lessons* (Whispering Angels Books 2010). She is also a member of Sisters in Crime, Inc. and the Florida Writers Association.

When she is not writing, she teaches law courses, creates educational game apps, and lives happily in sunny Central Florida. To learn more about Bridges DelPonte and her writing, please visit:

Author web site: *http://www.bridgesdelponte.com*

Amazon Author Central page: *http://www.amazon.com/Bridges-DelPonte/e/B00BW7BZYU*